Lightbringer

LAKEN CANE

ISBN: 9781793199522

FOLLOW LAKEN:

Amazon author page:

www.amazon.com/author/lakencane

Facebook author page:

www.facebook.com/AuthorLakenCane

Website:

www.lakencane.com

Subscribe to Laken's mailing List—which you can find on her website—and get a free book!

PLAYLIST FOR LIGHTBRINGER

-**RISE WITH ME** (IN THIS MOMENT)
-**NOTHING ELSE MATTERS** (METALLICA)
-**ANIMAL I HAVE BECOME** (THREE DAYS GRACE)
-**VOLCANO** (DAMIEN RICE)
-**WHO MADE WHO** (AC/DC)
-**WELCOME TO THE JUNGLE** (GUNS N' ROSES)
-**THUNDERSTRUCK** (AC/DC)
-**ZOMBIE** (BAD WOLVES)
-**THE CITY** (EXITMUSIC)
-**BONES** (IN THIS MOMENT)
-**MY NAME IS HUMAN** (HIGHLY SUSPECT)
-**THE UNFORGIVEN** (METALLICA)
-**GREY ROOM** (DAMIEN RICE)
-**THE SOUND OF SILENCE** (DISTURBED)
-**TOXIC** (2WEI)
-**HURT** (2WEI)
-**WICKED GAME** (FEAT. ANNACA, URSINE VULPINE)
-**DELICATE** (DAMIEN RICE)
-**VAMPIRE SMILE** (KYLA LA GRANGE)

Recap of Peacemaker, Silverlight book three:

Rifters break free from the prison in which the vampire elders trapped them—helped along by the Byrdcage warden's son Jamie Stone and his imprisoned witch mother. Trin will sacrifice herself to save the city, the humans, the vampires. In the end, she dies, burned by the dragon, and Amias brings her back as a vampire.

Characters:
Angus Stark: Alpha werebull. Trinity's protector, lover, heart.

Amias Sato: Master vampire. Raced to the island at the end of Peacemaker, carrying Shane, to save the one he loves.

Clayton Wilder: Finally retrieved his hunter status with his freedom. Has all the protection he needs in the sword made from his former tormenter, Miriam Crow.

Shane Copas: Hunter, Trinity's dark obsession. The end of Peacemaker saw him dead and slung across the shoulder of the master vampire, Amias Sato.

Rhys Graver: Tall, dark, and sexy. The dragon.

Miriam Crow: Taken to hell, forged into the sword Blacklight. Now she belongs to her former slave, Clayton.

Captain Frank Crawford: Captain of Red Valley Police Department, friend to the supernatural.

Leo Trask: Powerful half-giant that Trinity freed when she went after Angus. He's hers now—she just has to claim him.

Alejandro Rodríguez: Rhys's human assistant, badass extraordinaire.

Jamie Stone: Son of the warden of Byrd Island. His mother was an imprisoned witch. He helped her destroy the island. He's under the protection and care of Alejandro Rodríguez.

Jade Noel: Mysterious supernat. She's a lot of things. Nice ain't one of them.

Amanda Hammer: One of Jade's crew. There's some power in those hammer fists.

Derry Stark: One of Angus's daughters.

PART ONE

GROWING A VAMPIRE

Chapter One

The Way Station

It was like being born.

It was like being born, because it was a birth. A rebirth.

I clung to Shane, unwilling to release that connection to reality, and the vampire master pulled me from the awful, black despair that tried with greedy eagerness to hold me.

If I hadn't been turned, would I have had the same death, the same afterlife?

No. I was pretty sure not.

Time had no meaning. I absorbed the changes in my body and my mind. I grew from grasping infant to feral adult, and quickly.

Amias was unsure—I felt his doubt. It didn't scare me. Not then.

All I wanted was food.

Blood.

And I wasn't *me* enough to feel shame over that.

Amias fed me, cared for me, coaxed me from death to a different sort of death—my new existence.

He held me, stroked my hair, murmured meaningless words into my ear, and did his best to heal a body ravaged by vicious rifters.

A body he put back together.

"You must be prepared for scars," he whispered. "They will not disappear. Not all of them."

I did not care.

I'd had scars before.

There were other physical changes, as well. My fangs began to come in, and I felt them growing inside my gums the way I felt Shane's motionless, unresponsive coldness.

Shane's return to life was different than my own.

Because Shane had not been a bloodhunter. He didn't have my blood. He was not me. And when he stirred to life and began screaming, the master took him away from me.

Why? I'd wondered.

"Because eventually, he will hate me for forcing his turn, and he will hate you for seeing it."

I didn't know how much time I'd spent in the ground, with crumbly dirt like chocolate cake cradling me, the master feeding me, my mind slowly, so slowly, becoming something almost whole once again.

Time passed.

And when Amias bore me to the surface, I was changed from the girl I'd once been. New in some ways and ancient in others.

I was one of the bloodsucking parasites I'd hated and hunted.

I was undead.

I was a vampire.

Chapter Two

PRIMAL

I watched him as he revealed his body, watched him the way he watched me, with anticipation and hunger.

He never fed me without fucking me.

He never fed *from* me without fucking me.

I was his to do with as he pleased. He was my master. And sometimes when he said my name, *"Trinity, Trinity…"* it took me a minute to realize he was speaking to me. Trinity was my name.

At least it had been, once upon a time.

A million years ago.

I shivered, clenching my fists, my naked body tightening with…something. Dread, maybe, or anger. I couldn't tell. My emotions were too new and chaotic to be trusted.

"Do you want to taste me, my darling?" he asked, his voice low and full of promise. "Be still."

The blood of the master was something his vampires would crave until they were ended. It was a sickness, almost, eventually softening into a low level humming that would never really disappear. It became easier to control as a vampire matured.

But for new vampires, and especially for me…

"Yes," I breathed.

He stared down at me, waiting.

"Master," I added quickly. "Yes, please, Master."

Something sad wafted through his eyes. "Trinity," he murmured. "I do not want to break you. I do not want to see you broken. Do you understand that?"

I cared only for the blood. His blood. His words meant

nothing. I nodded eagerly, my entire body screaming with consuming hunger, unbearable need, and breathtaking anticipation. "Please, Master. Please."

He climbed into the bed, his bare body warm and comforting against mine. He drew me into his arms and we lay face to face, our lips almost touching.

I didn't dare move. I didn't dare do anything that might cause him to retract his offer. I stared into his eyes, unblinking and unmoving, my new fangs cutting into my bloodless bottom lip.

"Trinity," he whispered, at last, and brushed my lips with his. "Trinity."

He spoke my name often because he said I'd forgotten who I was.

I hadn't forgotten. I just didn't care.

I didn't care about anything but his blood, his body, his existence.

"Master," I replied.

He voice was suddenly sharp, almost angry. "Will you not fight me?"

I drew back, alarmed. *"Never,* Master. Never."

He sighed and rubbed my torn lip with the pad of his thumb. "Once upon a time you would have. You would have demanded your release. You would have wallowed in devastation at Shane's desertion. You would have been impatient to return to Bay Town, to your men."

"Now there is only you," I told him. "Nothing else matters."

He closed his eyes and didn't open them again until I patted his cheek softly, insistently. Then he stared at me, emotionless, blank. "You have to come back," he said, finally. "You have to return to us, Trinity."

"I never left you. I am here. I am always here."

But his eyes were full of frustration. "Only part of you," he muttered. "The blackest part. The broken part. The fucking *vampire* part." He squeezed my arm, hard. "Where are you? How have I lost you?"

I disliked his disappointment, his desolation. I wanted to do and be whatever he wanted of me.

I didn't know how.

"Time," he whispered, finally. "You just need more time."

I smiled. "Yes. Time."

He slid his fingers from my arm to my breast, and my nipple stiffened immediately at his touch. I shivered as between my legs, I began to throb. He had only to hint at what was to come, and my body responded.

I was a feeding, fucking machine.

And I did not care.

I had come back with parts of me missing. Perhaps someday they'd return. Amias was impatient—desperate, nearly—and that was the only reason I hoped I would become whole again. Not because I needed to feel something other than lust and hunger, but because *he* needed me to.

I gripped his erection, and a flare of jealousy streaked through me, there and gone almost before I understood what it was. He'd fed, of course he'd fed. He couldn't feed from me, because he allowed me to feed from no one but him.

His eyes widened and he tensed. "What did you feel?"

I squeezed his hardness. "Jealousy, Master. Your cock is filled with the blood of someone else. I don't…"

"Yes?"

"I don't like that you fed from someone else."

He inhaled sharply. "I fucked someone else, too, my love. Does that make you jealous as well?"

I only realized I was hurting him when he jerked and covered my hand with his. He didn't try to force my grip from his erection, but I eased up immediately. I was strong. Very strong. And I forgot that sometimes.

But he was the master. I was his servant. I had no reason for or right to my jealousy. He would take care of me. He knew what I needed, what was best for not only me, but his entire coven.

I relaxed. "I'm sorry, Master."

The spark in his eyes dimmed. "Trinity, Trinity," he said, mournful, dejected. Then, "It is a start."

"A start," I repeated, a good little blood-sucking parrot. I licked my dry lips. "A taste, please? I'm so very hungry."

But he wasn't quite ready. "You forbade your men from having sex with others," he murmured. "Do you not see me as yours?"

I understood, distantly, that he'd lied to me. He'd fed from another—he had no choice. But his cock belonged to me—as did his heart. "You didn't fuck anyone," I realized.

He turned me to my back and nudged open my legs, and with one sure, smooth push, he slid inside me. I was wet, ready, and eager. He pulled out, almost all the way, then slid back inside, deep, deeper still, his cock filling me up, rubbing against a million bundles of nerves.

I tingled with pleasure. Shook with it.

I groaned, but never took my stare from his. He'd taught me early on to keep my eyes open, to look into his as he fucked me. He liked that connection, that closeness.

I liked to be fucked. And fed.

Oh, how I liked that.

I wrapped my legs around his strong body and gripped his arms. "Master?"

He offered me his blood as he pumped his hips. "Take it, my love."

I struck without hesitation, my body trembling with desire and hunger. The hot, sweet magic of the master's blood exploded into my mouth, then slid down my throat and into my life, my mind, my existence, and as I drank, I grew stronger.

More alive.

Darker.

I would come back.

But I wasn't sure I really wanted to.

I wasn't just Trinity, and I wasn't just a vampire.

11

I was something unspeakable.
It lived inside me.
And I belonged to the darkness now.

Chapter Three

PAIN

Amias leaned over the bed, staring into my eyes as he always did, hoping to see the changes that would make him happy. He wanted to see something other than darkness and emptiness and hunger. He'd told me many times.

"Where are you, Trinity?"

"I'm here."

"No. Not yet."

A thousand times we'd had that conversation.

Someday it would end differently. At least, that was what he believed. What he waited for.

He wore a suit, fresh and crisp and smelling, somehow, of humans. Of the world outside the bedroom in which I'd been ensconced since he'd brought me to the surface.

I darted out my tongue to taste his skin, then nipped his bottom lip. Beneath the soft sheet, my naked body stirred. "You smell good. It makes me want to bite you."

The corners of his eyes crinkled when he smiled. "You are a greedy vampire."

I was stuck on the beauty of that smile. I slid my hands up over his arms, closing my eyes at the cool, almost unfamiliar fabric covering his flesh. "You are an irresistible vampire."

Every day, I changed a little more. I was maturing, but slowly. That snail's pace irritated my master.

I knew it frightened him, as well.

A spark of sadness lit my insides when I thought about it. I, as I was now, would never be enough for him. He wanted the old Trinity, even though he'd made me the vampire.

13

He sighed. "My love, I dislike the sadness I see in your eyes."

And before I could reply, he brushed my lips with his and continued. "But I am happy to see you…thinking."

"Changing," I whispered, into his mouth. "Growing."

"Yes." Then he pulled back, so he could stare once more into my eyes. Whatever he saw there seemed to please him.

And that was all I wanted. To please him.

Then he hurt me. "Soon, you will no longer be the shallow monster. Soon, you will be Trinity." He kissed my forehead, understanding my pain, but he never pulled his punches with me. "And I will force you out of the nest."

Fear, immediate and sharp, rose up inside me. "No."

He lifted an eyebrow. "No?"

My entire body tightened at his disapproval. "I don't want to leave you," I whispered. "Please don't make me."

"Only when you're ready," he promised.

Being ready didn't mean the same thing to him it did to me. I would never be ready to leave him. But he believed he would need to shove me out when the time came. For my own good.

Tough love.

"You'll always be mine," he said. "Wherever you are, whatever you become. You are mine."

"Always," I swore. "Forever."

I wanted nothing more.

Nothing.

But an image of Angus's face slipped into my mind and pain streaked through my chest. I gasped and concentrated on that pain, which was both familiar and strange.

Amias's stare sharpened. "Tell me."

"Angus," I murmured. "It hurt me to think of him."

He said nothing for a few seconds, and I couldn't read his face. "Good," he said, finally. "Slowly, like a turtle with one leg, but you will get there."

I didn't return his smile. "I don't want to get there. I'm

happy here."

He pulled away from me and went to stand in front of the mirror, where he straightened his tie and smoothed down his jacket. "You're happy to lie naked in bed, doing nothing but eating and fucking."

I flinched at the tired anger in his voice. "I'm happy being with you," I said. "You are all I care about."

He caught my gaze through the reflective glass. "Executioners are coming to Red Valley, Trinity. They're coming for the dragon."

"Rhys," I murmured, frowning. Then, I shrugged. "I'll be safe here with you."

He curled his fists, and I thought he might punch the mirror. Instead, he stared at the ceiling, and when he'd calmed, he turned to face me. "You're stuck, Trinity. Something happened when I brought you back. I must fix this."

Angry, I turned away from him and closed my eyes.

He placed a warm hand on my shoulder. "My love, my life. Whatever you believe, this is not who you wish to be."

"I know what I need and I know what I want."

"You do not." He sighed. "And as your master, your *maker*, it is my responsibility to take care of you. To see that you get everything you need, even when you are unaware that you need anything." He squeezed my shoulder. "When you are better, you will understand."

I flipped around to face him. "Better? I'm not sick."

He said nothing, just stared at me until I dropped my gaze. Satisfied, he leaned over and kissed my forehead.

A tiny flare of anger caused me to lift my hands and shove him away.

Not once since I'd returned had I touched him in anger.

But I was *pissed*. Disappointed. Devastated.

He crossed his arms. "Trinity."

I couldn't look at him. "What?"

"You are finished pouting."

15

I glared at the ceiling.

"Trinity."

"What?"

"Take the sheet from your body." His voice was stern, and a little cold, but there was no anger.

I hesitated, still upset, still pouting, and I hesitated. Should I make a push to disobey him, if he were planning to toss me out of his house anyway?

A gleam of surprise lit his eyes. "You will obey me. Take the sheet from your body. Now."

My entire body tight with anger, reluctance, and a deep, quick excitement, I grasped the sheet, pulled it off me, and flung it into the floor.

He smiled at my show of temper. "Good girl. Now open your legs for me."

I sucked my bottom lip between my teeth and concentrated hard, for a brief second, on keeping my fangs retracted. I didn't want to puncture my lip. That shit hurt.

He lifted an eyebrow.

Slowly, I bent my legs and let my knees fall open.

His stare caressed my body.

Heat, never far from the surface, burst to life as he trailed a finger over my thigh, and I moaned.

And just that quickly, I forgot my momentary spurt of rebellion. "Master," I said.

"I am pleased, my love. I am so very pleased."

As I was basking in the brightness of his words, he added, more to himself than to me, "You are in there. I see you."

"I am here."

I lay with my legs open and my arms flung over my head, giving him complete access to my body. I wouldn't move until he told me I might. He needed no restraints—his command was the chain that held me.

He ran his hands over my legs, my ribs, my breasts. I arched my back, urging him silently on when he lingered, needing more. Always more.

"Close your eyes, my love. Feel me."

I closed my eyes immediately. Without my sight, my vampire senses were even more intense, and my body tightened, gooseflesh erupting, when I felt his warm breath on my belly.

He didn't undress or climb onto the bed, and I knew there would be no blood this time. He'd fed me only a few short hours ago, though, and I could go longer each day without feeding.

"This time," he said, as though reading my mind, "You will orgasm without feeding."

I wanted the blood. I always wanted the blood. But he soon made me forget that I would be deprived of that delicious magic, because his tongue was creating a different sort of ecstasy.

He didn't touch me with his hands, only his mouth. I couldn't see, because he hadn't given me permission to open my eyes. I concentrated on the feel his mouth between my legs. There was nothing but his probing tongue, his firm lips, his hot breath.

And that was everything.

He brought me to the edge before pulling back, again and again, until the only thing that existed was his mouth on my throbbing, swollen, wet pussy.

He slid his tongue inside me, then wrapped it around my clit before licking me with long, slow strokes until I thought I would go mad from the pleasure of it.

I cried out at the pleasure pain, and he began to do other things with his mouth. His strokes became faster, then he sucked my clit into the warmth of his mouth, then he nipped the bareness of my lips.

And he let me come.

Finally.

I screamed with the pleasure of that release, and even before my voice had stopped echoing through the room, he was shoving me over the edge again.

He made me come until I knew it was no longer

possible for me to climax, and then he showed me how wrong I was by making me come again.

He left me there then, sprawled on the bed moaning and heavy in my own juices, and I did not open my eyes even after he'd gone, because he had not told me I could.

But I didn't need to see. I needed only to wait for him. He would return to me, and he would feed me, and he would fuck me, and I would be complete.

I sighed and sank into the soft, cradling arms of pleasure and dreams, where nothing mattered outside that room.

Nothing mattered outside my world.

And my world was Amias Sato.

Chapter Four

CLOSE ENOUGH

"They want to see you," Amias told me, two nights later. "Our werebull is not a patient man, my love, though he has shown remarkable restraint."

I said nothing, just snuggled deeper into the bed and smiled when he tightened his arms around me.

"He loves you, Trinity," he continued, his voice smooth and calm. "They all do."

"I'm not ready."

"You have a responsibility to them. To Bay Town, the way station, and—"

"I'm not ready."

He sighed. "You don't want to be ready. But this is no life for anyone, and you are physically stronger than you've ever been. It's time."

"I—"

"It's time."

There was a tone to his voice I hadn't heard before. He was done feeling sorry for me. Done feeling guilty for my…brokenness. All of it.

"I love you more than I ever loved life," he said. "I love you with a fierceness that makes me want to die at the thought of hurting you."

"Then don't make me go," I whispered, full of dread and dark, furtive things. "Don't make me go. If you do, I won't ever return to you."

"Sweetheart." His smile was as full of pain and tears as my heart. "You will always return to me, because you cannot do otherwise. My love. It is time to grow up."

He left the bed, despite my clinging arms, and stood waiting for me, his hand out. I wanted to ignore him, but he would have waited forever, my vampire master.

And I could feel it. He was right.

It was time.

I was scared. I wasn't sure what I was scared of, really, but it was time.

"Angus has decided it's my fault you have yet to return to them. He believes my love for you, my desire to protect you, has kept you from growing." He hesitated, then nodded. "He is right. To a point, he is right."

"Feed me first," I said, as I stood trembling in the circle of his strong arms.

"No, darling. Tonight you will stand in the city. You will watch the humans, you will allow humanity to seep back into your bones, you will feel your heart begin to beat with the magic of existence. You will not feed. You will learn control. And you will do this every night until you are…"

"Until I am what, Master?"

"Until you are Trinity."

"How will I know?"

He smiled. "You will know. We will all know."

"I'm not the same, no matter what you teach me. No matter what you make me do. No matter how much I grow, I will not be the same girl who died."

"No," he murmured. "But you will be close enough."

And after he'd dressed me, he walked me from our perfect, protected house, and he stood me on a street corner like a human prostitute and he left me there.

That was the first night I was forced out of the cocoon he'd created for me.

I would become a butterfly.

A butterfly that possessed tattered, scarred wings, fangs, and a taste for blood.

But I would never again be Trinity Sinclair, the girl who'd died.

Because she'd fucking *died*.

"God," I whispered, alone on my corner. "Help me to

care."

Then I laughed, because I did care, didn't I? If I prayed for it, then I cared.

And the humans walked by, tentative smiles and looks of horror and pity and some anger and hatred, and the reporters came, and I stood on my street corner and slowly, I began to grow. To change. To care.

To become Trinity.

Chapter Five

TEMPTATIONS

The city was different.

I wouldn't have known anything about it if Amias hadn't fed me information as he fed me blood. He'd held me in his arms, discussing events of the day and circumstances of the city, attempting to woo me back to life.

The changes had happened almost overnight, and the humans were not the same.

We had the rifters to thank for that. And the demons.

Himself and the supernaturals.

And me, I guess.

The city was different and the world was changing.

Changing once again for the supernats, but not only for them.

I stood on the street corner, unmoving and silent. I ignored the small group of human women as they trooped past me, hiding their giggles behind their hands, their pores releasing the stench of alcohol and cigarette smoke and sweat and food.

Food.

I didn't cry. I would never eat again, but I didn't cry.

The thought of consuming food made me ill.

The humans stopped walking and speared me with slightly drunken, almost shy gazes, and I closed my eyes as the scent of their blood overpowered their other, less appetizing odors.

I was slowly gaining control of myself. Amias had stood me on the street corner for the last two weeks with only one command.

"You will not feed."

I would either obey him, or I would be punished.

I would learn control, because otherwise I was just a feral animal. A parasite.

And I wanted it. I wanted, finally, *finally,* to dig myself out of the deep hole in which I'd hidden since the master had brought me back.

I began to mature rather quickly, now that I was given no choice.

I began to breathe again.

"Are you okay, Trinity Sinclair?" The woman addressed me as they often did since my transformation—by using both my names.

She was young, maybe twenty, her white-blonde hair wispy and clean, her cheeks red, her eyes bright and blue and full of life.

I shuddered and stared over her head, hopeful that my silence would encourage her and her friends to carry on with their night and leave me alone.

They were tempting. So tempting. And I was weak, hungry, and sick. Sick in my new vampire head.

"What's wrong with you?" one of the others asked. "Seriously. If you want a taste…"

Don't do it. Don't do it.

She waved her wrist under my nose, smiling. "Let me buy you a drink."

"We owe you," the first girl said. "The least we can do is feed you."

There was scattered laughter, uncomfortable and tentative. But they liked their fear. They liked their bravery. Their progressiveness.

Not all the humans were so changed, of course, but enough of them were that it made a real difference.

My fangs dropped in response to the aroma of the fresh blood that rushed teasingly beneath her thin skin, the way a starving human's mouth might water at the scent of a tantalizing meal.

The sharp fangs sliced into my tongue and I groaned at

the rich, tangy slide of blood. I didn't bleed much—Amias wouldn't feed me until after my long night of deprivation. Then, just before dawn, he'd draw me into his arms and reward me.

God, that reward.

A familiar figure stepped from the shadows of the alley across the street, waited for a line of cars to pass, then walked toward us.

He was quiet and smooth for such a big man, and the women continued tempting me, unaware a half-giant was right behind them.

"Trinity." His voice was a deep, dark rumble, and the eager humans gave soft squeals of fright and turned to look at him.

"Leo Trask," the blonde said, as though he might not know his own name.

He didn't look at her. Leo didn't often look women in the eye. He was too afraid—too sure—of what he'd see there. "Go on about your business," he told them. "You don't need to be here."

The blonde lifted her chin. "I want to feed her. She died to save us. The least we can do is offer her our blood."

"Another time," Leo said, gently, calmly.

"I think it's up to me," she said, stubborn and brave in her inebriated haze. "And I want her to bite me."

"You have no idea what you're asking for." His voice was a little tighter. He pulled the neckline of his T-shirt down and showed them the jagged, still healing wound on the tender flesh between his neck and his shoulder. "She gave me this the last time I offered to feed her."

I swallowed convulsively as I stared at the forming scar. It didn't matter that he was lying. I smelled the blood of that wound.

And I wanted it.

Unintentionally, Leo was tempting me more than those humans, with their alcohol-laced blood, ever could.

Then he lifted the hem of his shirt and showed the horrified humans the scar across the side of his muscular abdomen. "She gave me this the first time I offered." He grinned, somewhat ruefully. "I have not offered again."

"But—"

"She's too new," he said. "She has no control. She cannot make it good for you like the older vampires can. You have been told this countless times. All the humans have." His face hardened, as did his voice. "You're hurting her. Walk the fuck away."

I trembled. I needed blood. Wanted it. Craved it.

But I wanted my control more.

Amias would be angry that the half-giant was interfering yet again. Leo didn't give a fuck. He was my self-appointed bodyguard and there wasn't a person on earth who could have made him stand down.

The humans did not test him further.

When they were half a block away, Leo turned back to me. "Come home, Trinity," he said, as he always did.

"When he releases me," I replied, as I always did.

"You've been gone for months," he said. "It's time."

I wanted to go home. I could no longer feel the visitors because another caretaker was there to help them.

Himself had appointed one of the vampire elders as caretaker of the way station in my absence, and while I should have been grateful, I was savagely possessive of my home and my station and viciously angry that a vampire elder had taken over.

But no one else could have.

"I'm not strong enough. I…"

"You're afraid of hurting us, I know," he said, bland and calm. "But we can take care of ourselves."

Hunger roared through my body and I put my hands to my ears, as though that might stop it.

Damn you, Amias.

I shuddered. No. I could not go home. Not yet. Amias was the only person in my life who could control me. I

25

would stay with him and only him until *I* became the person in control of me.

I hesitated, then slid my fingers over my chest, pressing lightly over my heart. I wanted to go home. I needed to be with my men.

I smiled at Leo, maybe the first real smile I'd managed since I'd turned, and his face softened. Leo wasn't pretty. His face wasn't pleasant to look at. I'd once heard a human woman say that if Leo were to put a bag over his head, she'd be happy to spend a few hours in bed with him.

No, Leo Trask wasn't a handsome man.

Sometimes though, the truth inside him shone through and he became something no one could ever have seen as less than beautiful.

"You're frozen." His voice was comforting and sure. "But you'll thaw. You'll come back to us, Trinity." His face reddened. "To the way station, I mean."

Then he dropped his gaze and stared at the ground. Leo trusted me, but he didn't quite trust me that much. He was afraid he'd see revulsion in my eyes.

He would never.

Not when I'd been human, and not now that I was turned.

I understood though, because I thought I might now see revulsion in his.

"Thawed," I said. "Maybe. But I'll still be a vampire. I'll still need to eat people."

Once upon a time I'd known what I was. I'd known my place in life. I'd understood myself. I'd been a vampire hunter. A caretaker. A woman tied to a group of men I loved dearly and a town I was born to protect.

Now I was a vampire.

And I had no idea what that meant for me. What would I do? What was my purpose?

"No sign of Shane?" he asked.

Pain streaked through me, stealing my breath, and for a few seconds I was caught up in the intensity of that pain.

"Trinity?"

I focused on Leo's face. "No. No sign of him."

He wanted to touch me, I could see it in his eyes. But he only cleared his throat, backed up a step, and crossed his arms. "He'll come back when he's ready."

I sniffed the air, my body stiffening as I caught a familiar scent. Even more than that, a familiar feeling.

"The master is coming," I murmured. "Go away, Leo."

He didn't hesitate. He jogged away and melted into the shadows, but I knew that no matter what happened that night, or where I went, Leo Trask would be lurking in the darkness, watching out for me.

Chapter Six

TESTED

Amias raked my face with a stare full of glass shards. I almost physically felt his regard, and I shuddered beneath it. His stare was heavy and warm and sharp, trickling over my psyche, cutting into me.

He opened his arms and only then did I move. I stepped into his embrace and wrapped my arms around him, a quiet whine escaping my mouth, and I pressed my face to his warm throat.

"Good," he murmured. "Better."

It had taken me many unsuccessful attempts to maintain control when I was in my maker's arms. I wanted only to be devoured by him. I wanted him to feed me, and I wanted him to bite me.

I wanted to taste him, to hold him, to open myself to him.

And in the beginning, I had cried with my need to be physically part of him. I hadn't dealt well with the horror of that separation.

But I was growing, changing, and becoming—once again—my own person.

Sort of.

"Master," I whispered.

His body trembled. "I will never tire of hearing that."

"Then I will never stop saying it."

His sigh was gentle. "You will, my love. And you will resent me for creating such need, such submission. But as I told you…" He waited.

"I will always be your heart," I said, obediently.

"Yes," he whispered, and kissed my forehead. "You will." He tightened his embrace for one quick second, then set me away from him. "Now. Tell me."

I ignored my need to touch him. That need was huge, but it didn't consume me as it once had.

We both disregarded the few humans who walked by us. They paused, some of them, curious and nosy, but eventually they slipped away, carrying on with their night.

"I was tempted," I told Amias. "I was offered blood. I didn't take it." I lifted my chin. "I'm stronger."

His smile was slow, his dark eyes glittering beneath the streetlights. "You are stronger than you know. I have made many vampires. You..." His smile dropped, suddenly, chilling me.

"What, Master? What's wrong?"

But he only shook off whatever was bothering him and took my hand. "The giant was here again."

I nodded, but said nothing.

"If not for his interference—"

"No," I said, resolute. "I would not have fed. I would not have taken their offers."

"You cannot be tested if he continues to interfere." His voice was full of frustration, and panic tightened my belly as he turned toward the shadows from which Leo watched.

I was afraid Amias would challenge him, and I would be forced to hurt Leo to defend my beloved master. I *would* have. I would kill to protect him—from anyone.

But finally, for the first time, I did not want to.

Amias saw the change in my face. He read the thoughts in my mind as though I'd spoken them aloud. And suddenly, another change grew inside me. I didn't want him to read me. I didn't want my mind to be an open thing through which he might rummage anytime he wanted to pluck a thought from my head.

Yes, I was changing. And part of me grieved to see it.

No bloody tears rose in Amias's eyes, but I felt his emotions as he felt mine. He grieved with me.

"I wanted the return of Trinity," he murmured. "It had

to be. But I mourn what I will lose."

I cried out at the pain in his voice and unable to bear it, I fell to my knees and wrapped my arms around his legs. "I won't leave you," I swore. "I won't ever leave you."

He put his hand on my head, but didn't urge me to stand. He remained silent, and that silence was loud. I was hurting him, and I would rather have died than cause him pain.

"Trinity," someone said, his voice full of gravel. And anger, but not for me. Never for me.

Amias patted my head. "Get up, my love, and greet your raging werebull."

He helped me stand, then we both turned to look at Angus Stark. Angus, my werebull. And Amias was right—Angus was raging.

But when wasn't he?

Angus and I stared at each other for a few heavy seconds until finally, Amias broke the silence. "Two minutes," he said, his voice calm but firm. "You agreed to leave her alone until she was ready for you. And I am not yet comfortable with being the focus of the city humans' attentions."

"I will take as long as I fucking want to take," Angus growled, then calmed himself—with an obvious effort—when I clutched Amias's arm and frowned.

"Angus?" I asked.

"Sweetheart. I—" He rubbed his face. "Are you okay, Trin?"

"I'm getting better," I told him. "Stronger." And then, surprising all three of us, I pulled away from the master and went to Angus.

He hesitated, unsure, then his stare softened as he gazed down into my upturned face. He held me to him, his arms like rigid bands across my back. "God," he groaned. "Trin." He buried his face in my hair.

And more of my resistance, the coldness, the *vampireness*, melted away.

"I'm here," I murmured.

He lifted his face and over my head at Amias. "Did you tell her the executioners are coming?"

"I mentioned it."

"Mention it again," Angus bit out, furious, but his grip remained gentle as he held me. "She needs to come home before the bastards get here."

Their conversation barely touched me. It awakened no curiosity inside me. I didn't worry about executioners, though I knew what it meant that they were coming.

They wanted to kill the dragon.

But right then all I cared about was Angus's warm hands on my body.

I'd needed his touch. I hadn't realized it, but I'd needed it.

Still, my control was not strong. I darted out my tongue to taste his warm, fragrant skin, pressed my fingers to his pulse, and closed my eyes as his blood, his precious, tempting, deliciously fragrant blood, thundered through his body.

Oh, I wanted it.

How I wanted it.

I wanted him.

Not just because I was hungry. Not just because I was a vampire.

But because he was Angus. He was my...

"Alpha," I murmured. "My alpha."

He shuddered and tightened his arms enough to hurt me. "You're back." His voice hurt my heart. "You have your control, don't you?"

"It's coming," I said.

"Trinity." The vampire master grasped my upper arm and urged me away from Angus. "Do not tempt her further, Werebull. It is not time, and she is not ready. She is still changing."

"Stop yanking at her," Angus snarled, "and give us a minute."

31

Amias was worried, and he was reluctant to let me go, but he would not argue with Angus. Despite the anger and fear and worry they felt, they loved each other.

And they loved me.

"Come home, Trin," Angus said, when Amias backed away.

"Soon," I promised. "Right now all I can think about is biting you. I'm not ready."

But he disagreed. "You're thinking about biting me. You're not doing it." He cupped the back of my head and eased my face to his chest. "But if you want to, I will be happy to let you."

"That's not the point," I said, almost unable to get the words out. His smooth flesh was right there under the thin fabric of his shirt, warm and familiar and mine. At that moment, I wanted nothing more than to taste him. My werebull.

He would taste like power. Like domination. He would taste like heaven.

"The point is," he said, his voice rumbling beneath my ear, "that you want to, but you aren't. You're not a wild animal, Trin. Come the fuck home."

My body tightened. His voice was dim, insubstantial, and did nothing to distract me from my cravings. One taste. He'd said I could.

He was mine.

I could eat him if I wanted.

And I wanted.

I turned my head and scraped his flesh with my fangs, not enough to draw blood, but enough to let me know that I was still not fucking ready.

I threw myself away from him. "Go," I muttered, desperate. "Please."

He closed his eyes for a second, but he didn't argue. "Soon then," he whispered, and strode away.

I shook with need. My muscles knotted painfully as I restrained myself from running after him. And in the end,

I would have gone after him.

I would have given in. I would have rushed through the night, thrown him to the ground and ravaged him, attacked him, *drained* him, but for Amias.

Something feral rose inside me, triggered by Angus's scent, by the night, by my unending struggle to grow into something normal.

A low growl floated from between my lips, but even before the sound slithered out, Amias was aware.

I snarled, and the master grabbed me into the unbreakable restraints of his arms and bore me away. In seconds he was slamming me to the ground in an abandoned lot and pressing my baby fangs to his flesh.

"Feed, my love."

He didn't attempt to hide the satisfaction in his voice. I was not ready. Not ready to leave him, not ready to become independent, not ready to stop needing him.

And though he wanted his Trinity back, he was not ready to set me free.

"You're mine," he whispered, and then there was only the sound of my eager sucking as I pulled the master's blood into my mouth.

But dimly, with a distant disconnect, I felt the half-giant, and I knew he'd followed. From the shadows he watched, and waited, and wondered, perhaps, what it would be like to have a woman need him as much as I needed the vampire master.

Chapter Seven

DEAD INSIDE

The next night was the same.

I was hungry, as always, but I would not eat. I would not kill.

I would gain my control.

I would prove myself worthy of once again taking the name Trinity Sinclair, and I would find my place in the society of Red Valley.

A familiar black car pulled to the curb, taking my attention from the noisy, bustling pedestrians. The sleek, purring car glistened with the mist of rain beneath the tall streetlights, and for a second I concentrated on the tightening of my stomach muscles.

It felt strange, almost painful, and distantly familiar. Then I realized I was nervous. Or uncomfortable. Or ashamed, maybe.

Frank Crawford climbed from the back seat, took a moment to murmur something to his driver, and then strode toward me.

The mayor of Red Valley.

Probably something he'd planned for all along. Everything he'd done had been with an eye toward power. Not that I could complain. He was doing good things for not only the humans and his city, but for the nonhumans.

For me.

He put people into positions of authority who had the supernaturals' best interests at heart. The new captain of the police was a woman named Wendy Knight. And she loved supernats. Her girlfriend was a supernat.

They weren't open about it, Amias had told me, but someday they would be.

I hadn't spoken to Crawford since the night of the rifter battle. I hadn't been alone with him. I'd barely looked at him. He hadn't forced the issue. He hadn't even tried to talk to me.

But now there he was.

He stood in front of me, his hands at his sides, calm and quiet. Deep in his gaze was a spark of horror.

I smiled, slowly, to see it.

I wasn't sure why.

He cleared his throat, his gaze flitting from my scars to the tangle of thick hair that hung over my face. "Trinity?"

I simply watched him.

He looked good. The bags under his eyes had shrunk, the lines on his face were softer, and even under the cold streetlights I could see he was less pale. He was even a little less grim.

"I came to see you when Amias…" He hesitated. "When he brought you out of the ground. They wouldn't let me in and I didn't want to insist." He rubbed his chin, then crossed his arms and glanced around the area, probing the shadows with a cop's stare.

He paused on the dark, bulky shadow of the half-giant, who stood watch in the alley across the street. Most people would not have noticed him.

"It's only Leo," I said.

He nodded. "I know." Again, he cleared his throat. "I brought flowers to the master's house," he blurted, then, "Hell, this is awkward."

I said nothing, but the beginnings of a soft curiosity grew inside me.

He clenched his fists. "Are you even in there? Is that you, Trinity?"

I shrugged. "Yes."

He snorted. "Sure it is. I want to tell you I'm glad you're alive. That I missed you. That I'm sorry you had to allow the rifters to tear you to pieces."

We stared at each other, neither of us looking away. "I

wanted to thank you," he continued, his voice soft, "for saving our lives."

"You're welcome."

He shook his head. "Do you care, Trinity? At all? Or are you just…"

"Dead inside?" I grinned.

He went pale and took a small step away from me, unable, perhaps, to understand my insensitivity.

I reached out to touch his arm, but dropped my hand when he flinched.

Guilt and anger flashed through his eyes. "God, Trinity. I'm sorry. Everything you've gone through and I…"

"You aren't hurting my feelings," I assured him.

"Because you don't have any? You stand there smiling and talking and nodding, but your eyes don't change. There's no life in them."

I thought for a second that he might cry, but he straightened his spine and slid his hand into his suit jacket pocket.

"Is this what you want?" he asked. "To live as a vampire?"

"Are you offering to end me?"

"Yes," he whispered.

All around us the night went on as normal, with pedestrians and honking horns and the swish of tires. But suddenly everything else faded and there was only the two of us.

"You can't kill me," I told him, my voice rough. "Not even a hunter could kill me." Then I pressed my fingers to my chest, unsure. How did I know a hunter couldn't kill me? I knew it. Without a doubt, I knew it.

"If I take your heart and your head," he murmured. "You will die."

"If you so much as twitch, I will take *your* head," Leo said, appearing suddenly behind the captain. He wrapped his fingers around Crawford's arm and eased his hand

36

from his pocket. "You won't want to come near her again until you get that shit out of your mind."

Frank held up his hands, both empty. He turned to Leo. "You want her to suffer?"

Leo frowned, puzzled. "She's our Trinity. She's not a zombie you can put down on the street."

I paid little attention to either of them. The night was waning and I had yet to feed. My constant hunger was growing larger. More painful. It wore me down.

Crawford wasn't wrong. I was suffering.

"There's no one in there," Frank said, and they both turned to look at me. "Trinity would never want to be this way. You know she wouldn't."

"She's different." Leo's voice rumbled into the darkness, making me shiver with need. "She'd have to be. But she's still behind those eyes."

A quick spark of anger shot through me. "Shut up, both of you. I'm here, assholes." I thumped my chest. "I'm here."

They looked at each other.

"Assholes," I muttered.

"See?" Leo said. "She'll be fine."

"Yeah," Crawford murmured, unconvinced. And fighting his reluctance, his distaste, even, he reached out to touch me.

And my attention turned from Leo to the captain. To the scent of his humanness, the sound of his blood, the salt in his subtle sweat.

I wanted all of it.

"You should go, Captain," I said. "My control is not good and the only thing I want to do right now is you." I flashed my fangs at him, but I wasn't playing. I wasn't trying to scare him.

I suddenly wanted to bite Crawford more than I'd ever wanted anything.

I was so hungry, and he was so...fresh. His blood would be warm and wonderful as it slid into my mouth, creamy with fear, his pulse fluttering like a bird's wings against my lips. An addict had never needed a fix more than I needed the captain's blood.

Giving myself permission to think about it made it a thousand times more intense.

I wanted his blood, and he was there, teasing me. Tempting me.

"I'm hungry," I murmured.

There was no reason I shouldn't take what I needed. Yes, the master would punish me.

But it'd be worth it.

It would be so worth it.

I reached for the captain.

His eyes widened the second before I touched him, but that wasn't what kept me from getting to him. What stopped me was a scream, a gunshot, and a human falling dead to the pavement across the street.

The half-giant grabbed me into his arms and folded himself protectively over my body as Crawford crouched and reached for a gun that wasn't there.

The drama unfolding around me didn't faze me. Leo's proximity did.

He held me in his arms and I inhaled, pulling his scent deep into my lungs. His smell was…indescribable. It sent shockwaves through my brain and scrambled my thoughts, and even as the few human pedestrians screamed and fled in panic, I struck like a snake, bit into Leo's neck, and began to drink.

Chapter Eight

CROSSROADS

Oh, the taste of him.

I didn't just taste his blood. I tasted *him*. His magic, his power, his sweetness, and there, hiding beneath the rest, I found his darkness.

And it was good.

His blood filled me up, completed me, made me something closer to whole.

I was going to kill him, because I hadn't the strength or sense to stop eating. In his blood was paradise, and I could not stop. Would not.

Leo didn't yell or scream or try to peel me off him. His breath caught, he murmured something unintelligible, and then he cradled me to him. He could no more resist me than I could resist him.

Then something breathtaking happened.

It was as though my maturity clicked into place the very second I pierced his firm flesh with my needle-sharp baby fangs.

Leo couldn't have said no if he'd have wanted to, because my naturally occurring vampire sway was abruptly out of control, and it held him like a flopping fish between a bear's claws.

But then, someone I couldn't shut out or brush off intruded into my hazy, hungry brain.

Amias flew through the night toward me, and though I felt him coming, felt his rage and his worry and his fear, I couldn't pull myself away from Leo's blood.

I wasn't strong enough.

The master was, though.

He tore me away from the half-giant and it was like

ripping a leech off a human's leg. Even before Leo had stopped reeling backward from the shock of the feeding, Amias was flinging me into our house—the very house the city—the *mayor*—had given to him after I'd died.

The guards gathered around us, questioning, sniffing the air, their dislike of me obvious, though they would have given their lives for me—not only because the master demanded it, but because I was their dominant, just as Amias was mine.

They didn't know why. *I* didn't know why. But we all knew it was true.

Amias bore me to the floor and sat half on top of me, his fingers hard against my face as he turned it this way and that, his stare sharp and primal. "You are unhurt." And then, before I could open my mouth to answer, he barked, "You fed."

"I was hungry. Get the fuck off me."

He jerked back in shock. "What?"

It was such a human thing for him to say that I wanted to laugh. I didn't dare. I softened my voice. "I'm okay. I'm fine."

But he continued to stare at me, and finally, I realized what he already understood. "I'm back," I said. "Amias, I'm back."

His expression didn't change. "Do not call me Amias. Call me master."

I curled my lip. "Get off me before I put you through the wall."

"Fuck," he said.

I did laugh then, but with tenderness.

Despite myself, I wanted to cling to him. I wanted him to carry me to the bedroom and undress me, to take me to a place where there was no fear or responsibility or uncertainty. A place where I was okay. A place of comfort.

I wanted to.

I didn't.

It was time for me to return to the city, Bay Town, and

the way station.

It was time for me to return to my men.

"It's what you wanted," I murmured. "I'm Trinity."

Amias lowered his forehead to mine. "You are," he agreed, but he sounded like I'd died.

Like he'd lost me.

And in a way, he had.

I turned my face and pressed my lips to his cheek. "I love you," I whispered. "And I need you. That won't change just because I've transitioned."

He rubbed his lips over mine, urging them open, then slid his tongue inside my mouth to taste the memory of Leo's blood.

I wondered if he realized that something in the half-giant's blood had pulled me from the dark quicksand. And I wondered, for a second, if he would take umbrage.

But I was too full of life and energy and satisfaction to care. Leo's blood sang through me, and it felt better than anything I'd ever known.

I certainly wasn't going to tell Amias that.

He stood, finally, offering me a hand up.

"I almost got clipped by some asshole's wild bullet," I said.

Amias smiled, but there was only death in his eyes. He turned to his guards. "Find him."

They nodded and disappeared through the doorway, and one of the vampires rushed to close the door behind them.

"I have to go home," I told him, abruptly urgent. "I've been away for too long."

He didn't move. "Yes."

"Will you come with me?"

He shook his head slowly, not taking his stare from mine. "You will go alone to reunite with the group and reacquaint yourself with…" He shrugged. "With your future. I will be here when you need me." He ran his fingers over my cheek. "And you will need me. Do not be

41

stubborn when the time comes."

I frowned. "Of course not."

He opened his arms. "Let me have one moment before you go. A moment that is only mine."

I stepped into his arms. "I am yours."

But I was different, and we both knew that.

It was like I'd been trapped in a thick, endless fog for decades, and had just found my way out. But I loved Amias Sato. I loved him with an ancient, consuming passion that went beyond a woman's love for a man. He was inside me. He'd brought me back. He was my maker. And that would not end just because I could walk away.

I had things to do. I had to let the supernaturals know I was no longer imprisoned inside my vampire head. I had to find Shane. I had to contribute to the quickly changing city, court the humans, protect the vampires. I had to make sure the executioners didn't get to Rhys.

Most of all, I had to be with my men.

I realized something that sent a trickle of unease through me. I *wanted* to care more than I actually cared. I needed to feel something. I needed to feel alive. With Leo's blood inside me, I did.

It was more of an excitement, an eagerness to experience everything as a vampire, a craving to taste more than just Amias. More, even, than just Leo.

I drew back and searched the master's familiar black gaze. "It wasn't because I was turned that things were so bad with me—that I was lost and undeveloped and regressive. It wasn't just because I'm a vampire."

He said nothing, but his eyes wavered.

"Amias. Please."

"No, my love." He closed his eyes. "You're not only a vampire."

"What…" I cleared my throat and tried again. "What am I?"

"You know, but I will say it anyway. You were bitten by rifters. You've been turned by rifters. I am not your only maker."

He was right. I'd known. All the vampires had sensed it, which was why they looked at me with such distaste, even as they held me in esteem.

Amias tugged on a coarse hank of hair that snaked over my cheek. "Rifter hair," he whispered.

I left him, then. I rushed from the house and through the city, marveling at my awareness, my strength, my speed. I should have been devastated and broken and enraged because I'd died, because I was no longer human, because I was a vampire, for God's sake, a fucking vampire…

And even worse than anything else, I was a savage, horrifying rifter.

But I was not upset. I was not human enough to be upset.

And Leo…

Leo had yanked me from the fog.

The half-giant would be mine.

He just didn't know it yet.

Too soon, I stood outside the way station, softly swirling snowflakes sticking in my hair, and stared at the house.

They were in there. My men.

The werebull, the freed hunter, the dragon.

And Leo.

Leo was in there.

He was going to feel something about me, about what I'd done to him. I'd attacked him, had taken his blood without asking.

No matter what he said, he was going to be affected by that.

Light poured from uncovered windows, as though they'd thought I wouldn't find my way back otherwise. Strangely reluctant to go inside, I continued to stand there, watching.

Once I walked through those doors, there was no

going back.

Once I went inside the way station, I was going to take my rifter to the men, to the path wanderers, to the city. And the small part of human that remained rebelled against that. Because I was afraid I would hurt them.

I would hurt them all, in the end.

I was a vampire woman full of darkness.

And I was about to take it to them.

I strode across the yard and up the porch steps, and I flung open the door.

"Honeys," I called. "I'm home!"

Chapter Nine

STORM

They'd been gathered in the kitchen, of course. I heard the sharp sounds of chairs scraping the floor, then heavy footsteps as the men I loved rushed to greet me.

Angus was the first one through the doorway. "Trin," he bellowed, and yanked me into his massive arms.

Clayton and Rhys reached us a second later and I found myself looking around for Shane before I remembered that Shane had fled.

Leo hung back with Jin the Jikininki.

I closed my eyes and pressed against the three warm bodies holding me. I was where I belonged. Undead or not, I was incomplete without them.

"She's not the same," Jin said suddenly, his voice strident and accusing. "She came back as something ev—"

Rhys drew back, just a little. "Shut the fuck up, man."

I kept my eyes closed, unconcerned, concentrating on what I would feel, what I *could* feel.

Jin wasn't telling me anything I didn't already know.

They wrapped me up in their arms, holding me so tightly I couldn't breathe, but I didn't need to breathe. I only needed to be.

Finally, they released me.

"It's like I just woke up," I said.

Angus snagged my hand, then squeezed my fingers. He smiled, but his stare was sharp and serious. Probing.

All of them wondered if their Trinity was really inside the familiar body.

"You shouldn't have come here alone," Leo said.

"Don't worry, Leo. They can't hurt me with their guns and they can't catch me with their stakes."

45

Even if they did manage to stake me, not even that would kill me, unless they did as the captain had threatened to do and deprived me of my head and heart.

And at the very least, I'd make them work for it.

"Things will be okay now," Rhys murmured. "I have to say, love, that disappearing right after I won my freedom to have sex wasn't very nice of you." But there was no smile in his voice.

And I flashed suddenly to the night I sat atop his back, the dragon's back, wind screaming past my ears as he carried me to the island. To my death.

In his eyes was the same memory, dressed in guilt and sorrow.

"No," I murmured. I touched his cheek. "We all did what we had to do. No more guilt."

He grabbed my fingers and pressed his lips to them. "Trinity," he whispered. "I still need to say I'm sorry. I need you to know."

"I do know." I caught them all in my gaze. "And I know the world is a better place because we cared enough to change it."

"We killed you," Angus said, his voice rusty and full of pain. "We let you die."

"It was always meant to be," I told him. "And I'm here. Because of all of you. Right now. This moment is what we have." I hesitated. "But Jin's right. I'm not the same."

Angus shrugged. "We're all changed, Trin."

Clayton patted Blacklight, the sword forged from Miriam. "What happened to Silverlight?"

"I don't know," I told him. "If she's still inside me, I no longer feel her. I can't call her."

"You're home," Leo said. "And that's all that matters. The rest will sort itself out."

I looked at him then, my gaze going to his neck. "Did I hurt you?"

He looked everywhere but at me. "No."

"What happened?" Angus asked, frowning.

"I bit him." My voice was calm but excitement swirled inside me at the memory. I wanted to do it again. I wanted his taste in my mouth, my memory, my body. Wanted it, because I'd never felt anything like it—not even in the master's blood. "He's the reason I came back."

Leo did look at me then, surprise in his eyes. "What?"

"Your blood..." I shook my head. "I don't know. It did something to me. It made me well. It made me whole." I shrugged. "As whole as I'm going to be, I think."

"You're cold," Jin said, unable, it seemed, to keep his mouth shut. "Your coldness will continue to grow as your humanity shrinks."

I knew what he meant. I could feel it. "My softness is gone."

He nodded, his stare on the floor. "But you cannot be soft and lead the vampires."

"I'm not leading them. That's what the master is for. That's what the council is for." I looked around. "Speaking of the council, where's the elder Himself replaced me with?"

"He's in Willow-Wisp," Clayton said. "Now that you're back, he can return to his place with the council." He didn't add, *"I hope,"* but it was there in his eyes.

"Is he an irritation?" I asked.

"He's a vampire elder," Angus answered.

I frowned, confused. "So?"

"So he believes the supernaturals are part of the vampires, and therefore under his thumb," Rhys said. "He's extremely..."

"Bossy," Leo said. "And the supernaturals will never allow a *vampire* to rule them." Then he blanched as he realized what he'd said. As he realized he was openly contemptuous about the very creature I'd become.

"I see," I said.

"I didn't mean it that way," he told me. "I didn't mean you."

"It's not the same," Angus said. "You're not—"

"I'm a vampire," I interrupted. "And we all have things to get used to." I patted my pocket. "I'm going to need a cell phone."

"Trinity." Clayton squinted at me, unsure. "Are you truly not traumatized by the fact that you're now one of the undead?"

And they wondered if I had allowed myself to think about the horror of being torn to pieces by rifters, of sacrificing myself, my humanness, for the city.

I shrugged. "Guys, I'm fine. I'm no longer human. I'm not going to cry over my circumstances. I'm *immortal.*" I looked around at all of them, showing them my truth. "I won't have to leave any of you. I'll live forever. I'm a powerful woman. What's there to be upset about?"

I'd experienced life as a human—a weak, puny, ineffectual, vulnerable human—and I'd experienced the despair of a vampire's afterlife. Both those things would make a person appreciate the hell out of life as a vampire.

As they frowned at me, realizing I really *wasn't* the same as the old, emotional Trinity, the girl they'd had to handle with such care, I heard the crunch of tires on the way station driveway.

"Someone's coming," I said.

Someone was bringing news to the way station, and I knew without a doubt that it wasn't going to be good news.

I felt it in my strong, cold vampire bones.

Jin rushed to open the door and peer out into the night. "It's a friend."

He was right. Alejandro Rodríguez slipped through the doorway, his stare going straight to me.

"Alejandro." I held out a hand to him, but he ignored the hand and pulled me with unflinching joy into his arms.

"I'm so glad you're back," he said, a smile in his voice.

"You're not disgusted," I realized.

He drew back, his eyebrows high. "I'm never disgusted by heroes. I'm humbled by them. And I'd be honored if you'd accept me as your human assistant."

I squeezed his hand. "The honor would be mine. Thank you, Al."

Rhys clapped him on the back. "Good to see you, man, but I get the feeling you're not here to welcome our girl home."

Alejandro sobered, squeezed my hand, and nodded. "The executioners that were being sent to Red Valley? They'll be arriving soon." He looked at Rhys. "We need to prepare for the storm that's coming with them."

Chapter Ten

RESURRECTION

Fear, immediate and sharp, flooded the room. It tasted like metal on my tongue, and for a moment, dizziness overwhelmed me.

It wasn't *my* fear, though. It was the fear, knowledge, and unending horror that took up residence in a supernatural's soul at birth and never left.

My hyperawareness was excruciating.

But it dimmed as I swayed on my feet, and I eagerly shoved it away and grabbed huge handfuls of the cold hardness I preferred and wrapped it around my heart.

Being a vampire wasn't all fun and games.

"Killers," Clayton murmured.

"Mercenaries," Rhys said, and when I narrowed my eyes and looked at him, he refused to meet my stare.

"Little bitches," Angus said, but his voice was raw.

There were always going to be covert, top secret, dark and dangerous government organizations. One of them—probably a branch of Homeland Security, though that was not known for certain by anyone other than the government—took it upon themselves to declare certain supernaturals a threat to humankind.

Those supernaturals were executed, caught and used as weapons, kept alive for the curiosity of scientists, or, if the stories were true, sold to wealthy humans with dark agendas.

That branch of human government had sent people after the dragon.

"They won't get Rhys," I said.

"Who knows the dragon's identity?" Al asked. "Besides

the people in this room, of course."

"Crawford," Angus said. "Most of the vampires."

"The vampires are not a risk," I said. "But Crawford might be."

They looked at me.

"Would you kill Crawford to keep me safe, Trinity?" Rhys asked, a curious glint in his eyes.

"Absolutely," I replied, without hesitation, and did not miss the quick, furtive glance the supernaturals exchanged.

Al frowned. "It'll take time," he told them.

There was nothing I could do about their worry. They'd have to get used to me, just as I'd have to get used to me.

"Apparently I'm not very sweet," I said.

Jin snickered. "No," he agreed.

"Which group?" Angus asked.

Alejandro's expression didn't change when he spoke, but his eyes did. "Mikhail Safin and his crew."

"I thought they were chasing down a witch in Europe," Angus said. And there was something in his voice that I could barely comprehend.

Fear. There was fear in my werebull's voice.

"They were," Alejandro told him. "For nearly two years. But they caught her, and they're back."

"Darkness," Jin whispered, and his hissing voice made me shudder.

Rhys put his hands on his hips and turned up his lip. "I am the darkness," he said. "My dragon will burn them all."

And for a moment, Rhys's inner assassin peeked out and I wasn't the only stone-cold killer in the room.

I gave him a wink when he looked at me, and he took a step back.

I shook my head, disgusted.

Angus took out his cell and stared unseeingly down at it, and I understood why he was so very afraid.

His children.

They'd walked through hell. And it only ever got worse.

"They're government sanctioned," Leo said, his voice calm but concern in his eyes. "And somewhat leashed. They don't come in to take out every supernatural they see."

"One is too many," I said.

And though I didn't feel fear the way I once had, it was there, in the pit of my stomach. I was being affected by their dread, and I was suddenly afraid for all of them.

Darkness really was coming.

And we might not be able to stop it. Not this time.

"I'm *afraid*," I whispered, with something close to amazement.

Angus pulled me into his arms. "I'll protect you, Trin."

"We all will." Clayton caressed Blacklight's hilt.

I didn't explain to them that I wasn't afraid for me, because I didn't want them to think I saw them as weak and vulnerable.

I wanted Amias. I could have called to him. I could have opened my mind, reached through the distance of the dark night, and let him know I needed him.

Instead, I sighed and reached out a finger to touch Clayton's mystical sword. To touch the demons' magic. To touch Miriam.

And with that touch, something screamed to life inside me.

It was like an attack. It was like my legs had been hacked off and I was left bleeding and agonized on the floor. It was like someone cut open my chest and chopped my heart into hamburger with a sharp wooden stake.

Silverlight was waking up.

I reeled away from the men, blind to all but the redness of my pain, my cries guttural and unthinking as I was battered by my magical, beloved sword. Silverlight was a part of me I could not exist without—yet I was. Or had been.

"What's happening?" one of the men shouted.

His voice was strange and distant and unfamiliar.

She was waking up inside me and she was…

She was everything.

I screamed, but the sound was only in my mind. And the awfulness was replaced by something worse—death. Hatred. Rage like I'd never known.

Those things battled themselves inside me, and it took me too long to understand the truth.

The vampire was battling the silver and the rifter was battling the vampire. I was tearing myself to pieces.

And Silverlight was coming.

She was transforming, rising from her death.

And surely I could not survive the resurrection.

Coldness surrounded me, suddenly and inexplicably, then sank inside me. I was frozen. I was ice.

I was dead.

I was *dead.*

But Silverlight was not. And she needed out of that death.

So she came. No matter what her return would do to me, she came.

When she finally expelled herself from the confines of my body and was no longer part of me, she blazed with a power so fierce that she blew out the living room windows.

She didn't shrink and her light didn't deaden, even when she finally quieted. She flew into my grip and I closed my fingers convulsively around her huge, warm hilt. My pain eased.

The vampire inside me had felt the agony of the silver, but the rifter had embraced it.

The rifter won.

Silver did not hurt me.

And Silverlight was once again mine.

I had a feeling I was going to need her to deal with Mikhail Safin and his executioners.

I opened my eyes to find myself on the floor and everyone gathered around me, their eyes a little wide, faces tight with concern.

I squeezed Silverlight. "I'm going to need a sheath."

"Well," Leo said. "Trinity's back."

Chapter Eleven

MINE

Rhys wouldn't run, and he wouldn't hide out until the executioners gave up and found another city to torment and another power to capture or extinguish. He wanted to be where he could help protect the city and the supernaturals.

We just had to make sure Safin didn't discover his identity—and that meant Rhys would once again be forced not to shift into his dragon.

He could shift into anything else—literally—but he couldn't call his dragon.

He wanted to. He wanted to shift and fly and burn. It was a longing that shone from him like the hidden beauty of Leo's face.

We'd all moved into the kitchen to discuss the executioners, except for Clayton. He'd pulled his phone from his pocket and walked outside without a word to any of us.

It was almost as though I'd never left. The comforting familiarity of talks in the kitchen with my men warmed me. There was safety in the kitchen, and there was love.

A memory of my men surrounding me, touching me, *filling* me flashed into my mind and I shivered, then rubbed at the gooseflesh on my arms. Oh, if I could go back to that time...

I shook off the memory and put my attention on Rhys. "If the time comes when you need to run, you will run."

We stared at each other silently, neither willing to back down.

"You can't risk your life," I said, finally, softly. "Even if they don't kill you outright, they'll capture you and hand you over to…" I shuddered. Covert government organizations were the deepest, darkest fear of supernaturals. "You can't risk it."

Rhys's dark stare softened. "They will never take me, love."

"They have ways." I told him. I looked at Angus. "Tell him, Angus."

But Angus shook his head. "No, Trin. If Rhys doesn't want to run, he won't run. We won't let the bastards force him out of his home. We'll fight them. We'll always fight."

"I hate this." My voice was sharp and I clenched my fists hard to keep myself from punching—and breaking—the table. Silverlight lay gleaming and deadly in front of me and I wanted to snatch her up, run to meet the executioners, and slice them all to pieces.

The urge to kill was as intense as my urge to feed, and I was still not strong when it came to self-control. The need battered my brain, overwhelming me with its sudden fierceness. Eat and kill. That's what a rifter was created to do.

I trembled with dark bloodlust and deep hunger and slid my fingers around Silverlight's hilt. I would find them, and I would destroy them.

I would *eat* them.

Al's calm voice pulled me back from the edge.

"You don't want to go after them, Trinity. They'll be coming to you soon enough. Right now there's a chance they'll nose around, smash a few heads, find nothing, and leave again."

None of us believed that. The executioners' reputation preceded them.

I squeezed Silverlight and forced down my need to kill something evil. To kill something.

Control.

I would maintain control. Build it, strengthen it, own it.

And for that moment, I succeeded.

"No one saw who became the dragon," I said, finally.

"He wasn't here for long. He left, and we haven't seen him since."

They nodded. It was a simple story we'd all stick to when the executioners came with their questions.

Clayton walked into the kitchen and sat down across from me. "Tonight, rumors will begin that the dragon was sighted in China. It'll be glimpsed in a dozen other places over the next week. The executioners will hear."

I nodded. "Good. And if that doesn't work, we'll kill them all."

They watched me silently, and it took me a minute to realize they were a little shocked at my coldness. And maybe they were a little sad, but that couldn't be helped. I wasn't their little bloodhunter princess anymore. They might as well get used to it.

I stood. "I'm going to talk with the elder, then stand inside Willow-Wisp and watch the sun arrive before I sleep." Oh, God, how I wanted to see the sun. For three months I'd lived in darkness, and now I wanted the sun. I wanted it more than just about anything.

Angus stood as well. "We built you a protected room in the basement. It's shielded from the sun and requires a code to enter. It's also as hidden as we could make it. Unless someone knows what to look for, they won't find it."

Sleeping was the most vulnerable time for a vampire. Hunters could stake a girl while she slept, and she'd only know she was dead when she woke up in the despair.

I put my hand to my chest. "You knew I'd come back."

He stared down at me, unsmiling. "Of course we knew, Trin."

And something other than hunger or the cold blackness of evil flared to life inside me. It was weak, but it was there. And the more I thought about it, the stronger it grew. It wasn't just the fierce protectiveness I naturally felt for my men. It was the connection we'd had from the very beginning.

It was deep, true love.

Confusing to a rifter, but completely consuming to a vampire. People thought vampires had no heart. But that was wrong. They were *all* heart.

Poor bastards.

And I felt love. True fucking love.

I was a rifter, and I would need that coldness, that power, but I was also a vampire. And I could love.

"God," I whispered, and reached up to touch his face. "I love you, Angus Stark. I *love* you."

He did smile then, a tiny smile, his eyes crinkling at the corners. "I know, girl."

"I don't know who I am anymore," I murmured. "But I know I love you." I looked around, grabbing them all in my hungry gaze. "All of you."

When I looked at Leo, his stare was on the floor.

Al cleared his throat, then headed for the door. "We'll be watching the way station."

"Al," I said. "When do you think they'll arrive?"

"Maybe a week." He didn't stop walking. "I'll let you know when they're spotted. Rhys, Jade wanted a few words."

Rhys nodded, then gave me a quick kiss. "I can't tell you how happy I am that you're back, Trinity."

"Me, too," I murmured, and watched him follow Al from the room.

"You have a couple of hours before dawn." Clayton stood and walked to me. He ran his fingers down my arm, then took my hand. I was caught for a second on an immediate sting of lust, but my body must have been confused, because my fangs dropped into position. I ran my tongue over the sharp edges, shuddering with hunger.

Leo's blood was still inside me so it wasn't really that kind of hunger. It was just the hunger to taste my men. The hunger for sex. For warm, hard cocks and eager tongues and familiar touches.

The seductive scent of arousal hit my nostrils, slid into

my brain, and dropped to the suddenly wet and ready place between my legs.

Not the scent of my own arousal, but the scent of theirs.

"Shit," I whispered. I closed my eyes as my fingers tightened convulsively around Clayton's. Unable to resist, I took my hand from his and pressed my palm against the front of his pants. I gripped and rubbed the bulge straining beneath the fabric.

"Mine," I murmured. "Mine."

His body jerked and he groaned, a sound that bumped up my excitement to a whole other level. I wanted to devour him. I wanted to devour all of them.

I craved blood with an incomprehensible need, but at that moment, neither my longing for the sun nor my thirst for blood could compete with my hunger for scorching hot supernatural sex.

My control was gone.

"Trin," Angus said, his voice soft and caressing. "God, I missed you."

The half-giant strode from the room, his footsteps heavy and somehow grim as Angus and Clayton began to give me a proper welcome home.

Chapter Twelve

BONDING

I wanted to call Leo back. I wanted to taste his blood while I fucked Angus. I wanted to bite him as I sank down onto Clayton's hardness. I wanted to lap up his sweet, strange power while Rhys showed me what he'd dreamed of doing to me.

But Leo wasn't ready to come to me and Rhys was occupied with Alejandro and Jade.

And Shane was gone.

I made a quick mental note right then and there. I was done waiting for Shane Copas. I was going after my hunter, and I was bringing him home.

Whether he wanted me to or not.

Later, though. Much later. Right now, there were two men about to make my brain explode with pleasure, and there was no room for anything else.

I couldn't get enough of touching them, tasting them. I wanted to devour them even as I wanted to stretch out on the floor, close my eyes, and lie like the dead as they swarmed over my body.

They took me to the basement, to the secure room they'd created for me, because before we were finished, dawn would come. And I would rather not have burst into flames with one of them inside me.

I wasn't the only one whose need was extreme.

We'd been deprived of each other for too long, and a connection such as ours was never meant to be severed. Not even for a little while.

Angus was right—no one would find the hidden room if they didn't know to look for it. Clayton kicked a switch hidden behind a panel near the floor, then pressed his palm against the wall at waist level. A numerical pad was hidden behind that small section, and he punched in what seemed like a dozen numbers.

"Derry's birthday," Angus took time to murmur, then went back to kissing my neck.

Derry was his daughter, and I knew well her birthday, but his lips were distracting me so much I couldn't remember.

After Clayton put in the code, another panel slid open, and I had to duck to get through it. Once we were inside, Angus pressed a button beside the door, and it shut with a quiet, solid *thunk*.

The room contained a huge bed, a mini fridge, a desk, and a small, doorless alcove which held a shower and a toilet. There were no windows. A tall floor lamp shoved back the darkness and a thick area rug relieved the cold hardness of the concrete floor.

It was perfect. I'd be safe there.

I placed Silverlight on the desk and turned eagerly to Clayton and Angus.

Angus lifted me and placed me on the platform bed, and then my two hot, passionate, sexy men climbed into bed with me.

When I'd been human, no matter how much sex I had or with how many men I'd had it, there was always some sort of low-level hang up. A subtle feeling, even if I hadn't really been aware of it, that the type of sex I was having was sort of...*wrong*.

That feeling was gone. And it was only because of its complete absence that I realized it'd been there at all.

In its place was heat and eagerness.

I wanted to do every bad thing I could think of.

Mostly, I wanted it done to me.

In the dark distance of my mind, I felt the master's sorrow.

I kicked off my boots as I ripped Clayton's shirt open, unable to wait to feel his smooth skin against my palms.

Angus took my lips and I kissed him with greedy abandon, licking off the blood when my fangs cut his lip.

Both men were as eager as I was—neither had fucked anyone for the three months I'd been absent—and there would be no taking it slow.

None of us were in the mood for foreplay.

I wrapped my fingers around Angus's rock-hard cock and squeezed, and he groaned into my mouth.

Blood and sex.

There was absolutely nothing else.

Not for me. Not then.

Clayton snaked an arm around my waist from behind me, then grabbed my hair and pulled my mouth from Angus's so he could kiss me, and the second he did, Angus lay down, grabbed my hips, and set me atop him. He speared me with his hardness and for a second I thought that maybe he was too big, maybe I couldn't take him, maybe it was going to hurt a little.

I gasped into Clayton's mouth at the exquisite pain, and then Angus was thrusting up into me and I shuddered at the almost unbearable pleasure of it.

I needed more, always more—more feeling, more pain, more pleasure, and Clayton seemed to sense it. As Angus held my hips in a punishing grip and shoved his hugeness into me, Clayton bit my shoulder.

At the sharp pain of the bite my body went limp. I liked it rough. Oh, so much. Clayton muttered, "Fangs," and I had a millisecond to retract those damaging teeth before he grabbed my head and yanked me forward, shoving his dick past my lips and into my mouth.

If Angus hadn't held me so fiercely, pinning me in place with his thrusting cock, Clayton might have yanked me off the hot mountain of the werebull's body.

I gobbled Clayton's dick like I was starving, but I needed him to come. I needed to taste him, to drink him, to get him off, because more than I wanted to suck him, I wanted to bite him.

He climaxed abruptly, ejaculating with such force that I could barely swallow fast enough. Even before the last groan was out of his mouth, I tore myself from Angus, flipped Clayton to his back, and fell upon him with a hunger I had no way of controlling.

On my knees, I leaned over Clayton's body, wiggled my ass in invitation to Angus, and bit into Clayton's groin.

I knew what it would do to him. The ecstasy of that bite would linger, making him come when he touched it. The same thing had happened to me the first time Amias had bitten me.

And it was heaven.

Angus didn't wait. He got to his knees, slapped my ass—hard—then once again shoved his hugeness into me. I clenched around him, wet and hot and eager.

I bit Clayton.

With Clayton's blood hitting my throat and Angus's cock thrusting into me, hard and fast, I climaxed so fiercely that there was a breathless moment of nothing. Then a wave of pleasure roared through me and spilled out of me, and I was quite sure every single one of my men, there or not, would be taken by the overflow of that vast, consuming pleasure.

We were connected, and they would feel it.

They would be part of it.

The master, who'd refused to interfere with my first night back home.

Rhys, whose absence was perhaps lucky, because the executioners were coming and sex would likely bring his dragon, and he would sprint from the house and light up the sky with his screams and darkness and enormous power, and they would hear, those horrible executioners.

Even Leo, for his blood was inside me. My bite was part of him. He might not understand exactly what he was feeling, but he would feel it. He would climax, his cock in his hand, me on his mind, and he would wonder, perhaps, what the hell was happening.

And Shane, miles away, holed up in some dark, angry place, would feel it. Would feel me.

I'm coming for you, Shane Copas.

And as I climaxed, and climaxed again, and again, and again, I kept an image of my hunter in my mind, and he was there with me.

I'm coming for you.

I felt his resistance.

But his resistance would not matter.

He was coming home.

Chapter Thirteen

HUNGER

Seconds before dawn came, I slipped into sleep.

I didn't dream—I didn't think vampires *could* dream—but on the fringes of my mind lingered the perfection of that night.

It was like the blink of an eye. One minute I was sinking into darkness and the next, I was fully awake and ready to take on the night.

I sat up, my first thought on eating. The men had left as I'd slept. When I'd lived with the master, I would awaken every single night to find him watching me.

He would feed me seconds after I opened my eyes, except for after he'd decided to start standing me alone in the city to teach me control. Waking up without him felt wrong.

And I didn't like it at all.

I was covered with blood and sex. I took a shower, and when I stepped from the shower to peer into the mirror above the small sink, my gaze wandered curiously but dispassionately over my scars, and I wondered what the guys had thought of my marked face and body.

I'd had scars before, but not like the ones I now possessed. The rifters had torn me up. Still, most of the scars were silver and thin and swirly, almost pretty, maybe, decorating my face and body. They told the story of everything that had happened to me.

They were part of me, and I didn't mind them. Trinity the human would have. Trinity the vampire did not.

Amias had kissed every single one of those scars, even

the ones he'd given me when I'd been human. Especially those.

"Master," I whispered, morose.

It was too quiet, and I was too alone.

Hunger had taken up residence in my brain during my sleep, and when it hadn't been satisfied after I'd awakened, it began to grow. There were things I'd have to get used to, now that I was back in the real world.

Some of my clothes had been transferred from my bedroom to the sleeping room, and I dressed hurriedly, eager to leave the confines of my basement grave. I needed to greet the moon, to embrace the night, to feed.

Most of all, I needed to see Amias.

I rushed up the stairs, through the house, and to the one place I knew I'd find a warm body. The kitchen.

I placed Silverlight on the countertop. "Hello."

Jin peered into the oven, from which the rich scent of cooking meat wafted, and he barely glanced at me. "Good evening," he said.

Clayton sat at the table, reading something on his phone, unsmiling and serious as always. He stood and I walked into his embrace with a sigh, then buried my nose against his throat. I inhaled the vanilla scent of him. The cake scent.

But now, there was something even more appetizing mixed in with the cake. Blood.

"Mmm," I murmured, and touched my tongue to his skin. "You smell good, and you taste even better."

"Hungry?" he asked, and I didn't have to look at him to know he smiled. And he wasn't awkward in the least. There'd been no real introductory phase. No dark times when they had to get to know Trinity the vampire. It was as though I'd always been the person I'd returned as.

"Not here," Jin demanded, damn persnickety for a man who ate corpses.

I ignored him and concentrated on Clayton.

My belly tightened with anticipation. Hunger churned

through my body like an angry river, consuming everything in its path.

And then I was just the ravenous undead.

Clayton's body was like a warm loaf of bread, and his blood was the mouthwatering stew in which I wanted to dip it.

My appetite had taken over, and the man I loved was nothing more than walking, breathing food.

I drew back my lips and prepared to pierce his flesh, my mind empty of all thoughts but eating. It was that consuming. That important.

That *good*.

Then the door flew open and Amias yanked me from the hunter.

"No, my love, my greedy love. Your night will begin with your master."

I wrapped my arms around his neck and he carried me out of there. One second I was in the kitchen, Jin's annoyed voice beating the air like ineffectual butterfly wings, and the next I was inside Willow-Wisp. I rode Amias to the ground and straddled him, my mouth already forming a seal around his skin, pulling in the one thing a vampire needed to thrive.

His blood carried the essence of the woman who'd fed him last, and a hot streak of jealousy competed with my hunger.

That was something I'd need to get over. I was possessive of all my men, but Amias had to eat, and he could not always eat me. I was the servant, he was the master. He could be my only food source—at least for a while—but I could not be his.

That time, my jealousy lingered.

Amias shoved my pants over my hips and pushed his hand between our bodies, sliding a finger inside me. I moaned as I fed but didn't try to help him as he freed his cock, grabbed my hips, and shoved himself inside me.

He thrust into me and the familiar routine of fucking

and feeding from my master finally shoved everything else from my mind.

There was excitement in that encounter, but there was also comfort. I didn't realize how much I'd needed it until it was over and I was lying wrapped in his arms.

"I didn't like waking up without you," I told him, lacing my fingers with his.

"You did well." He kissed me, gently. "I wish you needed me as much as you believe you do."

"Amias. I—"

"I will go now," an unfamiliar voice said.

I gave a startled shriek but Amias didn't react. He'd known someone was there, of course, would have heard the man approaching.

For some reason, I'd been blissfully unaware that an audience of one was watching.

"Son of a bitch," I said, sitting up. "Who..."

But the second I glimpsed him, I recognized him. Deep in my vampire brain, I knew him.

The vampire elder.

I grabbed my jeans off the ground, unable to take my stare from the ancient power who crouched a few yards away, his faded eyes holding a grim sort of interest.

"Bring her," the old man told Amias, and then he floated to his feet and just...disappeared.

He was that fast.

I looked at Amias. "Did that just happen?"

The master's face was completely blank. His eyes didn't hold so much as a spark. I understood that he'd shut down. I didn't understand why.

"What's wrong?" I asked him, as he got to his feet and straightened his clothes.

He didn't look at me. "Nothing is wrong."

But I could feel his fear.

"Why does he frighten you so much?" I was genuinely curious. "Can he hurt you?"

He gave a sharp bark of laughter. "Oh, my darling. The

elders are back, and though they are taking some time to settle into their places, they are very, very powerful. And very old. They rule the vampires." He looked at me expectantly.

"Yeah?" I said. "So? Himself rules the supernaturals, but they don't shrink away from him or fear the very thought of facing him." I frowned at him. "I feel your fear, Amias. I don't like that he scares you."

"Not just fear, Trinity."

There was the slightest note of impatience and disapproval in his voice, as though he disliked that I hadn't grasped the situation. As though I'd insulted him by pointing out his fear.

He took my hand and led me in the direction the elder—I assumed—had gone.

I said nothing, just waited for him to continue as we walked.

"It is respect," he said. "And the knowledge of what they can do to those who break the rules they've set for us. It is the realization of what is to come, what will be."

While the elders had been occupied with the rifters, the vampires had lost their guidance, their rules, their place in society. They'd been left unmoored and had drifted quickly into the dark waters of a human's world. They'd become hated creatures the humans—and even the supernaturals—hunted, despised, tortured. Their lives had been…difficult.

But the elders were back to help change all that. The vampires would once again have rules and discipline and support.

And punishments, apparently.

"What is to come?" I asked, my voice barely above a whisper.

He stopped walking and took my shoulders, then leaned in to kiss my lips, once. "The changes with the humans and their reactions to us. That is not just because I have charmed them, or because you gave your life for them. It is not just because we swore to protect them and their city against further invasions."

I held my breath, waiting.

He hesitated, but finally, he told me what he needed me to understand. "It is because the elders hold a subtle sway over the humans. They influence a human's thoughts." He fell into silence and watched me intently, wondering how I would take that bit of information.

"You're saying," I murmured, "that by being here, the elders automatically mesmerize the humans? They make the humans…more accepting of the vampires?"

He inclined his head. "It is a complicated process, but yes. Somewhat. Just as your sacrifice was part of the process. The humans are influenced in certain ways by the very existence of the vampire council. It is a natural occurrence that is not truly understood, not even by the elders. Certainly not by me."

"They are priming the humans for change."

He nodded. "If the elders had continued to guard the rifters and were not here to influence the humans, I could not have posted you on the city streets to teach you control. Vampire clubs would not have sprung up overnight. No matter what we did to protect them from the monsters, the humans would have been unable to accept us."

"So it's all a lie," I realized. "They're…brainwashed into accepting us."

He smiled. "Us. It brings me joy to hear you say that."

I shrugged. "I'm part of you now. I'm a vampire." How easily that rolled off my tongue. And suddenly, a fierce pride clawed its way through layers of cottony coldness inside me and I knew it would be there forever.

And I understood how very hard it had been for the prideful vampires to be reduced to the contemptuous, ugly, hated creatures they had become.

No one had loved the vampires.

I clutched my stomach, only realizing I was crying

when Amias kissed the tears from my cheeks.

"I'm so very sorry," I whispered, finally. How had he borne it when I'd hunted and killed his kind? How had he borne it when I'd tortured them, staked them, sent them into the horror of their afterlife? And now, with the knowledge of what I'd done, how would I bear it?

"I helped create you," he said, sternly and with absolutely no doubt or judgment. "What you did, what *we* did, Trinity, was what we needed to do at that time. There will be no regrets or guilt or sorrow over that tiny moment. Just as you explained to Rhys that he was not to wallow in his guilt. Do you understand?"

But I'd felt his sorrow when he'd watched his people die. I'd felt his rage, his despair, his horror.

Now, I understood it.

And I was crushed beneath the weight of that knowledge. "Your pain will haunt me forever. *That* is what I understand."

His stare softened. "I know."

He did know. It was the same way he felt about me and my pain.

I didn't care at all that the humans were being gently manipulated. We needed all the help we could get convincing them to accept us.

At last, Amias took my hand and we walked on through the way station graveyard, and I felt somehow changed, yet again.

"How did you know what I told Rhys?" I asked.

He smiled. "I will not be far from your side until you are older. Until you are in less danger of being hurt."

My tense body relaxed and I gave a long sigh of relief as something inside me melted into the ground and left only serenity in its place.

"What does the elder want with me?" I asked.

"To know you." He squeezed my hand. "To speak with you."

"Cool," I said.

71

But fear colored his words as he gave one last entreaty. "Be careful, my love. Please. I would not like to see you disciplined."

I curled my lip. "If he tries anything, I'll tear him to shreds."

Amias only sighed.

It took us ten more minutes to find the elder.

In front of us was a clearing, free of tombstones, debris, and foliage. The clearing was bathed in moonlight, and a bright beam of it shone directly down on the two people who sat on the ground, their heads together as they discussed things I could only imagine.

One of the people was the elder. The other was Himself, the King of Everything.

I hadn't seen him since he'd sat behind me on the back of the dragon, and I was strangely reluctant to see him now.

I couldn't have said why.

Maybe just because I didn't know how I should feel about him anymore. Should I be angry? Should I feel betrayed? Should I kowtow to him, as always, now that he was no longer my king?

But then, he'd never really been my king.

The elder, though. He was my king.

"You're wrong. Your king will be the one with whom you rule."

I cried out and clutched my head as Himself invaded my mind, and anger, fierce and vast, bubbled like a spring inside me.

"Get out…"

To my utter shock, he obeyed me. No, I realized, immediately. He hadn't obeyed me—I'd simply expelled him.

Somehow, I had expelled the King of Everything from my mind.

And when I lowered my hands and opened my eyes, Himself and the elder were both looking at me. Himself lifted his hand and beckoned me into their circle of light.

Amias melted away and I walked reluctantly into the clearing to join the two ancient beings—and my future—alone.

Chapter Fourteen

LIGHTBRINGER

"Is this the end?" I asked, as I knelt with them.

"Oh, no, child," Himself said, his black eyes nearly lost in the folds of his skin. "It is the beginning."

I swallowed past the dryness in my mouth. "What happens in the beginning?"

"There is light," the elder replied.

He looked at me, waiting. In the waiting I saw that he was not a male. He wasn't female, either. He was both, and neither, and something beyond my comprehension.

"What do I have to do?" I whispered, dreading his answer.

He surprised me. "You have only to be, in one way or another."

"But my purpose—"

"Is to be," he interrupted, firmly.

Himself was more willing to elaborate. "The nonhumans have lived in darkness for such a very long time," he said. "It has crept upon them so subtly they began to accept their torment as a matter of course. But you. You and your sword. You will be their light."

My palm itched with the need to squeeze Silverlight's grip, but I'd left her in the kitchen with Jin. "How?"

They both smiled, as though I was a child they were tolerating. "Exactly as you have been since the beginning," Himself told me. "You protect the secrets, you connect the powers, and you bring the light."

I looked from one to the other. "By being nearly killed by a sick, mad vampire? By getting my entire family slaughtered? By standing by as Angus was beaten, his children tormented, my men subdued? By hunting and killing because my blood says that I must? By dying?" I curled my fist and hit the ground. "By becoming a *rifter?*"

The elder flinched at the word *rifter*. But his reply was immediate and impatient. "By *being*. You do not have to understand or accept it. It is so. You have decisions to make now. Leave me to my peace. It was hard-won and well-deserved." He lifted his nose into the air, closed his eyes, and dismissed me.

Himself's smile was almost mischievous as he watched my frustration. "Come, Lightbringer," he said, climbing to his feet. "We will leave him to his peace."

"Child," the elder called, as Himself took my arm and began to walk with me from the clearing. "You will tell the occupants of the way station that my job there is done. I shall remain in Willow-Wisp. They needn't fret overmuch. They are to continue bringing me warm blood, and I will not again darken your doorstep."

I gaped at Himself. "The supernaturals have been feeding him?" No wonder they wanted him out of the way station.

Himself urged me to continue walking. "The elders do not require human blood. They prefer the magical blood of the supernatural—the more powerful, the better."

His glance was expectant, as though I should understand what remained unspoken. And I did.

"He'll want to feed from me," I said, shuddering.

"Perhaps," he murmured.

"He needs to leave Willow-Wisp," I said. "Shouldn't he return to the other members of the council, wherever they are, and help them whip unruly vampires into submission?"

He frowned, angry at my flippancy. "Do not interfere with an elder, or presume that you might," he rebuked. "Your status will allow you much, but not even I could stop an elder if he decided to punish you." There was something stern and dark in his black stare, but there was

75

also a spark of concern. "You *must* understand this."

He reached out and before I could move, he touched my forehead. Immediately, something that had been unfinished inside me rushed to completeness.

I shivered and my entire body tightened with terror and immediate realization. My men hadn't really grasped the danger, or they would never have asked me to expel the ancient vampire.

Amias had known, though.

Now, I did, as well.

Whatever had failed to flourish inside my vampire body was now alive and aware. There was fear, respect, and even a certain freedom in the knowledge.

The elders were my gods. My rulers. I belonged to them, and I would obey them. In all ways and for eternity.

Just as all the vampires would.

And the elders would take care of me.

They had returned, and the world was changed.

At least, that was how I should have felt—and I did, until the rebellious rifter, enemy of the vampire, rose up to dispute the issue.

Still, I was not a stupid woman.

"Yes," I murmured. "I understand."

Once again, he urged me away from the elder's clearing. "The elder has relinquished his post as way station guardian. The path walkers are once again yours, my dear."

I nodded, then changed the subject. "The executioners are coming. The dragon won't run."

He said nothing, just walked on, his spine straight. He didn't want to discuss the executioners or the dragon, apparently. Not with me, anyway.

He looked well. Healthy. His hair was flowing and bright, as bright as his little raisin eyes, and his stride rivaled mine.

I didn't understand.

"Sir," I said, as we left the graveyard, "the last time I

saw you, you were…"

He smiled. "Poorly?"

"Yeah."

"I was dying and filled with useless reluctance to feed and heal myself. But it is not yet time for me to sink into the softness of my eternal bed."

I didn't ask how he'd healed himself. How one minute he was near collapse and now he appeared stronger than ever. "Where's Nadine?" I asked, instead.

I glanced at him when he didn't reply, then gasped and clutched his arm. "Sir?"

He'd shriveled, in the instant of my question, into a dark, grief-filled, faded old man. He didn't answer my question, and I wasn't going to ask again.

I had a bad feeling that I knew where Nadine was.

I didn't know the half of it.

"I consumed her," he murmured, finally. "And though it was expected—indeed, demanded—by my dear Nadine, I was weak and deprived myself until it was very nearly too late."

I felt myself go pale. "You…ate her?"

"Yes. She was a vessel of power and life, and her only true purpose was to take care of me. When I neared my end, she gave herself so that I might live on."

There was no guilt in the admission, just grief.

I could only gape.

"It was why she existed, Trinity," he said, gently. "When she gave herself over to me, she understood that one day, she would die so my power would survive."

I would never look at the King of Everything the same way again.

"I didn't say goodbye," I murmured. "She scared me, she irritated me, and I didn't care for her. But…"

"She's part of me now." He stopped walking and turned to face me. "She will hear your goodbye."

"So you'll never have to…" I gestured. "Do that again with someone else?"

His stare sharpened. "I will. I must acquire another assistant soon. I was waiting for you."

I took a step back. "No."

So this was the decision the elder had been talking about. On the plus side, he'd said *decision* like I had a choice. And if I had a choice…

"No," I said again, and more firmly, just in case he hadn't understood me the first time.

He was a few inches shorter than me, but his presence was so overwhelming he might have been a giant. He stared down his nose. "It is a great honor. You shall be the female to my male, the coal to my fire. You will be gifted with huge amounts of power, as Nadine was, and you will assist the King of Everything with all his needs."

I swallowed hard. My throat was so tight I could barely speak, but finally, with the weight of his arrogance crushing the life from me, I began to rebel. To get angry.

And I could thank the rifter for that.

"I'm not willing to be eaten by a man so he can keep his power."

His own anger began to rise, rolling from him in waves, but beneath it was stark disappointment. "It is an unmatched honor. You will be part of me and will rule forever."

I put my hands on my hips. The longer I stared into his black eyes, the angrier I got, and the easier it was to stand up to him. "Yeah? Let me eat you then. I'd rather rule that way."

He clenched his fists. "The master has left you no honor."

"The master has left me no fear." And I turned on my heel and marched away from him, leaving him to stare after me with his lonely desperation.

He would find someone else.

He'd have to. Or he could die.

Chapter Fifteen

DONORS

I walked into the kitchen and paused in the doorway, my sad stare on the empty table. No men were gathered around it, laughing and boasting and eating. The large, once warm kitchen was just quiet and stale.

Then Angus walked in behind me and the entire room brightened.

"You okay?" he asked, watching me. He understood my melancholia. "The future will be good. We all just have to fall into our roles."

"We have to deal with the executioners," I said. "Once they're no longer a problem, we'll be okay." I looked at him. "Won't we?"

He didn't hesitate. "Of course we will, Trin."

Jin crept into the kitchen and went to his stove. "I will cook for those who can eat."

"Thanks, Jin," Angus said.

"Jin and Trin," the Jikininki said, and giggled.

Angus lifted an eyebrow.

But I was abruptly overwhelmed by the quiet and the absence of people. I did not like the cold, silent kitchen. It depressed the hell out of me. "We need more people, Angus." I clutched his hand. "Bring the children."

"Okay," he agreed, but when he reached into his pocket to pull out his cell phone, it rang. "It's Leo."

He listened for a few seconds. "We'll be there." He hung up and looked at me. "Leo says Amias is in the city, and humans are gathering. He wants us there. Now that you're ready—"

"I can help court the humans."

"Yeah. We've been inching our way toward them, but Leo says Amias wants to bite one of them tonight."

I lifted an eyebrow. "That's risky." But I shivered. "Maybe I can bite one, as well."

He peered at me. "I can't tell if you're joking or being serious."

I laughed. "Maybe a bit of both. Jin, my sword."

But biting a human wasn't really a joking matter. If I bit one, I could turn him—immediately. At least that was what Amias and I believed. I could test the theory eventually, and I would. If my bite created more rifters, I could drink from only humans I wanted to kill. Unless I wanted to build my own little army.

I stared into space, my eyes narrowed, thinking.

"Trin?"

I jerked my attention away from the possibilities and took Angus's hand. "I'm ready."

I was happy enough to have something to take my mind off my sudden dejection. A girl needed a purpose— just not one that entailed being munched on by Himself.

When Jin returned with Silverlight, he held a sheath, as well. It was old and ugly, but it would do until I could find a proper one. I slung it over my shoulder, then went with Angus to court the humans of Red Valley.

In the end I ran all the way to the city, unable to make myself get into the confining hunk of metal that Angus drove. Soon, maybe.

We stood, vampires and supernaturals, in the city square, and humans stood around us, unsure, but I could almost smell their excitement.

"We'll always protect the city," Amias said. "We will always protect you."

The human crowd watched us, some of them more suspicious and angry than others, their faces pale, bodies stiff. Hope peeked through, nonetheless. They wanted to believe. They knew they needed us.

Could they trust us to take care of them?

Yeah, they could. Even if they weren't sure of that fact, they needed to believe it. And they were primed and ready for us to *make* them believe it.

"We'll be your bodyguards," Jade Noel told them. She'd been standing beside Amias when I'd arrived. She stood with her arms crossed, confident and bold, and there wasn't a single human there who didn't believe Jade could kick his ass.

We'd traded nods when I arrived—nods that were almost friendly. "Where's your sidekick?" I'd asked. It wasn't often Jade Noel was seen without Amanda Hammer by her side.

Worry softened her hard gaze. "She's in the Deluge."

I frowned. "Amanda's been hurt?"

The Deluge was a swamp at the far edge of Bay Town, a place of healing for the supernaturals. The reclusive healer Sarah Marston and her two sisters lived deep inside the swamp, and though I'd never been there, I'd heard the stories.

Not all of them were good, but there was one thing the supernats agreed on. Sarah Marston could help you—supernatural or not.

The problem was convincing her she should.

"She's fallen ill," Jade answered, and that was all she was willing to tell me.

Excitement hung in the air and mixed with the scent of hot dogs, popcorn, and perfume. Beneath that was a subtler scent of alcohol and cigarette smoke. People shivered and pulled their coats a little tighter around them. They stood in little groups as uniformed policemen threaded their way through the crowds, ready for trouble.

"It's like a county fair," I muttered.

"Maybe one in an alternate universe," Alejandro said, grinning.

He'd arrived with Rhys, but Jamie Stone was conspicuously absent. I didn't ask after the warden's son. Al would take care of him.

My men spread out behind me, silent and watchful. "We understand the importance of keeping the humans safe," Leo said, his voice rumbling out into the chilly night air. "If you allow it, we will protect you with our lives."

"You matter to us," I told them. "This is our city, too. You are our people, and we won't let anyone harm you."

They looked at each other, uneasy, but needing to feel secure. It had been months since the rifters had torn the city apart, but the humans were still shell-shocked, full of grief, and looking for some comfort.

And with the executioners coming, we needed the humans on our side more than we ever had.

Amias stepped forward, and as one, they recoiled, tiny sparks of fear flaring in their eyes.

"Vampires," a man called. "You want us to trust the vampires."

"Yes," I said, leaving the line to stand beside the master. "You've already begun to accept them. Now you need to trust them. Trust *us.*"

"I and my vampires will protect you from future attacks," Amias told them. "We will keep the city safe at night. The supernaturals will keep it safe during the day. You will be protected. We will not hurt you."

"They have already protected us," a woman said. "They killed the rifters. Trinity Sinclair is one of us, and she now stands with them. We *need* our own supernatural protectors. Other cities have them."

Heaven help me if they found out I was a rifter.

"Vampires eat people," another woman said, but she shrank back even as she said it, as though Amias might fly into a rage and attack her. "You *have* to eat people."

"No," he said gently. "We need to sip your precious blood, but only a little. We do not eat you."

"Think of it as being a blood donor," Jade said.

"Do we get paid for it?" a human asked. She was an older, grandmotherly type, and she did not shrink away when Amias looked at her. "I think we should get paid if we donate our blood."

"You will get paid for it," Jade answered, and there was only a whisper of anger in her words. I doubted the humans even noticed. "You'll get paid for it in protection. In order to protect you, the vampires need to eat." She hesitated. "I mean, to *sip.*"

"So you expect us to let the vampires just grab us out of the shadows and bite us?"

The captain held up a hand.

No, not captain.

Mayor.

I needed to remember that.

He'd gotten what he wanted, but so had we, really. Crawford would help create a city of peace. He'd work toward a city where the humans and supernats lived together in harmony, and he wouldn't allow the supernats to be abused.

I hoped.

I really hoped.

I was one of them now, and I would not stand by and watch as they were hurt. When I'd been human, I hadn't had a lot of choices. But now I was a vampire, and I could rip off heads with the best of them.

"The vampire council has returned," Crawford said. "The very council that gave up their freedom and their lives to protect us from the rifters. The vampires will be policed by this council. Believe me, their punishments if they step out of line or cause harm to you is worse than any punishment you can imagine. The vampires are not going to take your blood without your permission."

"Who the hell," a boisterous man yelled, "is going to give the bloodsuckers permission?"

The crowd began muttering and nodding, their fear masquerading as anger. They didn't want to feel as though they had no control. I understood that.

"Things have changed," Crawford told them. "You no longer have to live in fear of the vampires. If they're taken care of, they will take care of us. Plans are already underway for a club on Montgomery Street, one in Bay Town, and one inside the Sunset Mill Hotel. Some of you spend a lot of your weekends in the club on Park Street. Don't tell me you're not enjoying yourselves."

"Clubs," a man said doubtfully. "I haven't gone into any vampire clubs."

"You should try it out," I told him, "before it gets expensive."

"What do they do there?" another older woman asked, clutching her purse. "I haven't been there. I heard it's dangerous."

"It's not so dangerous," I said. "It's a place where you can go for a few drinks, some dancing, and an opportunity to share your blood with those who need it."

"A place where you can get to know the vampires as individuals," Rhys said.

"Vampire clubs," Jade said. "Feeding clubs. And believe me, once you're bitten, you'll want to go back for more."

"Allow me to demonstrate," Amias said. "May I have a volunteer?"

The crowd gasped. *"Fuck,* no!" someone shouted.

But a woman, maybe thirty years old, stepped from the crowd of humans. "I'll volunteer," she said.

Amias held out a hand. "Thank you."

She smiled, a little nervous, but mainly excited. She was attracted to Amias—with my newly heightened senses, I could smell her desire. And despite the fact that those were the types of humans we needed, I had to force down a sudden wave of jealousy. Possessiveness.

He was *mine.*

Amias looked at me, ever aware of my emotions. His smile was tiny. And pleased. Then he put his dark stare back on the volunteer. She gave him her hand and he pulled her to him, then brushed her hair away from her neck.

"Will it hurt?" she asked, breathless.

"Oh, no," he said, his voice smooth and creamy. "No, it will not hurt."

My heart slammed against my rib cage, and my stomach tightened with the knowledge of what was about to happen. What he was about to do to her.

For her.

I trembled with the force of my emotions but stood still and silent as he drew her into his arms.

"What is your name?" he asked, his eyes only for her.

She swallowed hard as she stared up at him, then clenched her hands together, likely to keep them from shaking. "Alicia."

"Alicia," he murmured. And her name on his lips was everything good, everything dark, everything sex.

She began to shiver.

I looked away—I *had* to look away because I didn't yet have the control I would eventually grow into, and I couldn't trust that I might not rip her out of his arms and bash her head off the ground—and found Crawford watching me.

Stuck for a second in the mystery of his gaze, my automatic instinct was to catch him. To mesmerize him.

His eyes widened and he jerked his stare away. I groaned silently, humiliated, angry, frustrated.

I hated that I was a baby vampire.

The only baby I wanted to be was Shane's baby hunter.

But Shane was gone.

When he'd realized his situation, that he was no longer Shane Copas, vampire hunter but Shane Copas, vampire, he'd gone a little crazy.

Almost the very moment Amias released us from "the womb," the dark burrow in the ground where he'd fed us like baby birds and coddled us like infants, transforming us from dead human to living vampire, Shane had fled.

Our growth had been accelerated, and it was a good thing, because up top, as I'd begun to think of the world, we were needed.

The vampires needed their master, my men needed me, and the humans needed everyone.

"Is he hypnotizing her?" a woman asked.

"Tell them," Amias said.

Alicia took her stare from his to look out at the crowd. "I'm not mesmerized. I just want this to work. I want the vampires to protect us. The youth of our city are open to them. They're visiting the clubs. They're *safe*." She looked at Amias once again, and her voice softened. "I want to trade blood for protection."

"That's disgusting," another woman said. "Vampires are gross. Like getting sucked on by a lizard."

Alicia turned up her nose. "Can you truly look at this man and call him anything but..." She blushed, but kept her voice steady. "Hot? He's the sexiest man I've ever seen. I don't know how you can look at him and think of him as anything less than beautiful."

She wasn't lying.

Amias smiled. "Are you ready?" he asked her.

"It won't change anything if you bite Alicia," I said, unable to keep my silence. "You need someone who isn't already convinced." I pointed at the woman who'd called him gross. "You need to win *her* over."

"Not going to happen," the woman said.

Angus put his arm around me and I leaned into his warmth. "I'll give you five hundred dollars," he told the woman.

"*I'll* do it for five hundred bucks," a young man said, and then there were several cries of, "*I will!*" before the woman shrugged and swaggered to Angus.

"You'd better be good for it," she told him.

I glared at her. "Go to the master."

Alicia reluctantly stepped away from Amias and the new woman took her place.

"Later?" Alicia asked him. "I don't need money to let you bite me." She smiled, already half in love. "Anytime you want me, come find me."

Amias looked at me.

"Absolutely not," I said.

And then, before anyone could say another word, Amias struck. He didn't give the donor time to waver. He didn't even look her in the eye. No one could say later that he'd mesmerized her.

She screamed, but it was a scream of surprise, and even before the sound was completely out of her mouth, it changed.

The scream became a wail, tapered off to a groan of delight, and finally, she moaned, and it was the sound of sex. She orgasmed as he sucked, and I shuddered against Angus, my legs trembling, my thighs pressed against the sudden wetness and zings of hot desire that very nearly made me come right there in front of a huge crowd of humans.

Because I knew how it felt.

I felt everything. Smelled everything. I was not the same.

The girl groaned, and a sigh floated from between my lips. The master's bite didn't bring only physical ecstasy. It could make the mind float on a sea of bliss. The vampire bite was better than any drug.

Only a master could have such an extreme effect on a human, but the humans didn't need to know that. The lesser vampires could make it good, as well. Just not *that* good.

It could also, in a master's hands, be the most painful thing a human could imagine, but they wouldn't be shown that, either.

I'd received both pleasure and pain from Amias. I knew well what he could do.

"Trin." Angus tightened his arm around me. "You okay?"

"I'm a vampire," I whispered.

There was a world inside my mind that hadn't been

there before. I'd survived the despairing wastelands of the afterlife. I now knew the fear of death, as did every immortal in existence.

So I would live forever.

Amias pulled his fangs from the side of the human's neck and licked the tiny wound, sealing it. The human tottered away, her cheeks red, her chest heaving, her hand to her mouth.

She was pulled into a little group of her friends. "Oh my God," she told them. "Oh, my *God*. So fucking good. He's…amazing."

She didn't have to say it loudly. I heard.

As did Amias.

He shot me a look, a quick glance full of pure male ego and satisfaction.

The joy of that bite would fade for her very quickly, and when it did, she might very well hate him for it. She'd forget the hugeness of her pleasure.

But that was okay.

Those who'd witnessed it wouldn't forget her reaction.

There was something so taboo in what had just happened—in the city before, a vampire boldly biting a human—no matter what the reason—would have gotten him tortured and staked. In the city before, a vampire wouldn't have stood in the square talking with humans like he were a regular person.

But Crawford was right. Things had changed.

And Himself had been right. It was time.

We waited, our little group of supernaturals and vampires.

And finally…

"Where did you say those clubs are?" someone asked.

"And so it begins," Jade muttered. "No human can resist a good time."

Chapter Sixteen

RIFTER

A week passed, then two, and still the executioners did not come.

Bay Town began to relax.

And I began to darken.

There was enough humanity left inside me to make me dislike that growing darkness.

"Your coldness will continue to grow as your humanity shrinks."

Jin had been right.

Amias was worried, but we both knew that only time would tell us exactly what I would become.

"You're part vampire," he said. "It will balance you. I am sure of that."

Perhaps he was right.

I missed Shane with an obsessive fierceness that consumed me. I couldn't let him go.

He wasn't dead—I'd have felt the absence of him.

He was out there, somewhere, without me. Without us, his...his *pack*. His crew. His people. He needed us, even if he didn't want to.

And god, we needed him. Part of us was missing.

"I'm going after him." I sat around the table with Angus, Rhys, Clayton, and Leo, watching as they ate their dinner, and just that suddenly, I made up my mind. It was time. I stood. "I'm bringing him home."

They stood with me, at once.

"We're coming with you," Angus said.

I shook my head. "I'll track him alone. I'm running."

"You can't go without at least one of us," Leo said. "I'll go."

"I can't track in a car." I watched him, unsure and a little wistful. "I can't take you with me, Leo."

I wanted to.

He said nothing, just waited for me to make a move so he could follow, no matter what I said.

"Amias will follow you," Angus said, finally. He grasped my shoulders and leaned forward to give me a kiss.

I could feel his anxiety. "You don't have to worry about me, Angus."

He snorted. "I've been worrying about you since the day I met you, Trin. I can't stop now."

"They can't hurt me," I told him. "Not really."

His frown was deep and held a tiny glint of anger. "You can be hurt, girl. You might heal from it, but I've been hurt enough times to know. It will mess you up. Don't be fucking careless."

So I promised him.

I couldn't wait a second longer. Once I'd decided to drag Shane home, I simply had to go. "I'll bring him back," I murmured.

Then I strode to the back door, the half-giant at my back, and I ran. I left Leo behind in a matter of seconds.

I didn't waste time looking for Amias. We were connected. He'd find me if he thought he needed to.

When I ran, it was like becoming a streak of energy that exploded through the air, quicker than a thought. There were no legs or arms or eyes, just a streak of magic that had none of the limitations of a human body. It *was* magic. There was no other word for it, no other explanation.

I had no idea how I'd track Shane, until suddenly, I did. I opened myself to him. I followed my senses, and I had no doubt they'd lead me straight to the love of my life. My obsession. As much as I was the master's obsession, Shane was mine.

I *would* find him.

I did, and it took me less than three hours.

I tracked him to a club in a town called Chesterton, and I stood outside the bar, my head down, my hand to my chest, trying to control my tears. I was overwhelmed by the nearness of him. By him.

"Shane," I whispered.

And then, I let go of the softness, because soft wouldn't get him back.

Soft would get me hurt.

Soft would make me let him go.

The club was bursting with music so loud it hurt my ears. It scrambled my thoughts as my new vampire ears sent it into my new vampire brain. It fucked me up.

But I felt Shane, and I didn't care about my ears.

I weaved my way through the throng of dancing humans, my senses leading me onward, and when a heavy-eyed human got in my path and slowed me down, I shoved him out of my way.

People were starting to pick up that it was the recently dead vampire Trinity Sinclair in their midst, and that something interesting was about to happen.

What were they going to do?

Not a damn thing.

Shane knew I was there. He knew, just as I knew *he* was there. He wouldn't come meet me, but he wouldn't run, either.

When I finally saw him, he was sitting at a round table, his back to the wall, with two half-naked girls on his lap. Another one was smashed up against his side, whispering into his ear, and two rather large men sat across from him.

He hadn't fed in a very long time. He would resist feeding, of course, even though it hurt him.

He was so very hungry.

He looked up, unable to resist, and met my stare.

I smiled.

His shudder was completely unintentional and unstoppable, and the girls on his lap glanced at him, then followed his stare to me.

I didn't look at them, but they were on my list of humans I might need to fuck up that night.

I felt like I moved in slow motion as I walked toward my heart, my vampire, my hunter.

Then I was standing at the table, rage, hunger, and lust screaming through my body. I wanted to kill, to hurt, to fuck, to eat. I wanted all those things, and I wanted them so badly I knew he'd be choking on the scent of them.

I was a feral animal.

Or maybe that was just the rifter in me.

I grasped the edge of the table and leaned over it, never once taking my stare from Shane's. "Get the fuck up."

One of the girls screamed in pain and Shane jerked, then looked almost unseeingly to where he gripped her arm. He let go of her and shoved both women off his lap.

"Get out of here," he told them.

They didn't need to be told again.

But he didn't move, just sat watching me with that dark, dark stare.

Two bouncers grabbed me. One pinned my arms to my sides, and the other grabbed me by the throat.

"You need to leave," the throat-grabber said.

I flung them from me so hard I figured they were dead as soon as they hit the wall. Then I grabbed the table and sent it sailing through the air after them.

It didn't matter if I hurt them. It didn't even matter if I killed them.

Not to me.

Not then.

Shane was suddenly cradling a shotgun, but he made no move to aim it at me.

"Are you going to make me carry you out of here?" I asked.

The other men had scrambled away as soon as I'd dealt with the attacking bouncers, and it was just the two of us.

I felt the crush of humans, smelled their fear, their interest, their sweat, but they might as well not even have been there.

"What the fuck *are* you?" Shane asked.

My grin stretched across my face, fake and deadly. "I'm your one and only." I took a step closer to him. "And I've come to take you home."

"No."

"Don't fight me, Shane. I will kick your motherfucking ass in front of all these tasty humans and in the end, you'll still be going home with me."

He shot me.

Lifted his shiny new Betty and blew me away.

He was fast, the bastard. So fast.

It took me a couple of minutes to pick myself up from the filthy floor and shake off the damage, and by then, he was gone.

That was okay.

He couldn't hide from me.

I should have left him, but I couldn't.

God help me, but I couldn't.

The vampire master found me as I ran, and he ran at my back, following me as I followed Shane.

I stopped once to get my bearings. "What are you going to do?" I asked Amias, my voice thick with tears. "Will you stop me?"

"I will do whatever you want, my love. I will help you catch him, I will kill him, I will bury him inside the earth and grow him all over again. I will do whatever you want me to do."

I grabbed his face and pressed my lips to his, hard, and only for a moment. Long enough to taste him, to tell him without saying a word that I loved him.

To thank him.

There was no right or wrong.

Not among vampires.

"Let's go get him," I murmured, and I followed my love for miles. All the way across the city, into the woods, into the bogs. Up hills, through swamps, across lakes.

93

And in the end, I got him.

Amias and I slammed his frail body between ours, and we held him, silent as he struggled, for hours.

We wore him down.

It was one of the saddest nights of his life, of my life.

Amias, he was old. He'd done that shit before.

When dawn came and we sank into the earth to sleep, Shane was sandwiched between us. And even in my sleep, I continued whispering love into his ear, begging him to accept what he'd become, to allow us to tend him, to let us love him.

To come home.

He knew he had no choice.

I wasn't giving him a fucking choice.

I was no longer that girl.

And as I belonged to the darkness, Shane Copas belonged to me.

Chapter Seventeen

SACRIFICE

I took away his will.

Maybe he needed me to.

That's what I told myself on the long walk home. He didn't try to run. He only put one foot in front of the other, his stare on the ground. And when I stopped in the middle of nowhere and pressed his fangs to my flesh, he drank, tears from his broken sobs mixing with the blood.

"Will you forgive me?" I whispered, once. "Ever?"

He didn't answer, and I didn't need him to.

I knew the answer to that question.

I only needed him to know I cared.

He would have died out there, eventually. He would have gone angrily into the despair, but first, he would have suffered unimaginably for a thousand lifetimes.

I'd saved him.

I'd fucking *saved* him.

Neither Shane nor Amias comforted me when I burst into tears.

We walked on, walked until the sun threatened to set us on fire. Once again, we slept.

The next night he seemed a little less bleak. I looked at Amias, who gave me the tiniest nod of agreement, and my heart leapt.

He was less bleak.

He would be okay, my hunter.

But then he turned to me, as though sensing my hope, and slammed the stock of his shotgun into my face.

Shane had been strong as a human. As a vampire he was a fucking train.

When I fought my way out of the darkness and dashed blood from my eyes, Amias had Shane on the ground and was beating him to death.

Shane was strong, but he was no Amias.

I threw myself at the master and tried to pull him off Shane, but it was as though I wasn't even there.

And despite the urgency, I calmed myself, leaned forward, and whispered into his ear. "You told me you'd do whatever I wanted you to do with him."

He turned his head to look at me, and I swear there was nothing in those icy eyes but madness. I'd seen it once before, when he'd nearly killed me. A lifetime ago.

It was the same.

And I had no idea how to bring him back.

"Master," I murmured, and ran my thumb over his lips. "Don't leave me."

He sat straddling Shane, his fist raised, madness in his eyes, and God, I couldn't bear it. I couldn't bear any of it.

Vampires had a hard fucking life. It was the price we paid for immortality.

I leaned forward, carefully, and pressed my lips to his. I covered his fist with my hand, kissed him, whispered into his mouth, let him feel my love, my need.

"I cannot be without you," I told him.

He tilted his head and opened his lips, tasting the blood from the injury Shane had given me. When he pulled back to look at me, his gaze was tender. "Do you hurt?" he asked. "Do you hurt, my love?"

"I'm becoming friends with pain." I closed my eyes and leaned my forehead against his. "It's the only way I know I'm alive."

Maybe I was the mad one. How could I not be?

"Your hunter loves you, Trinity."

We looked down at the fallen, battered vampire who lay healing and agonized and unfinished, and simply watched him as he watched us, with empty, cold stares and overflowing hearts.

"Don't do that again," I told Amias, without taking my stare from Shane.

He said nothing for a few seconds. Then, "If he hits you again, I will bury him."

"Amias, I—"

"No." He waited until I looked at him, then spoke slowly and clearly, not only for my benefit, but for Shane's. "If he hits you again, I will wrap him in silver and bury him in the fucking ground for eternity." He dropped his hard stare to Shane, and Shane, bloody and broken, began to tremble. "If you can't touch her in love, you will not touch her at all. Do you understand my words?"

Shane parted his battered, swollen lips. "Yeah. Fuck you both."

And he sounded almost…normal.

Shane had been a hunter, as had I. Perhaps he could have killed Amias by staking him. Perhaps I could have killed Amias by yanking Silverlight off my back and shoving her into his chest.

I bent over at the thought, crying out, the ends of my hair brushing the ground.

No. I could not kill him.

God, no.

Amias lifted me to my feet, then dragged Shane from the ground and stood him in front of me. "No more. She would die for you. What would you do for her?"

I lifted a tentative hand to touch Shane's bruised face, but he growled and jerked away from me. He was like a wild, savage dog, full of fear and rage and confusion.

"You shouldn't have let him run," I told Amias, suddenly angry. "He's half-cooked. We're never getting him back."

Amias only shrugged. "We will see. Let's go home."

With Shane between us we strode through the city, and we were halfway to Bay Town when we saw the executioners driving down Main Street in a slowly moving procession of armored black SUVs, spotlights on the roofs, with a battered containment van trailing them.

"They'll be heading to Bay Town soon, the bastards," I said, and as one, we slid into the shadows to watch them go by.

Shane grabbed my arm. "Executioners?"

I took the opportunity to cover his hand with mine. "Yeah. They've come for Rhys's dragon."

He let go of my arm and shook my hand from his. "Rhys?"

"That's right," I said. "You don't know. You…"

"Died," he growled, when I couldn't say the word.

I nodded. "He's a dragon, Shane, and he is magnificent. As big as the sky, and unbelievably beautiful. He shoots fire for miles. I don't know what else he can do, but *God*, that dragon. When I was on his back, I could only think of how much you'd have loved to…" Once again I trailed off, but only because I was too full of tears to continue. "I love you so much," I whispered, finally. "So fucking much."

We stood in silence for a while, watching the executioners crawl down the street. Then Amias spoke, his words for Shane, his voice hard.

"She went willingly to her death," he told my hunter. "She led the rifters to her blood, drew them out of the city, and let them tear her to pieces. I got to her seconds before the dragon set the island on fire. Look at her scars."

Shane would not, so Amias grabbed his jaw and forced him to. "*Look* at her. Look at her sacrifice. I made her one of us. They made her one of them. But she does not wallow in sanctimonious rage and self-pity."

Shane said nothing, and stared unseeingly over my head.

Amias released his face. "You disgust me."

"You shouldn't have brought me back," Shane snarled.

"No," Amias agreed. "I should not have. I did it for Trinity, but you will only ever hurt her. I should have left you in your darkness."

But Shane didn't hate me, not really. Shane hated himself. He hated what he'd become.

I knew how he felt. There was a battle inside me—part of me wanted to embrace my coldness, and the other part of me was terrified I would. If I became a block of ice, I would feel no joy, would I? No love. Nothing but the need to feed and a savage, primitive need to kill.

I'd felt some of that when I'd gone after Shane.

The rifter wanted to take over, and I couldn't let him.

I shuddered, and Amias slipped his arm around me. He said nothing, but he was there, and that was enough.

Chapter Eighteen

DARKNESS

Angus knew Shane wasn't right.

They stared at each other for a few seconds, then Angus turned away from him and took my shoulders. He sent his frowning gaze over my body, lingering on the bloodstains that crusted my shirt and colored my face.

"Are you okay?" he asked.

Amias crossed his arms. "The hunter cannot seem to control his anger. I have given him a final warning."

Angus turned to look at the silent, closed-off Shane. "We're here for you, bud. But I add my warning to the master's."

There wasn't so much as a flicker of emotion in Shane's eyes.

Rhys and Clayton, always with a tiny, undeniable connection that belonged only to them, watched Shane, regret dark in their faces. I wasn't the only one who loved Shane, and it broke all our hearts to see him suffering.

"Where's Leo?" I asked.

"He hasn't returned," Clayton told me.

I sighed. There was no way Leo could follow me when I ran, but that knowledge wouldn't stop him from trying. "I don't like him out there alone."

"I'll check on him," Rhys said, sliding his cell from his pocket. "And let him know you've returned."

"Thanks." I touched Angus's huge arm. "We saw Mikhail Safin driving through the city."

He nodded. "We're ready for them, sweetheart."

I smacked my palm with my fist. "They'll come while Amias and I are asleep and useless."

Jin slipped out onto the porch. "Tell them that dragons are inclined to appear in darkness."

Angus shrugged. "Can't hurt to try."

"I'll get that rumor started," Clayton said. But first, he walked to me and pulled me into his arms.

I sank against the heat of his body and rubbed my lips against his throat. "Cake. You always smell like cake." And even though I was forgetting the taste of it, I hadn't forgotten the scent.

I felt him smile. "It feels good to touch you," he murmured.

I lifted my lips for his kiss, then unintentionally glanced at Shane. He watched Clayton and me, and there was such a look of longing in his eyes that I couldn't breathe. It hit me in the chest, that look, that need, that loneliness, harder than any shotgun stock could.

"Shane," I cried, and pulled away from Clayton. I held my arms out as I strode toward him. "Let me hold you. Let me help you."

But he was once again blank and cold. "Get the fuck away from me."

I stopped and lowered my arms. "My hunter," I murmured. "What can I do?"

His face did not soften as he included all of us in his contemptuous gaze. "She is no better than Miriam was when she enslaved Clayton. Those two—" He pointed at me and Amias, then closed his hand in a fist that wanted to smash something. "They forced me here, like an animal. Like a child. Whatever I do, whatever I am, that's my business and I should be left to it." Finally, he pinned me with a fierce stare. "You had no fucking right."

"You were suffering," I said. "Someone would have sent you into the despair. I had to save you. You belong here. You were hurt. You were alone."

"I was *free,*" he snarled, then walked away.

I put my fingers to my mouth. "He's right. My God, what have I done?"

"It's the rifter," Angus said, trying to comfort me.

The flood of emotion shocked me—perhaps not even the rifter could smother the vampire when it came to my men.

I shook my head, fiercely. "No. No. It's me. I've made a mistake and I have to fix it." I started to go after him, to apologize, to free him, but Clayton's words took my mind off Shane and put it on something even more sinister.

"Executioners are here," he said.

"Looks like they're here to feel us out," Angus said. "Only one car."

We stood side by side and watched calmly as the black SUV rolled to a stop. The occupants were hidden behind darkly tinted windows, and they sat without moving for a few interminable minutes before finally, they opened their doors and began stepping out.

Four people in total—three men and one woman—and only one of them was dressed in a suit. The others wore combat gear. Vests, weapons, hats, hard faces and cold, cold eyes.

They were killers. Simple as that.

The man in the suit stood with his three crew members fanned out behind him, and he flicked his empty gaze at me and my people, and he seemed to see…everything.

He settled that cold gaze on me.

"I have come for the dragon. I believe he's here. In three days, I'll return, and you'll be prepared to give me his name and his location."

Darkness.

He was aptly named.

He was slender, medium height, short dark hair…unremarkable. Until you looked into his eyes. They were like pieces of twinkling yellow glass, offset by thick lashes. Above them, his brows slashed like dark gashes.

Death lived in those shocking eyes.

Not so much as a flicker of emotion, or softness, or curiosity.

Just death.

"Darkness," Jin whisper-screamed, then turned tail and ran into the house.

Shane stepped from the shadows. He said nothing, but it was enough that he was showing his support. He could have left us to the executioners, but there he was, blank eyes and all.

I suspected my blood had helped speed his healing, both physical and mental. He'd be fine. Changed, yes, as I was, but fine. He had to grow into his new circumstances.

And I could only hope that in the end, he'd choose to grow with me.

Maybe he'd heard me admit I was wrong, because the worried look he shot me was a little less dark. A little less hate-filled.

"Copas," one of Safin's crew said. "We'd heard you were in Red Valley."

We all stared at Shane, surprised.

"Shane?" I asked. "You know the executioners?"

"Shane used to be one of mine," Safin said. "Long time ago, for a little while. He was a good scout."

"He's one of ours now," Angus said, no judgment in his voice. And the dominant alpha he was couldn't be hidden.

Safin immediately focused on the werebull. The human alpha stared down the shifter alpha for a good two minutes before finally, I took a couple of steps toward the man Shane apparently used to work for.

"We don't have the dragon, Mikhail."

Darkness glanced at me, then back at Angus. He studied him for a minute before he decided to put his attention back on me.

But I'd seen what was in his eyes when he looked at Angus. There was going to be trouble between the two men.

Angus wanted to protect his territory. Safin wanted to take it.

And something else—something instinctual and ancient. There was immediate hatred and a rising challenge between the two of them.

"I expect resistance," Safin said. That was all, nothing more.

The woman in the crew stepped up beside him. Thick black braids fell over her shoulders, and she stared at us with bright hazel eyes, icy in the darkness of her face. She was stone cold, and she didn't care who knew it.

Even beneath the bulk of her clothes, I could see the bunching of muscle when she moved.

And her stare lingered on Shane.

"Fuck you," I said.

I felt her knowledge of him. Intimate knowledge.

And I didn't like it at all.

She put that cold stare on me and her smile spread slowly across her face, widening even as I clenched my fists, an almost silent growl floating from my lips.

"Shane went and got himself a vampire girlfriend," she told Safin, as she lovingly fingered one of the stakes in her belt. "Impossible as that seems, he has got himself a vampire girlfriend." She paused as she studied my face. "You must be Trinity Sinclair. We'd heard you'd come back with a face like a road map."

"A lot of things are fucked up," I said, calmly. "Not just my face. I used to be a vampire hunter." I paused. "And Shane?" I smiled. "He used to be human."

Her eyes widened and she took a quick, unintentional step back. Then she strode toward Shane to see for herself.

I was already moving. The second before she reached him, she found me standing in front of him, my body blocking hers.

"He's mine," I told her.

She was fast, too. Not vampire fast, but fast. Almost before I realized she'd moved, she had a stake pressed to my chest. "You made Shane Copas? You *turned* fucking Shane Copas?"

I held up a hand to stop my men from doing something that might get them killed. "I did not," I told her. "But he's mine, nonetheless."

"Aspen," Safin said. "We're not here to fight over a man."

"He's no man. He's a fucking soulless bloodsucker." She leaned a little closer to me. "I could tell you stories about the vampires he's killed. Tortured." She grinned. "I could tell you about the bad, bad things we did together."

"Get away from him," I snarled.

"Both of you get the fuck away from me," Shane said.

Aspen smirked and went back to her group. When I looked away from Aspen, I found Mikhail with his cold stare pinned to Clayton.

"What are you, sir?" Darkness asked him.

But we weren't willing to stand like children and allow Mikhail and his crew to interrogate us.

"We're done here," Angus said. "Take your bullies and get the fuck out of Bay Town."

Once again, Safin's stare clashed with Angus's.

I wanted to jump between the werebull and the executioner's deadly stare, but I didn't move. No one spoke.

When the silence became too hurtful, I broke it with a lie. Darkness would not believe it, but I'd stick with it for as long as I could. "The dragon was here long enough to burn the rifters, Safin. We haven't seen him since. We don't have a dragon living in Bay Town."

He looked at me, and it was like being looked at by a reptile. A cold, hissing snake or an ancient lizard. I resisted the urge to rub the goosebumps from my skin.

Apparently he didn't think my words deserved a reply, because he didn't open his mouth.

Mikhail Safin was the scariest human I'd ever met.

He looked at me, and all I saw in his face was something raw and primal. Something freaking scary.

He kept his silence and continued to stare at me, as

though I might be so freaked out by that stare that I'd break down and tell him everything he wanted to know.

Before I'd died, I might very well have.

He can hurt us.

That phrase ran through my mind, over and over, until finally I swallowed the dryness in my mouth and was able to speak without fear coloring my words.

"There's no dragon here." I thought I sounded relatively normal. "You stick around long enough, you'll figure out you're just wasting your time."

His golden eyes glittered like hard, pale diamonds. He was a machine—analytical, methodical, and unemotional—but finally, I saw something besides emptiness.

There was passion behind the hard glassiness of his eyes. Passion for killing. My savage bloodlust recognized his savage bloodlust. The coldness of my rifter understood the chill in his gaze.

We were alike, Mikhail Safin and I, with maybe one important distinction. I could love. I was nearly certain he couldn't.

"What happened to you?" I murmured. "What happened to turn you into such a psychopath?"

We stared at each other for so long that finally, Aspen cleared her throat. "Mikhail?" she asked, a little uncertain.

He ignored her. "I would ask the same question of you," he said to me.

"A lot of shit happened to make me what I am—I was torn apart and put back together as..." I shrugged. "As this. A couple of times, actually. So...what happened to *you?*"

And finally, he smiled. It was a tiny lifting of one corner of his lips, and a spark of genuine humor lit his eyes. He understood a person's need to understand why he was so...dark. He understood, and he found it amusing. "I have no excuses." He paused, as still as a master vampire. For a human, that was no small feat. "I was born this way."

There was no way to tell if he was lying. And in the end, it didn't really matter. He would do what he'd come to do, and before it was over, some of us would suffer, and some of us would die.

And that was the only truth in his eyes.

Chapter Nineteen

RAW

He left.

He gave us three days to deliver the dragon, and then he walked away.

Headlights appeared as another car turned onto the way station drive and sped toward us.

"It's Crawford," Angus noted, but his stare lingered on Safin's taillights.

I nodded. "He must've heard that Darkness was coming to Bay Town."

"I'm not sure what he can do," Rhys said.

His voice was strained. The executioners had him worried, and understandably so. He caught my concerned gaze and sent me a wink. "I'm okay, love."

"We won't let them take you, Rhys."

"I know."

But he was afraid—doubtless for the supernaturals and Bay Town more than for himself. He could shift and flee and they would never catch him. Even though that would mean he'd have to leave us, the ones with whom he belonged.

He could run and he could hide.

But if Safin attacked us, and he *would* attack us, Rhys would never leave us to him and run to save himself. If Safin began torturing supernaturals, Rhys would hand himself over to Darkness.

As Crawford's car and Safin's car drew even, they rolled to a stop, muttered a few words, and then Crawford continued on toward us.

He climbed out, motioning to someone else in the car

to stay put. He'd brought backup, just in case. Probably a couple of off-duty cops.

"Frank," I said.

He gave us a nod. "Everything okay?"

"Yeah," I told him. "He played nice, sort of."

"He came to give you his terms." Crawford hesitated, and finally, he looked at me. "You should go away for a while, Trinity."

I lifted an eyebrow. "You think I'd take off and leave the supernats to those assholes?"

His stare drifted over the scars that decorated my face. The scars that few people ever mentioned. The scars most people pretended not to notice.

Crawford didn't pretend not to notice. He lingered on them, and there was more than just pity and horror in his eyes. There was admiration, as well. "No," he replied, finally. "But if you take the ones you care about and hide out for a few weeks, it could save you some grief."

I gestured to include all of Bay Town. "I care about them all. And I can't hide the entire town."

He took a breath, then let it out in a tired rush. "Safin knows the dragon is one of you."

I shrugged. "And all we can do is try to make him believe he's wrong."

He watched me, his expression changing from frustration to worry to tenderness. It made me uncomfortable enough to look away.

"Be careful," he said. "You don't want them sending word back to their employers that you are as interesting as the dragon."

I laughed, but sobered when I saw he was completely serious.

"She will not be taken, Mayor," Amias said. "Trust in that."

He smiled and the captain visibly relaxed. Then he stiffened, frowned, and narrowed his eyes at the master. "If you try to mesmerize me, Sato, I will have you thrown into a cell."

Amias put a hand to his heart. "I would not dream of it."

"We'll face the enemy as we always do," Angus said. "Only this time, we'll have the city at our backs. And Trin will have us at hers."

It didn't matter to him that I'd become undead. That I'd become a rifter, a vampire, a monster. He still wanted me, as he always had. He loved me.

I looked at Shane. Did he love me, as well? Was there love mixed in with the disgust, the sorrow, and the self-hatred?

"You *worked* with them," I said, half disbelieving.

"There's a lot you don't know about me, baby hunter." And even as I gasped and my heart filled with joy, he growled and turned to stride away. But he'd been there, in those cold eyes, for one brief second. His *"baby hunter"* lingered in the air, and I closed my eyes and soaked it in.

It didn't really matter what he'd done or been or even how he felt about me.

Shane Copas would always be my dark obsession.

We turned quickly at a sound like a stampeding herd of horses, which grew louder by the second. The very ground seemed to shake with it.

"What the fuck is that?" Angus muttered.

Then Leo burst out of the trees and I watched him come with something close to awe. Giants were huge—even half-giants—and they could *run.*

No wonder he'd thought he might have a chance at keeping sort of close to me.

"Wow," Crawford said. "We could use him on the force."

I laughed. "I vote to give him a badge. You start hiring supernats, Captain, and things will change a hell of a lot faster."

He smiled at me, and for a heartbeat, I lingered on that smile. Then we both put our attention on the incoming giant.

When Leo made it to our little gathering he leaned forward, rested his hands on his knees, and attempted to catch his breath.

"Hey," I said. "Where's the fire?"

He groaned, then straightened and glared down at all of us. "Safin is coming to the way station."

I pressed my lips together to keep from smiling. "Been and gone, Leo."

"Fuck," he said.

I laughed again, and noticed the men watching me, softness in their eyes and tiny smiles on their lips.

Crawford cleared his throat. "Trinity, could I have a moment?"

"Sure, Captain."

"Come on, Leo," Angus said, giving me a wink and clapping Leo on the back. "After all that running, you'll need some dinner."

"I *am* hungry," Leo said, tossing once last glance at me before walking toward the house with Angus, Rhys, and Clayton. "I could eat a few chickens."

Amias said nothing, just melted away into the shadows to give us some privacy, but dawn was near. He wouldn't go far.

I turned to Crawford.

"Has Rhys considered running?" he asked, getting right to the point.

"I asked," I said. "He refuses."

He shrugged. "I doubt it'd make much difference to Safin anyway. He's going to believe the dragon is right here until it's proven otherwise."

"Or until we kill him," I said, my gaze steady on his.

"Killing him is an idea," he agreed, surprising me. "But I doubt it's possible. Executioners can't do what they do without protections in place. Safin is better protected than most."

I needed to know my enemy. "What kind of

protections? I know they have the US government behind them—what are we thinking, Homeland Security, maybe?"

He shrugged. "Maybe. But that's not what I'm talking about. They have actual physical protection. I don't know what's true and what isn't, but I've heard that they're surrounded by magic." He hesitated, and I knew whatever he was going to tell me would hurt. "Some of their victims were taken because of what they could do for the executioners. What they could give them. I heard they have a witch on their team who casts circles of protection around them when they face their enemies. I am certain he or she was with them tonight. Safin wouldn't have come to Bay Town unprotected."

I shook my head. "I didn't see a witch."

"She wouldn't have to actually be with them," he replied, dryly. "Only her influence. And there's more. Safin doesn't face down supernaturals with human weapons. He has weapons of power that even vampires have a hard time recovering from."

"Like Jade's wand?"

He nodded slowly. "Yes. Like that. Trinity…"

"No. I will not turn Rhys over to be killed. We'll fight for him, even if that means we'll die."

"*You* won't die." He didn't look away from me. "But they will. Think about that before you put them on the front line, Trinity."

"That's a little hurtful."

"But true."

"I love those men, Captain."

His eyes didn't waver. "Do you, Trinity? *Can* you?" He gestured at me. "As you are now, can you feel love more than you feel the need to conquer and kill and eat?"

I recoiled. "Fuck you."

"I spoke with the vampire master about rifters and their character. What's inside them is lust, he says. Bloodlust, pride, the need to devour. To kill." He hesitated, even as I stood frozen and devastated. "Can you really do what's best for the supernaturals?"

"Did the master say I couldn't?" I whispered.

And finally, he looked away. Maybe he looked away from the pain in my voice, or maybe he looked away from a lie he would tell me. "He didn't know."

"He'll stand with me regardless," I snarled, as rage covered the pain.

"Yes. He will." He turned to leave, then stopped. "We all will, Trinity. Despite what I said, we need you. I don't think I realized how much we needed you until you were gone."

There was something raw and embarrassed in that confession, but he put it out there anyway, even if he couldn't quite look into my eyes as he said it.

"Captain," I murmured. "I'm not going to let the monster take me over."

Maybe he believed that. "Call me when you need me." He walked away, climbed into his car, and drove away.

"Come," Amias said, appearing as suddenly as he'd disappeared. He took my arm. "Dawn is near and I would like you in my bed. We will sleep in your way station room."

I didn't have to glance at the sky to know dawn was coming. I could feel it. Nervous energy swirled in my stomach, heavy and full of acid. Protective, innate anxiety shivered through my mind. My skin began a subtle crawling, as though ants were climbing my legs, and my eyes grew heavy as my brain grew sluggish.

Dawn was no place for a vampire.

We had to fall into the safe arms of nothingness until the sun was chased away by the moon.

I wanted to talk with Amias about the captain's fears, about what he'd said, but it would serve no purpose.

Amias didn't have the answers. He just didn't.

"Let's go to Willow-Wisp," I said. "We'll sleep there." I hesitated. "I'm eager to see the sun again."

It was his turn to hesitate.

"What?" I asked.

"My love, not many can watch the sun arrive inside Willow-Wisp. Did you not wonder why I was the only vampire to sleep in the graveyard?"

At my silence, he hurried on. "The elder and I are old and powerful. Willow-Wisp would be crowded with vampires if they could watch the sun. You must come into the way station."

But I couldn't. "No," I said. "I have to try."

That I might not be able to withstand the sun inside the way station cemetery hadn't entered my mind. There was always the realization that I would have Willow-Wisp. I would have the sun.

And now he wanted to yank that hope away from me.

"It is not safe, Trinity," he said.

"I have to fucking try."

He followed me as I ran, and I felt his fear. His terror. He was afraid I'd die there, burning beneath a sun that did not want me.

And when we stood inside the gates, waiting amongst the crumbling tombstones, the sky began to lighten, too subtly to see, but strong enough to feel.

Pain roared over me as my skin began to crisp and smoke, but I didn't move. It couldn't be true. I would see the sun. I would.

I rubbed my arms as they began to blister, but didn't take my stare from the sky. "Give me the sun," I begged. "I belong here. Give me my sun."

But it was not my sun, and it would not see me as anything other than a vampire to burn. I was a creature of the night, and I would never see daylight again.

Amias wrapped me in his arms and took me into the ground, because there was no time, not even for someone as fast as him, to get me into the sleep room.

If he'd have waited another second, not even the ground would have accepted us. Vampires could sink into the earth to sleep, but only before the sun touched and claimed it.

So there was that one second, and he took it.

And I was certain I would lose myself to the darkness, because the light did not exist.

Not for me.

Chapter Twenty

COLD

When I awakened and came out of the ground, I was calmer.

But Amias was dark and sober as he studied me. "You have made your choice," he said, finally. "You have chosen the rifters."

I flashed him a grin, then wrapped my arms around his waist. "I've simply chosen to embrace who I am. Not just the vampire, but the rifter, as well. I don't have to let it make me a killing machine." I pressed a kiss against his throat. "Until I need to be a killing machine." I pulled away and peered into his face, willing him to believe me. Willing *me*, perhaps, to believe me.

"I will not become careless with those I love, Amias."

He leaned forward to kiss my forehead, and it didn't make me feel better. It made me feel like he was indulging me. Like he pitied me.

Later, I stood alone outside the way station and watched the moon. I let her bathe me in that soft, magical light, and I sent my thanks skyward. I would forget the harsh, burning sun, and I would appreciate the moon.

The sun was my enemy.

I made a decision not to let my reality distress me. I would embrace what I had, or I would go crazy longing for what could never be.

It was all in how you looked at things.

I would rock darkness.

The moon and my men were all I needed.

And blood.

And sex.

And…

I shuddered and pressed my palms against my eyes. "Shut up."

Bay Town was quiet—too quiet—as the supernats prepared for the trouble Safin and his crew had brought to Red Valley.

The trouble the dragon had brought.

I shrugged off the worry over my inner rifter and stood in the still, cold darkness, soaking in the night and its muted sounds and scents and emotions.

Four vampires slipped from the line of trees behind me and crept forward. I couldn't smell them and I didn't hear them, but I felt them.

"Why are you here?" I asked, without turning around.

"The master sent us to guard you," a woman said, holding her palms up when I faced them. "He wanted us to help when Darkness returns."

She stared in my direction but didn't directly look at me, and neither did the three males with her. I walked to them, and could feel their desire to move away from me even as they forced themselves to stay put.

"Angela, isn't it?" I asked.

She looked at me then, surprise in her eyes. "Yes."

"I appreciate the help. I need vampires at my back." I gestured at the house. "Come in, please. The place is too silent. It bugs me."

Not that the vampires would liven it up any. They were nervous, quiet, and quickly suspicious. The humans and supernats would come to relax in a changed world long before the vampires would.

She glanced at the three men with her—all four of them were older, experienced, and deadly in a fight, but they were not ready to settle into a house full of supernats. Or me, because they still felt the rifter inside me and that screwed with them.

"If it's okay, we'll keep watch out here," she said.

I nodded, unsurprised. "You'll be welcome inside if

117

you decide to enter."

They needed their invitation, and now they had it. They could come into the way station whenever they wanted.

I stopped when I reached the porch and turned back to them. "You're not the only vampires Amias has patrolling the area."

"No. There will be dozens of us here each night. And Jade Noel is patrolling with her crew and Alejandro Rodríguez."

"What are your orders?" I asked, curious.

"To maintain your health," she said, flashing a quick smile. "To protect and defend you and your men."

I tilted my head. "And the executioners?"

She shrugged. "We will fight when we need to fight."

"Even if you can't win?" I asked, curious.

"Even then."

"I will, as well," I murmured, and my kinship with the vampires was undeniable.

I left them and went into the house to join the others and wait for what the night would bring. Executioners, maybe.

Death, likely.

Safin had given us three days.

I wasn't sure any of us believed he would keep his word.

There was no honor in Darkness.

Angus sat at the table, and Jin bustled at the stove, but still, it was too heavy. Too quiet. Too depressing.

I tried to shake off the melancholia but it did not want to budge. Things had changed too much, too fast.

Shane wasn't in the room, but as I'd felt the other vampires, I felt him. Only much more strongly. He stood in the backyard, staring into the sky, his thoughts as dark as the night.

He didn't run, even though I'd left him alone to give him the chance. He'd made his choice. He was staying with the group, where he belonged.

Angus opened his arms and I went to him. I wound my arms around his neck and pulled his scent deep into my brain. "Where is everybody?"

"They'll be here for dinner."

"Leo?" I asked.

"He's with Rhys."

"Good. I don't like him out there alone."

Angus laughed. "Trin, have you seen what Leo can do?"

"Doesn't matter," I said stubbornly. "Things can happen to supernats. You know that."

"Yeah. I know."

"Everything would be perfect right now if the executioners would disappear."

"Word of the fabricated sightings reached Safin," he said. "He sent some of his men to look into them."

"But he's still here."

"Yeah. The asshole is still here."

I began to pace, unsettled. I wished a visitor would come off the path. I was beginning to think I'd somehow failed to take back the reins from the elder since I hadn't had heard so much as a peep.

Angus walked to the fridge for a cold beer, and I grabbed his arm when he walked by me.

"Angus," I said. "Bring some of your children. Please. They can have their dinner here. Can they, Jin?"

Jin practically danced with joy. "I will prepare a feast."

"Or just throw in a couple extra potatoes," I said dryly. Jin tended to be overly dramatic at times. "Is it safe for them to come, Angus?"

Angus nodded. "I'll send word for the guards to warn me if Safin leaves the city. I can get my little ones to safety before he gets near the way station." He patted my ass. "Go on, sit. I'll call Derry."

I hesitated, but in the end, I sat down. Derry hadn't seen me since I'd turned, and I wasn't sure how she'd react.

"There's this tug of war," I said, after he'd murmured a few words into his cell, then slid it back into his pocket, "I feel this coldness, and that's okay with me, but at the same time, I'm jittery and uncomfortable and unsure."

"It'll take some time," Angus said. "You'll sort yourself out."

Abruptly, I was once again hungry. Amias had fed me when we'd awakened, but apparently, I was a stress eater.

My appetite grew stronger as I watched the pulse in Angus's throat jump, as my mind quieted and I concentrated on the roar of blood through his veins.

He lifted his beer bottle and downed the contents, and I watched his throat work as he swallowed.

Angus was one tasty son of a bitch.

He lowered the bottle and then froze at the look on my face.

"I'm hungry," I said, simply. I felt no shame in my hunger. I felt only eagerness, desire, and the certainty that in the next couple of minutes, I was going to feed.

From him, preferably.

But I was going to feed.

I was standing in front of him before I realized I'd moved. There was no fear in the alpha werebull's eyes. His stare sharpened and became bright with a different kind of hunger.

"So fast," he murmured.

I pressed my body against his swiftly hardening cock, and though my desire for his blood was foremost in my mind, my desire for his body was intense.

"Not in my kitchen," Jin said, banging a large spoon on the stove. "Out with you! The children will arrive soon." He chased us from the kitchen and we went, laughing and impatient, and I was as full of nerves and excitement as I'd been the first time I'd ever had sex, fallen in love, or fed.

I hoped I would never lose that excitement, but I was a vampire. I'd lose it someday.

But not this day.

Forgetting about executioners and the potential brokenness inside me, I hurried with Angus from the kitchen, my senses exploding with life, love, and the temptation of blood.

He took me to the basement room, perhaps because danger was close and no one was more vulnerable than when in the middle of sex and blood.

Angus opened the door, then pulled me into the room. He pressed my palm against his erection, groaning when I squeezed it.

"Get naked for me, werebull," I murmured.

He was out of his clothes in sixty seconds flat. He sprawled on the huge bed, grinning up at me, his stare both hot and brimming with love. "Play as you will, Bloodhunter."

He didn't have to tell me twice.

I shed my clothes and then jumped on top of him, wallowing around like he was a mountain of smooth, warm silk.

I licked my way down his chest and then slid his hardness into my mouth, careful not to let my fangs drop down and hurt him.

He groaned and buried his fingers in my hair. "I will never get enough of you," he murmured.

I could live with that.

Life was pretty perfect for a rifter.

Feed, fuck, and fight.

It didn't get better than that.

Chapter Twenty-One

MAGIC

I placed Silverlight on a side table and gazed happily around the crowded kitchen.

"Better?" Angus asked, smiling down at me.

I nodded, overflowing with the goodness of his blood and the joy of his noisy children.

"Trinity!"

I looked up just as Derry barreled into me, and returned her hug tentatively as I waited for her to realize that I was no longer the person she remembered.

It was as though she had no idea that I might have doubts, or that I believed she should. She was the same as she'd always been. To her, so was I.

"I *missed* you," she said, then grabbed my hand and pulled me to the table. "We all did. Dad, did you tell her that Shelby got his shift, and Lindsey was apprenticed to a witch?" She chattered on, and I sat soaking up the noise and laughter and warmth. That kitchen was brighter than any sun.

They dug into the food Jin placed before them, and when I glanced at his almost cheerful face, I realized I wasn't the only one who missed the sound of laughter around the kitchen table.

"I didn't get anything," one of the little girls said glumly, and Derry hastened to make her feel better.

"You will someday, sweetie."

"Daddy always says that too." The little girl—Natalie—picked up her fork and poked at a mound of potatoes. "But it never happens."

"You're only seven years old," Angus said, leaning over

to drop a kiss on the child's head before taking a seat beside me. "My girls are too impatient." He winked at me. "All of them."

But a sudden chill washed over me, and I didn't return his smile. "Angus," I said, without meaning to, "I love you."

Everyone quieted, then Derry rushed in to fill the suddenly uneasy silence. "I love you too, Daddy."

"Me too," one of the little boys pipped up, then everyone in the room decided that they loved Angus and should tell him so as quickly as possible.

I couldn't help but laugh, but the chill lingered.

Clayton and Rhys walked into the kitchen smiling, and Angus roared a welcome and thumped the table so hard the plates jumped. "Sit and eat," he demanded. "If you don't mind a roomful of noisy children."

Jin sat full plates before them almost before they were settled into their chairs, and I was sure, even over the noise, that I heard him humming.

"Where's Leo?" I asked, watching everyone eat, tempted to try a bite myself. If I hadn't been reasonably sure I'd throw it up immediately and ruin everyone's meal, I might have tried. "He likes to eat."

"I'm here," Leo said, from the doorway.

Shane was beside him.

I watched my hunter, thrilled he was joining us, afraid to speak up and spook him.

Angus had no such fear. "Jin," he called. "Find an extra chair for Shane and Leo." He lowered his voice. "I got Shane a phone," he told me. "He asked for one. He'll be okay, Trin."

My heart lightened further. Shane was using a phone, coming in to the brightness of the house, and so far, he hadn't killed anyone. Things were looking up.

Leo went with Jin and returned with two rather heavy patio chairs. "They will have to do," he said, when I lifted an eyebrow. "If this becomes a regular occurrence, we will need another table and more chairs."

"Scoot, children," I said, and two of the older ones pushed their chairs apart to make room for Shane and Leo.

I watched Shane from the corner of my eye, hoping to appear casual, pretty sure I was failing miserably.

He couldn't eat, was still mad as hell, and didn't seem overly eager to be in the same room with me, but he sat. He glanced at me once, then looked away.

Shane was lonely.

In the way station kitchen, at that moment, was only happiness. We all felt it. But things could change in the blink of an eye.

And I blinked.

Jin turned from the stove. "Darkness," he almost shrieked. "He's here."

The children immediately dropped their forks and stared at Angus, waiting for him to tell them what to do.

"How the fuck did they get here without anyone seeing them?" Angus roared.

Magic, that was how. Fucking magic.

I stood and strode across the kitchen floor, pausing to snatch up Silverlight and sling the sheath over my shoulder. All five men were warm and ready at my back. "Bastards," I muttered. They'd ruined a perfect night.

"Stay here," Angus told his kids.

"Daddy," little Natalie called. "I'm scared."

Derry rushed to comfort the child, but when I glanced back, what seemed like a sea of pale faces stared back at me.

Life was hard for a supernatural child.

"I'll be with you in a minute," Angus told me. He didn't have to tell the others to watch my back. He knew they would.

He rushed back to the children and I could hear him murmuring to Natalie as I left the kitchen and went to meet the executioners.

We didn't want to fight. Not right then. People would

die—likely *our* people—so we would put off that eventuality for as long as we possibly could.

"Rhys," I said, as the pounding began on the front door.

"No," he answered.

"They don't know Rhys is the dragon," Clayton reassured me. "He's safe."

"No one is safe," I said.

"Open the door," Shane said, his voice tight with excitement.

He was spoiling for a fight, and I knew exactly how he felt. That same excitement lived inside me.

Who could be afraid when they were brimming with cold, killing joy?

"Here we go," I muttered, and pulled Silverlight from her sheath as I flung open the door.

"Hello," Aspen said, smiling. "You didn't think we were going to leave you alone, did you?"

"I think you will when I deprive you of your head," I replied, way more calmly than I felt.

She laughed but I turned my attention to Safin, the only one who really mattered. Safin was my equal. His people were not.

Those eyes. They held me pinned to the spot, fascinated, afraid, intrigued. "I wouldn't have taken you for a liar, Safin," I lied.

"I would like to make sure there's no dragon hiding under your bed." He gave a deliberate pause. "Or in it."

"Move aside, Sinclair," Aspen said, "before we *make* you move."

Angus was suddenly there, his body pressing against my back. "Threaten her again," he said, his voice quiet, "and I will kill you where you stand."

Aspen paled.

No one doubted that the werebull could—or would—do as he promised.

"While I'm in Red Valley," Safin said, "Bay Town

belongs to me. If you prefer a show, I can surround this place with fire and bullets and force my way in." He waited.

Angus's children were inside. The last thing I wanted was bullets flying over their heads. I should never have asked Angus to bring them there. But it was the way station. It belonged to Himself, really, didn't it?

It should have been off limits to a bunch of assholes wanting to kill supernaturals.

It should have been.

Apparently, it wasn't.

"Make it quick." And I moved aside.

Aspen smirked, and I made a mental note that before it was all over, I was going to hurt her.

She saw that dark promise in my eyes and as she passed me, she bumped me with her shoulder like a bully in a school hallway. "Looking forward to it, vampire," she said. She pointed a thumb at her fellow bully. "This is Edgar, by the way."

"I don't give a fuck," I said.

Edgar peered into the kitchen, then quickly stepped through the doorway. "What is this, some kind of supernat school in your kitchen?"

The children were gathered into a knot of fear, the bigger children surrounding the smaller ones. They recoiled when the large human, covered in weapons and tattoos—sidled toward them.

But Angus planted himself quickly and firmly between the executioner and the kids. "They're off fucking limits, asshole."

Edgar narrowed his eyes, folded his arms, and glared at Angus. "You're awful brave for a supernat who has human authority in his house. You might want to step the fuck away, *asshole.*"

Angus cracked his neck and loosened his shoulders. "Safin."

Mikhail leaned against the doorway, his stare amused

but watchful. "Yes?"

"Do you want to control your goon or should I do it for you?"

Enraged, Edgar didn't wait for Mikhail to speak. With a growl, he went for Angus.

"Daddy," someone cried, and immediately Angus's attention snapped to his children.

Edgar punched him in the jaw, and Edgar was neither small nor weak. And even as Angus staggered back, Natalie broke free and ran screaming toward him. "Don't hurt my daddy!"

Angus shot Edgar a look that promised retribution, then leaned forward and scooped up his little girl.

The men and I faced off against the executioners as Angus assured Natalie that he was fine. Derry and one of her brothers waited to take the frightened child from Angus's arms, but she buried her face against his neck and sobbed as though her heart were breaking.

Most supernat kids grew hardened to the brutality they witnessed—brutality that was so frequent it was somewhat normal and always expected. But Natalie was different. Delicate. Shocked by violence and horrified that her precious father might be hurt.

Poor kid. She had an innocence most nonhuman children lost early, and as I watched Angus soothe her, an icy chill slipped down my spine.

Something had happened to me when Amias had brought me back. I was getting useless premonitions way too often, and I didn't want them. What good were they?

They were indistinct and confusing and told me nothing.

Still…

"Angus," I said. "Give her to me."

He frowned. "Trin…"

"I need to take her home."

He transferred the child into my arms. There was a question in his eyes, but I couldn't answer it. I just needed her with me. I needed to protect her.

"Gather the children, Derry," I said. "I'm taking you home."

"I'll go with you," Leo said.

Edgar held up his hands and shocked us all. "Wait," he said, his voice gruff. "I apologize for being a dick with children in the room. I…" He shook his head and ran a hand over his face, then eyed Natalie. "I'm sorry, little girl."

Natalie raised her head off my shoulder and looked at him. "You are?"

His face softened. "Yes."

"Okay."

He gave her a smile that transformed his face.

Darkness grew tired of watching a scene that was quickly turning soft and uninteresting. "Edgar, are you coming, or have you decided to stay here and be the baby minder?"

Edgar flushed.

With a last glance at the children, he left the kitchen.

"I'm taking the kids home," I told my men. "Don't let those assholes out of your sight."

"No." Derry said. "Harlan drove his car, and I drove mine. We'll take them back, Trin. I want you to…" She glanced at her dad, and I understood. She wanted me to stay there and take care of him.

Angus snorted and shook his head in disgust, but his stare was soft as he eyed her. "Get them home, then, girl."

Harlan, one of his older sons, took Natalie. "Call me if you need me, Dad."

Angus kissed the boy's forehead. "I will."

As the children hurried through the kitchen doorway, we went after the executioners, unwilling to let them explore the house without supervision. God knew what they'd get up to.

In my bedroom—my former bedroom—Darkness stood in the middle of the room, getting his impressions.

"Where do you sleep now?"

I curled my lip. "You know I'd never tell you that."

"Is it true," Aspen asked, "that you're banging all these men? Vampires and giants and weres…" She winked. "Oh my."

I smiled. "Jealous?"

"Maybe."

In another time, if she hadn't been an executioner, I might have liked Aspen.

Maybe I'd even have liked Edgar.

Darkness…no.

Not so much.

"Somewhere close," he said.

"She won't stray far from her bounty of warm flesh," Aspen agreed.

I crossed my arms and said nothing.

"Give me the name of the dragon," Safin said. He didn't raise his voice, didn't change expressions, but the command was strong.

And he had absolutely no doubt that I would give him the name. Maybe not right then, but eventually, I would cave.

But he didn't know me at all.

From the corner of my eye I saw Rhys stiffen just the tiniest bit.

"Finish your search and get the hell out of my house," I said. "I don't know who he is, and I wouldn't tell you if I did. You're wasting your time. And mine."

He studied me for a few seconds, his gaze considering. "I see a human peeking through those lovely eyes," he told me. "But I also see a monster. Which one, I wonder, will win when I start cutting little pieces off the ones you care about?"

Chapter Twenty-Two

RAGE

Not one of us could speak. Not at first, not while we tried to absorb the terribleness of the words Darkness had just uttered.

A trembling began deep in my belly and traveled slowly toward my chest. Right before my heart was overtaken, however, I reached down even deeper than the shaky terror and surrounded my heart with something fear couldn't penetrate. Ice. Black, cold ice.

Safin gave me a nod, his stare never leaving mine. "That's what I thought." Then he gestured to Aspen and Edgar, and they followed him from the room without a word.

But when Aspen looked at Safin, she had a spark of curiosity in her eyes.

No one spoke again until we stood outside, my line of supernats facing off against his line of executioners.

"The dragon," he said.

I shook my head. "We don't have the dragon. We don't know who he is."

He gave me a sharp nod. "All right. We'll do this the hard way."

"Do it any way you want," I told him. "It won't make a dragon appear."

His freaky golden eyes seemed to burn into my brain, but I couldn't look away. If I looked away, he would see it as weakness. And the last thing I wanted was Mikhail Safin to see any of us as weak.

"The mayor told us you're leashed by the very people who hired you," Rhys said, surprising me. Not because of his words, but because he'd spoken up at all. He was drawing attention to himself. "You're not permitted to stomp into Bay Town and start torturing nonhumans."

"I am not permitted to *slaughter* a town of nonhumans," Safin said, as though he took Rhys's words seriously and wished to better explain the facts to him. "At least, not without provocation. I am, however, free to torture a select few." His smile was polite.

It was still scary as fuck.

He waited a few seconds to see if Rhys wanted to argue.

Rhys did not.

Unable to resist, I slipped my hand into the dragon's.

He squeezed my fingers, gently.

Safin's stare traveled from my face to our laced fingers, and a whisper of a frown caused a line to appear between his brows, there and gone so quickly I thought I might have imagined it.

He looked up and caught me watching him, and there must have been something in my eyes he didn't like. When he next spoke, there was a thin undercurrent of anger in his voice.

"You'll force me to hurt your people."

Angus didn't wait for me to speak. Vibrating with rage and frustration, he faced down the executioner. "And you will force us to kill you."

Aspen closed her eyes and rubbed the bridge of her nose, as though she were too exasperated for words. "Don't make this into a war you can't win. If you care about the other trash in this town, you'll give us the fucking dragon." She shook her head and spread her hands, her voice almost cajoling. "We'll get him anyway. Why make us cause so much pain first? Hmm? Our boss won't like it, your boss won't like it…I mean, come *on.*"

Perhaps the worst thing was that she was dead serious and truly confused.

Her threat had the opposite effect on me than the one

she'd intended. She threw her words like poisonous darts, and the weight of them, added to Safin's cruel promises, was the tipping point.

Rage rose up like a tidal wave and washed away my fear. It also washed away my control. I felt the vampire-rifter coldness in that flood, and I embraced it. And in the end, if that was all that remained of me, I'd take it happily.

There was no fear, and there was no doubt. Only dominance and death.

"You won't take what's mine," I told Safin. "You want to bring a fight to me, Darkness?" I took a step toward him, then another, and he watched me come with a quickly sharpening stare and a tension in his body that hadn't been there before. "I'm ready for you."

He was unprepared, and he knew it.

Things had accelerated a little too quickly.

And that was his own damn fault.

Weapons appeared in Edgar and Aspen's hands. Not strange, magical weapons—just regular old guns. The two executioners crept sideways, widening the distance between them.

They wouldn't know it, but vampires—dozens of vampires—were a few yards behind them.

I couldn't help it. I laughed.

Cold joy filled my heart, excitement sang through my veins, and a hunger like I'd never known overtook my brain. I was bursting with energy, and though I didn't take another step, my body vibrated with the need to run, to slash, to bite.

Oh, how I wanted to fight.

I didn't have to look to know Amias was suddenly at my back. I felt him there, just as I felt the explosion of *life* inside me.

"Mikhail," Aspen muttered, her voice tight and ready and eager.

But Mikhail didn't reply, and he didn't take his stare from mine.

I sniffed the air, scenting his danger, but it didn't calm me. It excited me further.

"What are you?" he murmured, finally. "Not just a vampire in there."

"No," I agreed.

My body hurt. I needed to release some energy or I would surely explode. I had no idea what was happening, and I had no idea how I was controlling it. I didn't *want* to. I wanted to run through Safin's group and rip them to bloody chunks of meat, and I wanted to devour them.

I moaned, and it did something to my men. It called to them, brought out their monsters, and forced to the surface their own bloodlust.

Angus shifted in seconds, his perfect silver horn flashing as he tossed his head. Blacklight screamed to life in Clayton's grip, and blood ran down Shane's chin as his sharp fangs violently dropped and sliced his lip. Amias growled, unchanged—but the master was always ready.

Amias Sato was always his monster.

I couldn't find Rhys. He'd run from my call. From the risk of being seen.

If he shifted, did the executioners have something sneaky up their sleeves, some way to kill a dragon? I couldn't image they did. They needed the man to appear—not the beast.

But I could not underestimate Mikhail Safin.

I had a feeling that if anyone could strike down a dragon, at least one in the early throes of shifting, Darkness could.

Leo had dropped to one knee and raised his fist, but he didn't hit the ground. He didn't want to kill them.

And Leo's power didn't just kick ass. It annihilated.

The sound of abruptly discordant sirens grew louder as squad cars sped toward us. Crawford was coming.

Had I called him? I couldn't remember.

"Mikhail," Aspen yelled, flashing her gun from one supernatural to the other. "Kill them?"

133

And then, she got tired of waiting.

With no answer from her boss, she pulled the trigger. She was aiming at Clayton and she'd have hit him—if not for Blacklight.

Clayton's sword not only deflected the shot, but caused it to ricochet, and ricochet *hard*. Blacklight, otherwise known as Miriam Crow the necromancer, shot Aspen with her own bullet.

Her cheekbone shattered and she screamed, but despite being shot in the face, she didn't drop her weapon. Even as Edgar reached for her, she lifted the gun and once again took aim at Clayton.

"How the hell," she screamed, shock in her voice. "How the hell?" Then she turned on Safin. "Why didn't you protect me?" She cupped her cheek with one hand and held her gun with the other. "You fuck," she howled. "You fuck."

Mikhail didn't pull a gun—he reached under his loose coat and emerged with a coiled whip.

"Stand down," he said to his crew, and then he unfurled that whip and sent it streaking toward Clayton. It released sparks of golden fire as it flew through the night, and no one there doubted its power. The air was suddenly crackling with electricity, and I knew if Safin's whip reached Clayton, he was going to be in trouble.

Why everyone was picking on Clayton I couldn't have said—until I glanced at him.

Blacklight had surrounded him in a foggy black haze of smoke, and when he moved, the smoke moved with him. Demon smoke, demon fire. It swirled around him, leaving trails that reminded me somewhat of the vampire fog trails a bloodhunter would see.

The trails I used to see, before I'd died.

In that black, wispy smoke were…faces. Faces with gaping mouths releasing silent screams, screams I thought I would be able to hear if only I could listen.

Angus roared and charged Clayton to shove him out of

the way of Safin's whip, but when the werebull hit that smoke, it was like hitting a brick wall at full force.

There was no time to see if he was okay. The golden whip hit the smoke, and with a sound like the world cracking, the whip broke through.

It curled around Clayton's neck and was colored immediately with scarlet as it cut through his flesh. Still, Clayton had lived in hell for a very, very long time, and he didn't lose his cool—he whirled his sword and brought it down on the whip.

But Clayton would be decapitated by that evil golden whip long before the sword managed to sever it.

On my back, Silverlight woke up.

The first thing I saw after I ripped her from her sheath was Safin's eyes, bright and full of interest, and I knew he would try to take her. In the end, he would try.

I brought my blade up under the whip, joining Clayton and Blacklight in a desperate attempt to sever the wicked cord that held him. I felt it, through my sword. I felt power and coldness and strength and a sort of springiness, and it was like trying to cut through the tentacle of a monstrous, electrified octopus.

The whip was strong and full of magic.

But Silverlight, an ancient, mystical weapon forged in hell, was stronger than a dozen whips.

When his weapon began to split beneath her blade, Safin released Clayton and yanked the whip home. Immediately, Clayton reeled backward, one of his hands to his throat.

He radiated weakening puffs of black smoke as he stumbled toward the way station to recover, Blacklight still firmly in his grip. Jin would care for him.

Bracketed by Amias and Shane, Leo at my back, I whirled to face the executioners. If one of them had so much as twitched, we'd have torn them apart. We wanted to—I could feel Amias and Shane's desire to fight, to kill, to *eat* just as I felt my own—but Safin was not a stupid man.

He shoved his whip, once more coiled and quiet, under his coat.

"Mikhail," Aspen said, her mouth barely moving. "I *told* you it was a bad idea to come alone."

"If I had brought more people," he said, smoothly, "the vampires surrounding us would likely have eaten you by now."

She gasped and jerked around, her gun in one hand and a stake in the other, but there were no vampires to see. She whirled back to face me and the supernaturals around me, her face leaking blood, her eyes crazy. "Let's fight!"

"No." He didn't look at her. "Now is not the time."

"It will never be the time," I snarled, disappointed that I would not kill them all, yet relieved that I would not kill them all. I was torn between darkness and light.

I couldn't have said which one was stronger.

Doors slammed and whirling police car lights danced in the night.

Frank Crawford came cautiously toward us. Apparently, he'd decided he could be both mayor and cop.

"Safin," he said. He edged forward, four uniformed cops—guns drawn—at his side. He also held a gun, but kept it pointed at the ground. "I want you and your crew to get into your vehicles and drive the fuck away. Now."

For a breathless moment I was positive Safin would rebel against the order, but in the end, he inclined his head and relented.

But he had one last thing to say. "You all seem to be laboring under the misapprehension that you have choices in this matter. You do not. And the blood of the Bay Town supernaturals will be on your hands." He included us all in his dark glance.

"Safin," Crawford said, lifting his gun. "Take off."

"We're going," Safin said. "But you know we'll be back."

We watched him silently as he strode away. Edgar was

practically dragging Aspen as she began to feel the effects of her injury.

"How in the hell," Crawford said, watching them go, "did one of them get hurt?"

"Miriam," I murmured. "And the demons."

He looked at me, clueless. "What?"

"Blacklight," I elaborated. "Clayton's sword caused her bullet to ricochet. I figure that whatever protections she has in place kept her from dying tonight." I slid Silverlight back into the sheath. "And I figure she knows it."

"I'll talk with Himself," Angus said. "I don't see a way out of this."

He stood with his arms crossed, unconcerned with his nakedness and the cold temperature of the still night air. He sported a huge, spreading bruise across his right shoulder and chest, and watching him, I forgot about everything else and wanted only to go to him. To touch him.

His body would be as hot as a furnace, despite the chill, and I wanted him to wrap me up in that heat. I dropped my gaze from his bunching arm muscles to his tight, muscular abs, and lower still, to his heavy, hanging sex.

His cock twitched and began immediately to stiffen. *"Shit,* Trin," he muttered, and stomped away to find some clothes.

And then he'd visit the King of Everything to see if maybe we could get a little fucking help from the most powerful man we knew.

PART TWO

THE DARKNESS

Chapter Twenty-Three

SMOKESCREEN

"I called your shifts," I said. "I didn't know I could do that."

"It was a strange feeling," Clayton said.

We sat in the kitchen, Rhys, Clayton, Shane, Leo, and I, waiting for Angus to return. I hoped that somehow the King of Everything would know how to handle the executioners, but I was pretty sure that if he could have, he already would have. He wouldn't need us to ask.

"Yeah," Rhys agreed. "It was like you were inside me and had my beast by the throat. You were dragging him out and all I could do was run. And even then, I nearly lost control."

"But you're a dragon," Leo said. "Not even her call could force you to shift. But the others couldn't fight her."

They nodded. Maybe someday that ability would come in handy.

"You should leave town," I told Rhys.

Rhys shocked me by nodding. "I have a plan. It may not work—probably won't—but I'm going to take off and cause some ruckus far from here." He shrugged. "Maybe that will convince him the dragon doesn't live in Bay Town."

"Burn a path across the country," Leo said. "Make him think you're passing through and not settled anywhere. You don't want to bring trouble to another town."

That was Leo. No matter what was going on, he was concerned for other people.

"Agreed," Rhys said.

Neither of them seemed very convinced Rhys's plan

would work. Safin was a smart guy and he had his mind made up. He would know that the dragon would try to throw up a few smokescreens.

But it was a plan, and it was better than the nothing we currently had.

Clayton sat at the table, his throat wound still open and glistening, but it looked better than it had when I'd first walked into the room.

"Can I do anything for you?" I asked him.

"I'll heal," he murmured, his voice raw and low. It hurt him to talk, so I didn't question him further.

I nodded, then blew out a hard breath and pushed away from the table. "Shane," I said.

He looked at me, surprise in his eyes before he blanked them. "Yeah?"

"You're hungry." I held out my hand. "Let me feed you."

I could feel his hunger. He was starving himself, and it showed in his dull eyes, his dry, pale skin, and his sharp cheekbones.

He ignored my hand. "When I want to eat, I'll eat." Then he stood and disappeared through the back doorway.

"Fuck," I muttered, irritated, disappointed, and just a little hurt. I shouldn't have been—it was his right to refuse me—but I was. "He's stubborn."

"Give him time," Rhys said. "He'll come around."

"He's starving," I said, a little too sharply. "There is no time."

"All it will take is a drop of your blood on his lips," Rhys said. "He won't resist you then."

I thought about it. I'd force-fed him after I'd captured him. I could attempt it again, but any trickery on my part was going to drive him farther away.

I'd wait for as long as I could.

But he had to feed.

"When are you leaving?" I asked Rhys, changing the subject.

"I'll get a couple hours of sleep and head out in the morning. I'll be back before you awaken."

I nodded, but all I wanted was to beg him not to leave. I wanted to lock him in the safe room with me. "I have a bad feeling, Rhys."

"You've been through some really intense and quick changes, love. What can I do to help you?"

I looked at him, and almost before the last word fell from his lips I was tingling with need, desire, and hunger.

I rubbed at the gooseflesh on my arms. "It doesn't matter what else is going on, the mere hint of food and sex makes me..." I groped for the words, and finally, I found them. "Makes me insane with need. And nothing else matters."

I tried to fight the craving, but the more I resisted, the stronger it became.

"I need to find Amias," I murmured.

Rhys lifted an eyebrow and then took my hands. "No, you don't. I'm right here. I have blood. I have a cock. Both of those are yours." His eyes twinkled when he smiled, and just that quickly, there was nothing on my mind but Rhys Graver and his freely offered blood and cock.

"Yummy," I said.

He laughed. "Back atcha."

I had to give my inner vampire a break and let my rifter out to play. It was the only way I could duck all the bad shit flying around trying to knock my brains out.

Rhys was mouthwatering with his freaky dragon sex and his magical, scorching-hot blood.

And he was mine.

All I had to do was take him.

"Yes," I said.

Something dark flashed through his eyes. I wondered if he saw that same darkness in me. And suddenly, I wasn't the one with the largest need and lust and craving in that room.

I wasn't the one with the darkness.

Rhys was.

I hesitated, shocked by the abrupt zing of fear that streaked through me.

"Can we really do this here?" I tried to hide my shaking hands against my legs, but he knew. He felt my fear.

He was pleased by it.

"My dragon will not be restrained tonight."

"But...you can't shift in the house." The basement was big, but it wasn't *that* big.

He shuddered at the thought of shifting, then groaned and abruptly unfastened his pants. His cock sprang free, and I could not resist wrapping my fingers around his almost extreme heat. "I'll show you something," he said. "Are you ready?"

"I don't know," I answered, honestly.

"It doesn't matter," he said.

I had a feeling it might matter just a little. Especially to me. But what was I going to do? I was already swept away by my own desire and the excitement of knowing that every time I was with him, the dragon was going to show me something new.

Something incomparable.

I could only hope that he had figured out how to control his shift, because if he couldn't, there weren't enough Captain Crawfords in the world to make Mikhail Safin leave us the hell alone.

Chapter Twenty-Four

LOSS

"Can you not kill him?" I asked, as we slipped away from the house. "Sneak in and make it look like an accident?"

He looked at me.

I shrugged. "I've heard the stories."

He said nothing for a few minutes. "Funnily enough, Trinity, I wanted to keep the bad stuff away from you. I didn't want you to know my…"

"Darkness?"

"I suppose so, love."

"And now?"

"Now, you can handle it." He flashed me a smile, quick and white. "Now, *you* are the darkness. I think you always were," he continued, more to himself than to me, "but in a different way."

"I'm one of you."

"You are," he agreed.

Still, he seemed strangely hesitant to discuss his life.

"You killed people?" I asked, finally. "Humans? For money?"

I hoped I didn't sound like I was judging. Who among us hadn't killed a douchebag or two?

"Yes," he said. "When it was necessary."

"Necessary?"

"I kill people like Safin," he said. "But none were quite as powerful."

I snagged his hand. "Kill him, Rhys. If you can do it and make it not touch the supernaturals or lead back to you, then kill him."

He squeezed my fingers, his voice as dark as the night

through which we walked. "I'm good, love. But I don't know if I'm that good."

"Why not?"

"He has…" He shook his head, gathering his thoughts. "He has some sort of knowledge. I won't catch him by surprise, I don't think."

I curled my lip, easily and casually contemptuous of the executioner. "He's human, no matter how much power and protection he's stolen, bought, or borrowed."

"You don't understand, Trinity."

"What? He's *human*. And you can shift into anything. Cling to his shirt as a button and when he's alone, shift to the sharpest blade you can and take his heart."

I could feel his sudden pain.

I stopped walking, grabbed his arms, and stared up into his face, shadowed and mysterious beneath the moon. "Rhys, what's wrong?"

He didn't want to say the words, but finally, he did. And then, I understood why he was so reluctant to talk about something that not only made him ashamed, but broke his heart.

"The dragon requires all my power, Trinity. I am now a dragon shifter. Nothing more." He pulled himself free and walked on, leaving me to stare after him, stunned.

I caught up with him, trying to stomp down the pity I was drowning in. Rhys would not want my pity.

"You're a dragon," I said, my voice hard enough to hide my horrified disbelief. "That's *everything*, Rhys. Your dragon is such a big deal that the government wants to kill you."

He didn't look at me. "If I survive the executioners, I'll figure it out."

"You can shift and be free. You just have to leave."

"I'd be on the run forever. Do you not understand what that would mean?"

I did. I did understand. "We'll get through this," I said, finally. But there was no belief in my voice.

And while I could, before I lost him, I wanted—needed—to lose myself in the dragon. Because one way or the other, I would lose him. Mikhail Safin would force him out of hiding eventually. He'd either run, or he would die.

My heart broke for him. My heart broke for all of us.

"Becoming an unfeeling monster doesn't seem like such a bad thing," I murmured.

"I know exactly what you mean." I didn't know how he could still smile, but he did, and it was genuine.

"I love you," I murmured.

We were deep in the woods of Bay Town, and when I closed my eyes and buried my face in the fabric of the night, I smelled nothing but clean, fresh air, small animals, vampire guards, and Leo.

"Leo is watching our backs," I said.

He nodded. "I know." He reached out to touch my face. "He'll resist you, Trinity. He's afraid of losing himself. His power. He also wants to be loved and wanted for himself, despite his face. And he doesn't believe anyone can love him like that."

"Not even me?" I whispered.

"Not even us," he replied.

"We'll prove it to him."

But he shook his head. "Leo is good to his bones, but he will not let you use him."

I took a step back, frowning. "I don't want to *use* him."

He lifted an eyebrow. "Of course you do. You felt his power in that bite, didn't you? You felt what his blood could do for you, how powerful it could make you?" He paused, but went on when I said nothing. "His fear that you will want that power is not ungrounded, is it?"

"I don't know," I murmured, honestly.

"*He* does."

Biting Leo had given me the best high of my life. It had done something amazing to me. I wanted more of it. I wanted to see if it could make me strong enough to protect my supernats without worrying about groups like the executioners. I wanted that.

Did I want him for himself? Did I think about him when I was in the throes of sexual ecstasy? Did I love him so much I ached, the way I did with Angus, Clayton, and Rhys? Was I obsessed with him the way I was with Shane, and did I know I couldn't live without him the way I knew with Amias?

"Fuck," I whispered.

It was not the same with Leo as it was with the others.

Then I understood something else. I might not have felt an instant connection with Leo the way I had with them. He might not have been one of my fated loves. We might not have been meant for each other.

But when I thought of him, when I allowed myself to really think of him, closed my eyes and pictured his huge, hard body and his beautiful eyes, heard his laugh, felt his goodness, thought about his protectiveness, his humor, his pain, all I felt was love.

When I imagined what it would be like to touch him, all I felt was desire.

And when I imagined life without him, I was devastated.

Leo had sneaked up on my heart and planted himself firmly inside it. Not his power. Him.

I just had to make him believe that.

I opened my eyes and looked at Rhys. "I do love him," I said, simply. "How could I not?"

He grinned. "There you are, then."

Now I just needed to bond with the half-giant. I needed to make him believe I cared about him. I needed to make him mine.

When Rhys slid his full lips across mine, when I touched his smooth, dark skin, when I immersed myself in one of the men I loved with the realization it might be the last time, I kept Leo with me.

And even if he didn't know it, he was being loved by someone that night.

Chapter Twenty-Five

HEAT

"Thirty minutes," I murmured. "The sun is near. Make me come before dawn comes, Dragon."

I was hungry. Hungry for everything.

In seconds, I felt the air—scorching hot air—caressing my bare body.

I opened my mouth and his tongue slipped between my lips, burning my lungs when I inhaled, dripping down my throat when I swallowed.

He was heat.

Before Rhys, I'd had no idea how good it could feel to burn.

Heat came off him in waves and I began to shiver as that heat caressed me, penetrated me, consumed me.

He did everything a normal man would do, but it was like being touched by a god.

And then, there was only the sex.

It was like a drug, his sex, and I happily overdosed.

We lay bare and vulnerable on the hard ground, and I barely noticed the stones and sticks and other unfriendly objects that bruised my flesh and crunched beneath me.

But Rhys noticed, and he put me on top of him so I could use the sweetness of his body as my bed.

I tried to imagine what it would be like to be made love to by Rhys and Leo at the same time. To taste the perfect magic of Leo's blood while Rhys's dragon swallowed me whole...

It was unimaginable, really.

But it sure did get me hot.

Maybe Leo was in the darkness not with his back

turned, but watching us, longing for us, being a freak for us.

Rhys grabbed the backs of my legs, right beneath my ass, and held me still as he rubbed himself at my opening, groaning, whispering.

His breath sizzled across my skin like electricity, causing the fine hairs to stiffen, and as his dragon began to stir, the danger of it, and of discovery, took my excitement to a whole other level.

And then, I felt Shane.

I dragged my lips from Rhys's, and my body jerked as I sniffed the air, searching for my hunter.

I didn't have to wonder if he watched.

He watched.

"Is it Shane, love?" Rhys murmured.

"Yes."

"Do you want him here?"

I didn't hesitate. "Always."

"Then we will bring him." He reached up and buried his fingers in my hair, forcing my lips once more to his.

"How?" I whispered, into his mouth.

His voice was strained and raw. "I'll show you." He shoved himself into me at the exact second he raked a nail—a claw, rather—down the side of my neck.

Even as I cried out in surprise and shocked pleasure he began to move, and I met him thrust for thrust, my flowing blood beckoning to Shane.

He was so hungry.

And then he was there, behind me, and I sat up on Rhys as Shane pulled me back against his chest, tilted my head, and ran his tongue over my neck.

"Fuck," he groaned. "Fuck you."

He snaked his arms around my waist and slid his fingers over my breasts, squeezing a little too hard.

He held me as he drank, his warm tongue exploring my wound, as Rhys's fingers bit into my thighs, and I used my strong legs to lift and fall, lift and fall.

There was perfection in that union.

I stopped worrying about Rhys letting his dragon out to play. It was dangerous. It was risky—too risky.

We all knew that—Rhys most of all.

So Rhys could worry about it.

As we slammed against each other and Shane accepted the offering of my blood, I orgasmed. I orgasmed hard.

I orgasmed the way only a dragon could make a person orgasm. My whole world exploded.

And the dragon could not be contained.

Even as he began to change, to heat and smoke, he plunged inside me, began to grow, and the overpowering, vast pleasure grew with him.

I tightened my muscles around him and held him there. Maybe I was afraid if I released him he'd fly to the sky and the executioners would see him and that would be the end of everything.

But not even I, with my strength, could contain a dragon for long.

He spasmed inside me, releasing liquid fire that made me climax again, sending a path of ecstasy from between my legs to my belly to my brain.

I knew what it was like to be fucked by Rhys. I knew the extreme, almost unbearable pleasure pain, the extraordinary sea of emotions he could create inside me.

But that night, it was something even bigger.

I didn't know what.

I only knew that I had to taste him. Not Rhys—I'd already fed from him.

I had to drink from the *dragon*.

Still impaled by Rhys's growing cock, I ripped myself from Shane's mouth and pierced Rhys's neck with my razor sharp fangs. Then I formed a seal around the tiny wounds and began to suck.

The dragon screamed and his voice cut into me the way my fangs did him, and somehow, he began to feed from *me*.

I couldn't see, but I could feel.

And I felt the dragon. He rose up around me, inside me, under me, and flashes of red beat at my closed eyelids and I was consumed by a fire of primitive, unbearable pleasure.

I was ripped from him, flung from him, and the suddenness of it was so disorienting that I couldn't think. I didn't know what was happening.

Shane caught me and held me against him and I stared up at the vast darkness that was Rhys's dragon, a darkness that ate the moon, whirled like smoke, smoke that was so dark it stood out against the night sky.

I wanted to go with him into the sky. I wanted to cling to him, to ride him, to be part of him. Then, something on the ground a few yards in front of me moved, and I understood what Rhys had wanted to show me.

There was no dragon in the sky—there was only the spirit of the dragon.

I saw it, because...

Oh, for many reasons. Because he was mine. Because I was his. Because his blood was inside me and mine was inside him. Because he wanted me to.

I wasn't the only one to *feel* him. But I would be the only one to see him.

Then dawn was racing toward me.

The sun would kill me. Not even the spirit of a fierce dragon could protect me from that.

Worse, the sun would kill Shane.

So with my body still shuddering from the effects of dragon sex, and my mind stunned, overwhelmed, and completely disoriented, I still knew I had to get the fuck inside.

I grabbed Shane's hand, and I ran.

Behind me, the dragon screamed.

Huge wings beat the air, propelling us forward and him skyward. The night lit up with red and I moaned, sure the sun had come and we were burning, but it was only the dragon.

No. Not the dragon. The spirit of the dragon. I felt for those few minutes what Rhys felt every second of every day.

The chaos, the need, the primal longing…

How did he not lose his mind?

But then…something was wrong.

Now that the dragon wasn't the only thought in my head, I was able to feel other things—like the fact that something was fucking *wrong*.

I nearly broke down the kitchen door when I reached the way station.

Only Clayton was in the kitchen, standing in the middle of the room, his face pale, his hand pressed to his groin. The dragon had that effect on the supernaturals. All of them.

His throat was completely healed.

"Something is wrong," I told Clayton as I stumbled for the stairs, Shane right behind me. "I can't feel Amias."

"Sleep," was all he could manage, his voice thick and slow.

As if I had a choice.

Terror gripped me, but it didn't keep me from sliding into unconsciousness.

It was almost a relief.

For a while, there was nothing.

At least not for me.

But up top, the world carried on.

And sometimes, the day was no less dark than the night.

Chapter Twenty-Six

HORROR

Instantly awake, I shot open my eyes, sat up, and found Clayton standing beside my bed, watching me.

"Trinity," he said.

Panic, immediate and sharp, tightened my body.

I slid from the bed and began to dress, not taking my stare from his. "Tell me."

Shane stood as well, alert, quiet, and a little less...awful. The night had been good for him.

But it hadn't been good for everyone.

Clayton's voice was low and reluctant and his eyes were dark.

I was trembling even before he spoke the words.

"Nearly an hour ago Leo discovered a brutalized supernatural girl in the trunk of his car. He is..." He looked away from my horrified gaze, gathered himself, and continued on. "He didn't do it, Trinity."

"Of course he didn't do it." I pulled on my boots, my hands shaking. "This is Darkness," I murmured. "This is Safin cutting off little pieces of the ones we care about, just as he promised." I stood, and looked at him. "This is Safin forcing our hands. Where is Rhys?"

He stared blankly over my head. "He left Bay Town to show himself far away from here. He hasn't yet returned." Finally, he met my eyes, and for an instant, he was the Clayton of old—Miriam's Clayton—full of dark, scurrying things, crunchy, black torment, and most of all, a consuming hopelessness. "Darkness can win, Trinity."

He loved Rhys. Their connection was unbreakable. And Clayton was completely terrified, and completely sure.

In the end, Darkness would take Rhys.

He would take him, because we would hand him over.

I closed my eyes for a few seconds. "I have to feed. I need Amias. Where the hell is the master?"

Something is wrong.

"I'm here," Clayton said, then pulled me to him. "Feed." He held his hand out to Shane. "Come here."

And though Shane hesitated, he could not refuse Clayton's offer. Not with Clayton raw and agonized and afraid. Shane was an asshole at times. He wasn't a monster.

Not anymore.

I pulled back to look at Clayton. "The girl," I whispered.

"Eat first," he told me, and there was something in his eyes that told me I should do as he said.

I struck, and that was the first time since I'd turned that my feeding was methodical, clinical, and joyless. It was simply a necessity I couldn't ignore, not if I wanted to burst from that room and tear up the night, which I would absolutely need to do.

Shane fed from Clayton's other side, and we took only enough to get us through the next few hours. There was no time for anything else.

When I finished, Clayton put his fingers to his seeping wounds and there was no life in his eyes when he looked at me. "The girl is Angus's Derry," he said.

I pressed my fist against my teeth, unable to retract my fangs, unable, for a second, to function as the reality of his words sank in.

"Angus took her to the Deluge," he told me, before I had to ask. "Jade Noel is with them."

The healer was difficult and reclusive, but she would not turn away a child. Not ever.

Rhys was missing, Angus was shattered, and Amias was in trouble. The Bay Town supernatural children were in danger.

And I had a very bad feeling that the horror was just

beginning.

I was abruptly and completely overwhelmed. I swayed on my feet, my fingers to my temples. "Shit," I whispered. "Too much."

I did the only thing that made sense.

I reached into the blackness inside me and I yanked my inner rifter to the surface. It was the only way I could make things right. There were things I had to do, and I couldn't do them with worry, softness, or love.

I had to do them with rage.

When I straightened and opened my eyes, both Shane and Clayton recoiled.

"You're a fucking nightmare," Shane murmured.

I smiled and reached for Silverlight. "I'm about to become Mikhail Safin's fucking nightmare. See if you can find the elder in Willow-Wisp. He'll know where the master is. Do whatever he tells you to do. Clayton, make sure the children and the weak have been moved to the tunnels. Call upon the wolf pack to guard them."

He turned and jogged from the room without another word.

I dropped my phone into my pocket and turned to Shane. We stared at each other for a few seconds, and then I walked to him, took his face between my palms, and pressed my lips to his.

He didn't shove me away.

He didn't return my kiss or touch me or close his eyes, but he didn't shove me away.

Baby steps.

I rushed from the basement and left the house, my mind on Mikhail Safin. I slowed once so I could call Frank Crawford.

I explained that Derry had been attacked and left for us to find, and that I couldn't feel Amias.

That I was on my way to confront Darkness.

"Shit, Trinity," he murmured, trying to absorb my words. "Shit."

"Yeah," I said. "Where is he, Captain?"

"They hurt a child, Sinclair. *I* will be going after Mikhail Safin."

"They hurt a supernatural child," I replied, my voice even. "This is supernatural business. And we'll take care of it."

"He hurt a child," he repeated, firmly. "And that shit is not happening in my town."

"Frank, Bay Town is not yours. And we don't need him arrested. We need him dead."

I strode through the city streets, keeping my eyes peeled for a gathering of executioner SUVs. Frank didn't have to tell me where they were. I'd find them. But it'd make things a hell of a lot easier if he'd just give up the location.

Electricity danced across my skin, making me jumpy, and it took me a minute to realize it was the castoff terror and worry. Better dancing across my skin than living inside me.

"They'd better hope I find them before Leo does," I told Crawford. "At least I'll make it quick. Leo will slice them up an inch at a time."

I had no doubt that Leo was stomping through the city, searching for the monsters who'd messed with Derry.

"Do you understand what will happen if you attack the executioners, Trinity?"

"Captain," I replied, "ask me if I give a fuck."

He said nothing for a few heartbeats. Then, "Hyde Hill. They've taken over the old Hyde Motel."

I wasn't surprised. On Hyde Hill they could see who was coming up after them. There were also a lot of humans living on the hill. Safin would believe we wouldn't attack with humans surrounding him.

He was wrong.

I started to slide my phone back into my pocket, but called Leo instead. And when he didn't answer, I called Al.

"Alejandro," I said, when he answered. "It's Trinity."

"I heard about Angus's girl. I'm so sorry."

"Yeah," I said. "It's…" I blew out a breath and shook my head. There were really no words.

"I was waiting for your call. You're on your way to talk to Darkness?"

"Yeah," I said. "Talk."

"I'll meet you up there."

He hadn't needed to ask for their location. I figured there wasn't much that got past Alejandro.

I hadn't slipped into the city alone. Of course I hadn't. The vampires lurked, and though I didn't see them, I felt them. And as I slid my phone back into my pocket, I beckoned one of them toward me.

"Where is the master?" I asked.

But he didn't know.

I needed to know where Amias was, because if I let myself, I would crumble without him. I would live in misery and desolation, because he was the master.

My master.

And I really did not want to exist in a world without him.

Jade Noel called before I reached the hill.

"Angus wanted me to call. He said to tell you to stay the fuck home until he can come back." She hesitated, and her normally angry, aggressive voice softened. "Derry won't let him leave her bedside."

"How is she?"

"Not good, but the healer seems to think she'll recover. She's telling her dad she's too afraid for him to leave her alone, but the truth is, she's too afraid he'll face off against Safin and die."

"I'm going after Safin now," I said.

"Where is he hiding out?"

"Hyde Hill."

I could feel her surprise. "That's not exactly hiding out," she said.

"Safin is a little too arrogant. He doesn't believe he

needs to hide."

"Oh," she said, "it won't matter if he hides. As soon as he's secure in Derry's recovery, Angus is going after him. And he will kill him."

I curled my lip, rage making my body tight. "Not if I kill him first."

"He's Angus's kill," she said, her voice tight and judgmental. "You'd take that from him?"

"Yeah, I would. If I kill Safin, I'll likely save Angus's life. He can't hurt Darkness."

"It's good that you have such confidence in him."

"Fuck you," I said. "I don't care about his pride or his need for revenge. I care about keeping him alive."

And I went to find—and kill—Mikhail Safin.

Perhaps I was a little too arrogant as well.

Chapter Twenty-Seven

POWER

I raced up Hyde Hill, the sounds of the city providing the music that urged me on—sirens, roars of engines, blaring music and horns and laughter and screams—I heard it all. I felt it all.

The executioners were waiting for me.

They surrounded the old motel. And in a breath of tangled silence, Aspen's laugh, clear and almost sweet, rose above the cacophony of the city.

Shane was abruptly there.

Shane, angry and eager as ever to take himself out of his own head by fighting.

He patted his shotgun. "I wouldn't let you face Darkness alone, baby hunter."

He'd give me that, because there was a chance we'd die there that night.

And who could hold a grudge when death was blowing you kisses?

Then another figure strode toward us, his long legs eating up the distance, his towering figure at once familiar and foreign.

Leo the half-giant.

And he carried with him the memory of a battered supernatural girl.

"Come on," one of Safin's men yelled, and a streak of blue power hit the sky. "We're ready, motherfuckers!"

Yeah, they were. Still, they were going to have to fight hard, even with their stolen magic, to defeat us.

"Sinclair," Safin called. "How nice of you to visit."

"We're here because you attacked a child," I told him.

"We're here to free the dragon. And we are here to kill you."

The street and parking lot separated us. Still, I could see his frown.

"Free the dragon? You believe I have the dragon?" He sounded genuinely confused. "I can assure you that if I had the dragon, I would be long gone."

"The dragon will be free when you're gone," I told him. "And one way or another, we're going to make that happen."

And then what seemed like twenty cop cars came roaring up the hill, sirens shrieking. They slid to a halt on the street between us and the executioners, and cops jumped out and took cover behind open doors, guns drawn and aimed squarely at the executioners lined up in front of the motel.

I was thankful the earsplitting sirens had been cut. My ears continued to ring with the awful sound of them, and that made it a little hard to think straight. Damn vampire hearing.

Crawford, wearing a vest and holding a gun, stepped out of the lead vehicle and faced off against the executioners.

"Well," Safin said. "It's good to know which side you're on, Mayor."

"This is my city," Crawford told him. "I don't care *who* sent you—you don't come into my city and attack one of our children."

"*Your* children," Safin said, shaking his head, tsk-tsking. "You disappoint me, Frank." He held his coiled whip in his right hand, but made no move to send it streaking through the air. "If you really care, you'll convince the supernats to hand over the dragon before more tiny nonhumans are hurt." He paused. "And they will be hurt."

"One of the children was attacked?" Edgar said. "What do you mean, attacked?"

"Battered," Leo answered. "Beaten. Broken. Hurt.

159

Attacked." His knuckles cracked as he curled his hands into fists. "And you will die for it."

Edgar looked at his leader. "You had to hurt a kid? Already?"

"Edgar," Mikhail said, "you may be too soft for this gig. Remind me to revisit this conversation if you survive the night."

"I'm not too soft for anything," Edgar growled. "I just don't see the sense in hurting children."

"Shut the fuck up, Edgar," Aspen told him. "You *are* too soft."

"It's a weak man who'll use babies to beat his grown-ass enemies," one of the cops said. She kept her gun aimed steadily at the executioners.

Vampires poured from the shadows and stood at our backs, and even Safin's men quieted at the sight.

"Where have they all come from?" Safin asked, stepping from one of the motel room doorways. He did not sound worried, merely curious.

"From the ground," I told him.

Edgar and Aspen slipped up beside him.

"And you are here because you want us to bury them again?" Aspen said.

The executioners laughed.

"It doesn't matter," Safin said. "Allow me to demonstrate." His whip cracked through the air, curled around a vampire's leg, then dragged her across the street and into the parking lot.

She was screaming before she hit the ground.

"Silver is like the sun," Safin said, calmly. "And I always come prepared."

Safin had laced the lot surrounding the motel with silver. The vampires couldn't help us. They couldn't fight.

Shane couldn't fight.

"Fuck," he muttered.

And I knew he'd try anyway.

Safin flung the vampire back to us and then withdrew

his whip. And slowly, carefully, the vampires pulled back. Just a tiny bit, but enough so I felt their withdrawal. They didn't want to leave me to the executioners—the master would not be understanding—but really, unless someone tossed them an enemy to kill, they were pretty much useless.

And then Darkness turned his attention to me.

He unfurled his whip with a flick of his wrist, and sent it with deadly aim between two of the cop cars—and right at me.

The whip was as fast as a vampire. I barely had time to flinch before the thing curled around my throat and began to tighten with a gleeful and unbreakable grip.

I heard shouting—Crawford, I thought, and roaring—definitely Leo—and then I let my breath whisper through my lips and lightly brush the long line of whip that snaked from my neck to Safin's hand.

"What are you? Not just a vampire in there."

No.

Not just a vampire.

I followed that breath all the way down that unending whip, all the way to Safin himself. One second Shane was reaching out to try and rip the deadly lash from my neck, and the next I was standing in front of Darkness.

And it didn't matter that the whip was cutting through my throat. I drew back my lips and prepared to eat Mikhail Safin.

"No," he said, and flung me through the air, his whip sending me whirling as it dug in a little deeper.

There was pain, and a lot of it, but it didn't disable me—it made me mad.

I grabbed the whip with both hands as it slung me against the motel. If I couldn't bite Safin, I would bite his whip.

In some distant part of my mind I heard the others fighting—and I understood it was not going to be good for the city. If we couldn't run off a few humans, why would they believe we could protect them against invading supernaturals?

They wouldn't.

As soon as my fangs sank into the whip, I registered two things.

The whip wasn't a whip. The whip was a snake. A living, breathing, thinking *snake*.

And Safin was mentally connected to it.

When I bit into the whip, I was connected to it, as well. And to Safin, in a dim, confusing sort of way.

And I registered that Darkness wasn't simply doing a job for a shady government agency. He wanted the dragon more than he wanted, at that moment, anything else in the world. And he would do anything he could to get him.

There was a supernatural inside his room. A bound wolf with a spike through his penis and a missing eye. Darkness was cruel and hard and meant to get what he'd come for.

I felt him.

He felt me, as well.

He uncurled the whip from my throat at the exact moment I ripped my teeth from it, and I whirled through the air and slammed to the hood of one of the cruisers violently enough to dent the hood.

I was not okay—for about sixty seconds.

I rolled off the car, fell to the ground, knelt there long enough to shake off the fog, then climbed to my feet.

I'd seen other things when I'd bitten the whip. A chaotic flurry of images and thoughts and emotions, but there was no time to sort through them. Later. Later I would thumb through the images that remained after the whip had let me go.

I yanked Silverlight from her sheath, and I went once more for Darkness.

Safin and I clashed—whip versus sword, man versus woman, dark versus...dark.

He'd learned a lesson and didn't leave the whip with

me. He sent it in painful flicks, and that bastard licked the flesh right from my bones.

And with Silverlight, I gave as good as I got.

She sliced him up. Her light drowned him in molten liquid silver.

In the end we were two bloody, hurting fighters, neither willing to give up, and I knew no mere human could have stood toe to toe with me and my sword and very fucking nearly bested both of us.

No way.

Darkness was no more human than I was.

He'd been made a long time ago.

He hated it.

And he knew I knew.

That knowledge fueled the fire of his savagery, and he wanted nothing more than to kill me because he couldn't stand the fact that someone knew his awful, shameful secret.

His crew wasn't full of undead and supernatural—they were strong, fearless, and they held magical weapons.

But they weren't supernatural.

I hated the executioners, but I was amazed by them. I didn't like my admiration, but it was strong. As were they, the bastards.

The cops had fled with the fight, trying to find somewhere safe to watch—it was all they could do.

And finally, the half-giant sent the executioners and their stunning weapons running for cover, and Safin and I went to our separate corners to recover.

I was very nearly to the point of collapse.

Luckily, so was he.

The vampires melted into the shadows as Crawford and his men came slowly forward, wide-eyed and pale, though they'd seen supernaturals fight before.

I was pretty sure they hadn't seen a fight like that one.

There were seven dead executioners. They lay sprawled across the parking lot, their special, stolen weapons scattered across the cold, broken pavement, their magical protections long since severed.

Three of the victims had been sliced into neat sections by Leo. One downside to his power was the fact that in a crowd of fighters, his power didn't differentiate between friend and foe. It simply sliced up anyone it touched.

That had to frustrate the hell out of him. With Safin's whip flinging me all over the place, Leo would have been worried about accidentally hitting me.

And Darkness…

"Sneaky bastard," I muttered.

Darkness was a supernatural.

A supernatural who killed other supernaturals while working with, fighting for, and protecting a deadly group of humans. He hadn't been born that way. Someone had made him.

And that was when—and why—his hatred of supernaturals had begun.

I wondered if any of the executioners suspected that the protection surrounding them had come not from some fabricated captured witch, but from Darkness himself.

But now I wasn't worried that Safin would bring the wrath of his government organization down on us.

No. He wouldn't do that.

Bright spots.

"Trinity?" Leo asked.

He stood with Shane, both of them watching me, their faces gory masks of blood.

I frowned. "Shane? How did you fight with the silver protecting the lot?" Then I understood. "Silverlight touched you before. She made you immune."

"Could she do that for them all?" Leo asked, gesturing at the vampires who'd wanted to help.

"No." Shane said. "Only if they…"

"Only if they belong to me," I finished. "And I'm getting tired of having to convince you of that every five minutes, Shane."

He curled his lip. "I'm already convinced. But I don't have to kiss your ass and pretend to like it."

Crawford joined us. He took my arm, gingerly, and peered with concern into my face. "Are you okay?"

My clothes were in bloody strips, embedded in my flayed skin, and my body shook and trembled sporadically as it attempted to heal from that crazy powerful whip.

"The bastard nearly skinned her alive," Leo said, grim, angry, and guilty.

"You can't protect me from every little bump, Leo, though I appreciate you trying." I looked around, a little fuzzy. Okay, a lot fuzzy. "I saw Alejandro fighting. Where'd he go?"

"He was here a few minutes ago," Leo said. "I don't know where he went."

"There." Crawford pointed, and we all turned to look.

Al was rushing from the motel, his arm around the supernatural he was half carrying, half dragging from one of the rooms.

"He went in after their capture," Leo said.

Shane ran to help Alejandro with the shifter. He simply picked the big wolf up and slung him over his shoulder— and despite my half-dead status, I turned to mush at the sight of him. His strength, his willingness to help, his aloofness.

Everything he did made me want him.

Two executioners came to one of the doors and glared out, but they made no move to retrieve their tortured, half-conscious prisoner.

I continued to shiver.

I needed blood. Blood would help me heal a hell of a lot faster.

Leo caught my eye with his big, muscly body and his mystery and his delicious, special blood.

I needed to feed from Leo.

"Why doesn't he shift?" Crawford asked, and I turned my attention to him.

I would have loved to taste Crawford, as well. *Loved* to. And if I wasn't careful, I would lose control and bite him, and that would be the end of the Captain.

I tore my hungry thoughts away from him. "They've shoved a silver spike into his dick," I said.

Every man there shuddered.

Despite the silver, the supernat had been naturally and uncontrollably trying to shift, but he could get no further than some dull patches of fur and a slightly changed face.

"Poor bastard," one of the cops muttered, as Al slid his blade through the zip ties around the wolf's wrists. The second he was free, the dazed prisoner turned away from us, hunched over, and began to attempt to remove the silver.

He never said a word, but once, his breath hissed from between his lips and he groaned. Then the spike hit the pavement and he shifted, his howls drifting behind him as he loped away.

"Poor bastard," the cop repeated.

Crawford stared grimly toward the silent motel.

"What are we going to do, Mayor?" one of the cops asked.

Frank shook his head. "I honestly don't know. I would suggest you go in and arrest them all, but I have a feeling that wouldn't end well for any of you."

"Yeah," one of them said. "I don't think that's an option."

Then they turned, as one, to look at me, Leo, Shane, and Al.

I lifted an eyebrow. "We're working on it."

But I didn't see a way to kill Darkness.

And though I didn't say it, I was reasonably certain the only way we'd see the last of Mikhail Safin would be when he decided it was time for him to go.

Chapter Twenty-Eight

CRAZY

Across the lot, one of the fallen executioners groaned.

Leo growled, curled his hands into fists, and went for the injured human—as did I. We both wanted him. But I needed him.

"Sorry, Leo," I said. I stood over the human and stared up at the half-giant. "You can have him if I can have you. I have to feed."

He wavered. His feeling of responsibility to me was vast. But in the end, he turned around and let me have the human.

I felt them watching me—my people, the cops, and the executioners—as I leaned forward, grabbed the suffering human, and yanked him into the air. Even with my injuries and hunger, it was as though the fully grown man weighed next to nothing.

I tore his throat out with my teeth, drank down his blood—I'd never tasted anything like Leo's blood and I wanted to own the hell out of that magical red liquid—but human blood was almost as good. Just in an entirely different way.

So very good.

And I drained the son of a bitch.

When I was finished, even as he began to stir and reanimate as a rifter, I ripped his head off and flung it at the motel. One of the windows shattered and an executioner screamed a curse as the head of his friend landed at his feet.

I giggled and wiped my mouth, then turned to find Crawford staring at me with such horror that I wanted immediately to burst into tears.

The blood of the human filled me with everything—joy, life, energy, and emotion. I was like a pregnant woman with my hormones all over the place.

The others—cops and supernats alike—looked everywhere but at me, and for a second I was overcome with shame, loneliness, and a tiny bit of the same horror that wafted from Crawford.

But in the end, Shane came to stand with me, and though he didn't touch me, he stood beside me, crossed his arms, and glared out at the world on my behalf.

And just that quickly, my emotions swung to joy.

Being nearly ripped apart and then feeding from a human could make a girl a little crazy. Even a vampire girl.

Finally, we went home.

Back at the way station, I cleaned up as fast as I could, then went in search of some answers.

Amias hadn't appeared, nor had Rhys, and Angus was still in the Deluge with his child. The other children had been moved to the tunnels, and I could only hope they'd be safe there.

The swamp had no cell service and no landlines, so I couldn't contact Angus. I'd go to Willow-Wisp to speak with the elder, and if Angus hadn't returned by then, I'd go to the Deluge.

I also needed to speak with Himself, but I had no idea how to contact him. Angus sometimes called him—or he had, before Nadine's unfortunate end. I doubted Himself carried a phone. He really *did* need an assistant.

As I left the way station, I spotted Leo. He stood at the edge of the yard, his arms crossed, staring silently into the distance.

"Leo." I touched his arm. "Do you want to talk about it?"

He looked down at me, his face pale and drawn, his eyes bloodshot. "It's a bad time, Trinity."

I nodded. If he'd have been one of the other men, I'd

have wrapped my arms around him. "What can I do?" I asked, and kept my hands to myself.

"Angus." Then he stopped, swallowed hard, and tried again. "It was in his eyes. When I carried that little girl into the house, he…" He couldn't say the words.

"No, Leo," I told him. "If Angus thought you had anything to do with hurting Derry, he'd have torn you apart on the spot."

I knew Angus. If he'd had so much as a single doubt, he would have painted the walls with Leo's blood.

Leo shook his head, but said nothing more.

He absolutely believed Angus thought he'd hurt the girl.

Nothing I could say would reassure him. Angus would have to do that.

"We need to kill Safin," he said, staring once again into the distance.

"Kill him with your power."

"I tried. When he had you in the air, attached to that whip, I sent my power at him. It killed one of his men on the way, but when it got to him, it simply stopped. Like it hit a brick wall. I can't kill him."

"Leo." I hesitated. "Why didn't you—"

"Why didn't I put my hands on him? I'm a half-giant. Huge. Dangerous. Strong." He looked at me.

I nodded, half-ashamed without knowing why.

"He has some sort of protection. None of us can touch him. We all tried. Crawford tried to shoot him. Nothing can touch the man. It's like he's not really there."

"Of course he can be touched," I said. "*I* touched him. He had to run, in the end, because he was so injured. I would have killed him." I thumped my chest like an angry chimpanzee. "I touched the hell out of that motherfucker."

"No, Trinity. You didn't. Silverlight did." His devastated gaze drifted to my sword. "Silverlight will kill him. I believe she's the only one who can. But there's also a chance he might win. He might kill her." He watched me, waiting. "Or take her."

I recoiled, I couldn't help it. He was right.

He was *right*.

If I took Silverlight back to Darkness, he and his freaky snake whip might actually get the best of her. Might kill her. I didn't want to send her into that. I didn't want to risk her.

Still, I would. Of course I would.

But my fingers itched to soothe the strips of raw flesh that had yet to completely heal, and I wanted to run Silverlight far away from the man who might be able to kill her.

Worse, the man who might be able to take her. To possess her.

What if he took her and she turned on me? She'd turned on the demon who'd owned her before me. What if Darkness took her and told her to hurt me?

I pressed my fingers into my stomach, unable, almost, to bear the thought.

She was mine. Mine.

And I could not lose her.

"As soon as you recover," Leo said. "We can't wait for him to come to us, and we can't wait for him to hurt another child."

And he turned back to stare once more into the distance, at something only he could see.

It broke my heart to watch him suffer, but I didn't know how to help him. I'd refused to let myself really think about Derry. About what she'd gone through. Her fear, her pain...

Shit.

"Leo." I gripped his forearm, needing to feel something besides the blackness of Derry's nightmare. "Do you want to go to the swamp with me to check on her?"

He shook his head. "Angus wouldn't want me there. Not yet." He dropped his stare to where my fingers lay against his arm, then averted his eyes quickly, guiltily, even, as though he were taking a sneak peek into a woman's bedroom window.

I rubbed my thumb over his skin, softly. "I wanted to thank you."

"For what?"

"For taking care of me. For watching my back. For always making sure I'm okay."

"You saved my life." He gave a ghost of a smile. "It's the least I can do."

I slid my hand up his arm and over his broad chest, not even a little ashamed that I wanted him so much that I would try to seduce him, that I would make him mine because I needed his blood.

It wasn't like I'd hurt him.

His entire body tightened and I honestly couldn't read what was in his eyes when he stared down at me.

"Come here," I said.

He hesitated.

He *resisted*.

"Leo," I said. "Have you never—"

"I'm not a virgin, Trinity," he said, dryly, but with a hint of something I couldn't quite grasp. "I've taken women to my bed. I had to pay for every single one of them, but I've had sex."

I didn't move my hands. They lay there on his chest, wrong and awkward, but I couldn't take them away.

He continued on when I stayed silent and motionless. "I've never had what you might call a real relationship. I've never had love. I've never had a girlfriend."

"Leo…you could."

He shook his head. "Look at me." There was no bitterness in his eyes, just calm acceptance.

"I am. And I'm seeing you." If I'd been taller, or he'd been shorter, I would have kissed him. "I see you, and I want you." I moved my hands then, not up, but down. "I want to be yours, and I want you to be mine. Let me take

171

you."

His voice became a husky murmur. "You can break me, Trinity. I'm asking you not to do that." But he didn't grab my wrists, didn't stop me from inching my fingers down his huge, hard body.

"Let me take you," I whispered.

He lowered his gaze to my lips. "I'm not sure you *can* take me."

And in his voice was pride. Pride, heat, and the desire to let me in. To let me love him.

But larger than the need was the fear that I would crush him.

"I know it's my blood," he said, and finally, he grabbed my wrists, right before my fingers touched a stiffening part of him that might have killed me had I been human. He was a half-giant. There was nothing small about him.

I looked, gasped, and my stare flew back to his. Maybe he was a little amused.

Mostly, he was just sad.

He knew. He knew about his blood. He knew what it'd done to me.

Leo had been hurt enough.

"It's not just your blood," I said.

I'd have to prove it to him. Somehow.

He trusted me with his life—he didn't quite trust me with his heart.

And I didn't blame him a bit.

I left him there with his thoughts and his unbroken heart and strode into Willow-Wisp. I searched for the elder for an hour before finally giving up. He wasn't in the graveyard.

Or if he was, he wasn't showing himself to me.

I stood in the center of Willow-Wisp and closed my eyes, silently calling for Amias. In the midst of all the other horror, his absence was, somehow, the darkest. The hardest for me to handle.

He simply wasn't there.

And Rhys was probably flying over Hong Kong, hoping rumors of his sightings would reach the ears of the executioners and they'd rush out of Red Valley and begin to chase the dragon in another country.

I hoped for that, as well.

But I knew better than to believe it.

When I opened my eyes, Amias wasn't there, nor was Rhys, but the King of Everything stood silent and still before me, waiting.

I rushed toward him and would have grabbed his bony shoulders but at the last second, I thought better of it. "Tell me everything," I cried, instead. "Where is the master? Where is the dragon? Can I kill Darkness? What do I do?"

I only realized at that moment how utterly out of my depth I was. How utterly afraid I'd do the wrong thing and get everybody killed.

There was sympathy in his eyes, eyes almost buried in the wrinkled folds of his face. "I cannot tell you that, child."

"Cannot?" I asked, confused. "You don't know?"

"I know only that we must control what we can control. The rest is left to fate and is not ours to decide."

I stared at him. "What the hell does that mean?"

He sighed. "I am afraid it means that I cannot aid you at this time."

"You don't know?" I asked, again. "Are you saying you don't know?"

He relented, slightly. "You've already done something very important. Your victory over the executioner has ensured that an army of humans will not fall upon Bay Town—but his resolve will not weaken. He will have the dragon. He must." He lifted his chin. "Therefore we must turn our efforts toward protecting the dragon. That, we can do."

"We can?"

"We must."

Safin's determination went beyond doing a job for his employers. "Why does he want to kill the dragon so badly?" I knew I wouldn't get a straight answer. Himself danced around the truth like it was fire that would burn him if he got too close.

He surprised me. "For power. He has been ordered to kill the dragon—but he wants to *be* the dragon." He peered at me. "You saw what was inside him."

I gave an involuntary shiver. "He's not human."

"And there is nothing he wants more than power. All power. It is the only thing that motivates him. The only reason he lives."

And finally, I understood. "It's why he's so strong. Everything he has he's stolen from other supernaturals." I pressed my fingers against the sudden pain in my chest. "He wants to consume the dragon. He has the ability to..." I swallowed hard and looked away, remembering Nadine. "To absorb power."

He nodded. "And either way, the dragon will be dead. We must not allow that to happen. We must not."

"Then *help* me," I said. "I can't kill him on my own."

"You are the only one who can." His voice was bland, but his eyes blazed. "You carry the sword, and he cannot absorb *her*." He looked pointedly at Silverlight. "You bring the light. And you must banish the darkness."

"But he can take her," I said. "He can use her."

He said nothing, just watched me.

"Can't he?" I asked, desperate for him to say *no, no, child, he can't take your sword.*

"You must not allow him to," he said.

"I need Amias," I whispered. "Where is the master? Please, tell me that."

But he could not.

Or would not.

I curled my hands into fists and God knows what I would have done at that moment if the long-absent visitors, the path walkers, the lost, wandering spirits, hadn't decided at that exact moment to finally come knocking at the way station door.

I had forgotten what it was like to have them in my head, screaming for help. And by the time I lowered my hands from my ears and looked, Himself was gone.

I was on my own. And as soon as I tended the visitor, Silverlight and I would go after Darkness.

He was the only thing I knew how to do.

Chapter Twenty-Nine

CROSSOVER

Jin was so excited his hands shook. He kicked a chair away from the table and practically shoved me into it. "They're here," he said, as though I might not somehow be aware of that.

I pressed my fingertips against my temples, trying to stop the discordant sounds inside my head. And abruptly, the noise was gone.

I opened the walls between the way station and the path, between my world and the visitor's, and I brought the wanderer inside.

Disoriented, he stumbled back a few steps, but he didn't fall. "What the fuck is this?" he said. "More tricks?"

"Hello," I said. "Have a—"

"This isn't my world." He darted his stare around the room, as though he could see the entire world through the kitchen walls. "Place doesn't smell the same."

"Please," I said. "Sit. I'll explain."

He didn't sit, though, just stared at me from eyes that had seen a lot of really, really bad things. I wanted to flinch from the look in those eyes, because beneath the coldness was a sorrow so huge I was afraid it would engulf me.

His body—whether borrowed or his I couldn't have said—was whipcord lean and scarred, and his dirty hair, maybe a dark blond, though I couldn't really tell with the dust of his path covering it, snaked over his shoulders and down his chest.

"I'm the caretaker," I said, when he remained standing. "I'm here to help you find your way home."

His eyes widened then, and he strode to me, and before I could react, he'd grabbed my shoulders and yanked me to my feet. "You can send me home?"

Shit. His desperation was overwhelming. I could have broken his hold easily, but as my fingers pressed gently against his chest, I felt something.

"You're not human," I realized. He was the first nonhuman that had come off the path—during my time as the caretaker, anyway—and I wasn't sure what that meant. "What are you?"

He squeezed my arms, impatient. "That doesn't matter. I've been on that fucking path for..." He shook his head. "Forever. I need to go home. Can you get me there?"

I couldn't keep looking into his eyes as I crushed him. "You died," I told him. "You wouldn't be on the path if you hadn't died. I can help you find the path to your...your paradise. But you cannot stay in this world. You—"

"You're dead," Jin said, gleefully.

I glanced over the stranger's shoulder to where Jin lingered, his fascinated gaze on our visitor.

"I didn't die," the man said, irritated. "I went through the portal, got on the path, and somehow, I got off here. I keep getting the wrong fucking world." He shook me a little. "You'll put me on the right path?"

There was no arguing with him. "Yes, I can put you on the right path. I just need to find it." I patted his chest. "I need you to sit down and take my hands."

"Yeah," he said, then almost reluctantly, as though he thought I might make a run for it if he released me, he let me go and took a seat at the table. He stared incomprehensibly at the tray of food Jin had placed there, then grabbed the water and chugged it down like a man who'd been thirsty for a long, long time.

I waited for him to finish, then slid my hands across the table. "Please," I said, when he hesitated.

He laced his fingers with mine.

"I'm Trinity." I pointed my chin at Jin. "This is Jin."

He glanced from me to Jin and then back to me. "Owen," he said.

"Owen." I really, really hoped he found happiness, because his grief was overwhelming. "I'll help you. It's why I'm here."

"Hurry," he told me. "I need to get back before it's too late."

I was curious despite myself. "Where is home?"

He smiled, and my stomach tightened. There was something about him. "Home is with my crew and the greatest woman I ever knew. I made a mistake. All of us did." His voice had softened as he spoke and the mystery in his eyes hid the grief. "Find my path, Trinity. It's unkind, but it'll lead me home."

I believed him. I really did.

He wasn't the same as the others.

His paradise wasn't the afterlife.

"I will," I said. "I'll send you home."

He glanced down at himself. "This is the first time I came through without my clothes. And my hat."

Jin spoke for the first time. "I'll fetch you something to wear."

"Jin," I called, before he could rush out of the room.

He stopped and looked at me. "Yes?"

"He's not the same as the ones before, is he?"

He glanced at Owen. "No. He is the same as me."

I wrinkled my nose. "He's a Jikininki?"

He sighed. "He's not human. He never was." He spoke to the stranger without looking at him. "You may never find your way. You can stay here."

But Owen shook his head, his long hair sliding over his shoulders. "No," he said. "I can't."

Jin was back shortly, carrying a small pile of neatly folded clothes and an old pair of boots. He placed them on the table. "Clayton will not mind."

"The night is unseasonably warm," I murmured to Jin,

as Owen dressed. I politely turned my eyes away while he hurriedly pulled on his borrowed clothes, but I'd seen enough to know that the one who held his heart was a lucky woman.

Clayton arrived as the man was pulling on his boots. He stood behind me and placed his hands on my shoulders, then glanced at Owen. "Visitor?"

"Yes," I said. "And I'm about to send him home."

The two men exchanged nods.

"This your guy?" Owen asked.

"One of them," I said.

He lifted an eyebrow but said nothing.

"What?" I asked. "Your woman doesn't have more than one man?"

His laugh was rusty. "Yeah. She really does." Then he smoothed his shirt, almost nervously. "I'm ready. Send me back where I belong, Trinity."

If he were dead and had come through with a borrowed body, he'd leave it behind for Jin to dispose of.

I hoped that wouldn't happen.

I closed my eyes and began to search for his path.

"There are two of them," I said, confused. I'd never seen two paths for one visitor before. And I had absolutely no idea which one to grab. *Two* paths."

"Take the one that looks like it's full of blood and nightmares," he said. "That's the unkind path to my unkind world. And that's the one I need."

He would know. I just had a feeling.

I squeezed his hands, then opened my eyes and looked at him. "Good luck."

He gave me a half smile and parted his lips to speak, then disappeared before the words could form. Disappeared as he'd appeared, only quieter.

He left no body behind. Only a strange, almost sweet sort of sadness and an echo of a distant world I would never know.

"Find peace, Owen," I murmured.

But I wasn't sure such a thing really existed—for him or anyone else.

Chapter Thirty

PROMISES

I stood, shaking off my sudden melancholia. "What did you find out, Clayton?"

He stared for a few seconds at the spot the wanderer had vacated, then took the coffee Jin handed him and sat across from me. "Nothing. I found so sign of Rhys and no rumored sightings."

His worry was enormous.

"He'll be okay," I murmured. "He'll find his way back to us, Clayton."

He took a drink of his coffee. His expression didn't change, but I knew he believed something dire had happened to Rhys. "Still nothing from the master?"

"No."

And sitting around waiting for and worrying about my men was driving me crazy.

"I'm going after Safin," I said. "This time, I'll kill him."

"You're healed?" Clayton asked.

"I'm healed enough." I drew my sword and caressed her blade. "Her light is the only thing that can kill Darkness. And I have to do something. I can't just sit here."

"We need Amias and Rhys to help fight them. And Angus. Be patient, Trinity. There aren't enough of us to take on the executioners."

"You will make do," Jin said, staring blankly at the stove, as though he knew he should be cooking but there was no one there to eat. "Call upon all the supernaturals. They will keep the executioners occupied so you can tend to Darkness."

I was curious. "Do you think I will defeat him, Jin?"

He declined to answer that particular question, but told me something else, instead. "Himself and the elder are not at all certain."

Clayton narrowed his eyes. "What do you know, Jin?"

Jin glanced at me, and I could feel his uncertainty. I could also feel his fear. "I know nothing."

"Jin." I stood and went to him, then reached out to touch his arm. "I won't let anyone hurt you."

He looked down his nose at me. "You could not stop it."

A tiny zing of anger shot through me, and I realized that I was protective of the strange Jikininki. "I promise you I can."

He glanced from me to Clayton, who nodded. "We'll protect you," Clayton said. "Trust us. And tell us what you know."

"It would be disloyal," Jin said.

I frowned. "To whom?"

"To him," Jin whispered, and inclined his head toward the kitchen window.

I craned my neck to peer out the window, drawing back with a shiver when I saw Himself standing in the yard, staring toward the house.

He gave me the creeps sometimes.

I knew he had the best interest of the supernats at heart, but still...

"Jin," Clayton said, firmly. "If you allow Trinity to go blindly into danger, you won't have to worry about Himself harming you."

Jin swallowed so hard I heard the gulp. "She is aware of the danger."

"Is she?" Shane asked. He leaned against the doorframe, watching us.

I brightened, immediately and unmistakably. I didn't go to him, but whenever he wasn't near me, some part of me went a little cold.

Jin didn't like Shane. At least not the new Shane. An odd feral look crossed his face when he caught sight of Shane, there and gone so quickly I might have imagined it.

"Of course I'm aware," I said. "I know how powerful Mikhail Safin is. I know I might not kill him." I shrugged. "But I know I'll try."

Shane crossed his arms. "There's something wrong with Amias."

"Something," Jin whispered.

I sheathed Silverlight and went to Shane. "What do you mean?"

"You feel it, too," he said. "He made us." He stared at me. "You feel it."

I shook my head but couldn't say a word. Yeah, I felt it. I didn't want to, but I did. "Something's wrong," I said. And I'd known it when I went to sleep without Amias and woke up without Amias and walked through the night without Amias.

Something was wrong and it wasn't Derry or Rhys or anyone else. It was my fucking master.

"Clayton," I whispered.

He slipped his arm around my waist. "I'm here."

"I need you to track Amias."

And before he could say anything or doubt himself or believe that tracking the master might be impossible, I once again drew Silverlight from her sheath.

I ran my wrist over her sharp edge, opening a vein, then offered it to Clayton. "You'll find his trail in this blood—it's his blood. Follow it."

He didn't hesitate. He took the blood inside himself, and even before he stopped drinking, I could see a change in him.

Shane and I followed him from the house.

"Leo," I bellowed, as we followed Clayton. He wouldn't be far, and we were going to need all the help we could get.

He caught up with us before we'd left the front yard.

183

"News from Angus?" was the first thing he asked.

"No," I told him. "We're going after Amias. We're going to go get him, then we're kicking the shit out of Safin and his crew of assholes. Come with us. It'll be fun."

Shane laughed and took another step out of the black pit of his anger. "That's my freak of a girlfriend."

And despite everything, I smiled.

"I see the fog," Clayton murmured, not five minutes later. "It's black."

My chest tightened with hope I was half afraid to feel. As Clayton—and the fog trail—led us further into the woods behind Willow-Wisp, I lifted my sword into the air and she began to glow with a soft light that lit up the night.

"Killer flashlight," Shane said.

Then my cell rang. "Shit," I muttered. I dug it out of my pocket, then forgot my irritation when I saw whose name was on the screen. "Angus! How's Derry?"

"She's…" He blew out a hard breath. "Physically, she'll heal. I'm worried about her state of mind."

"How are you using your cell? Did you leave the swamp?"

"Just far enough to get a signal. Derry is sleeping, but she wakes often to make sure I'm here. I can't upset her by going far."

There was frustration in his voice, and I understood. Angus wanted to go after the person who'd hurt his daughter, but his daughter couldn't bear for him to go.

So he would wait.

But only for a little while.

"I want to visit her."

"She'd like to see you." Then his voice deepened. "I heard you took on the executioners alone." And there was the smallest thread of anger in his voice.

"Not alone." I shrugged. "Safin hurt Derry. And after we find Amias, I'm going to kill him for that."

"*I'm* going to kill him for that." His voice was dark enough to make me shiver. Angus was suppressing a hell

184

of a lot of rage while he was with Derry, and he wanted to release every single bit of it on Mikhail Safin.

I knew he couldn't. "Silverlight and I are the only ones who have a chance at killing him," I said. "He's got some sort of protection surrounding him. You won't get near him." I softened my voice. "I'm sorry. But believe me when I say I will make him suffer for what he did."

His voice didn't soften. "Trinity, I will kill him."

He could try. He *would* try.

I believed Darkness wanted to fight Angus—just two alphas beating each other senseless—but I didn't believe he would.

The only way he could fight the werebull was to dissolve or at least weaken the ring of protection surrounding him—and he wouldn't do that. He'd hurt Angus in other ways—like terrorizing his children.

Darkness wanted to live to take the dragon more than he wanted to see if he could defeat Angus in a personal physical fight.

But if I was wrong and Safin and Angus went at each other with fists instead of magic, I would be ready.

If he lowered his protection and took on Angus, I was going to sneak in and run Silverlight through his cold, black heart. I wasn't above a good sucker punch. Or sucker stabbing.

So I told Angus what he needed to hear. I told him I wouldn't face Safin again without him.

I didn't tell him we were tracking the master, that I feared something terrible had happened to him, or that Rhys was missing. He'd find out soon enough, and as he didn't want to add to Derry's stress, I didn't want to add to his.

I didn't want to consider that we might not find Amias. That somehow, someone had gotten to him. Had driven a stake through his heart and had taken him from me.

That he might be wandering in the despair, lost to me forever.

185

I didn't want to consider that.
But I really just couldn't seem to help myself.

Chapter Thirty-One

SEARCH

Amias had been part of me since the night he'd nearly killed me on the street in front of my sister's house. I could always feel him.

But I didn't feel him now.

And I had only two hours before dawn.

The longer we walked, the more worried I became. I walked beside Leo as we followed Clayton, and waited with grim hopefulness for him to announce that he'd finally found the master. Shane followed behind us, a little apart, as always.

My fingers brushed Leo's hand and after a tiny hesitation, he caught my hand in his, squeezing gently. "We'll find him," he promised.

I nodded.

Sure we would.

"You've tried to meet with the council?" he asked. "Surely they know where he is."

"I don't know where *they* are," I said. "They hide from me. Not even Himself will tell me where they...live. Or whatever they do."

"I think they're afraid of the part of you that belongs to the rifters."

"Belongs to the rifters," I repeated, quietly.

He glanced at me, then away. "I'm sorry. I shouldn't have said that."

"They're extraordinary and powerful," I told him. "They're not going to be afraid of me."

"You underestimate yourself."

I shook my head. "No. I know what I can do."

Shane walked up to my other side. "Clayton is leading us back to Willow-Wisp. We're going in from the back."

He was right. I closed the distance between us and touched his arm, causing him to jerk.

"He's in Willow-Wisp after all?" I asked.

He blinked and looked around. "He didn't start in Willow-Wisp. But this trail is fresh. It's like…"

My fingers flew to my mouth. "He's in the ground. He's moving in the *ground*."

Clayton pointed. "If you're right, his trail ends there. It's not just dissipating because dawn is coming. That's as far as he's made it."

"I'm going down," I said, releasing Leo's hand. "If I find him, there might not be time to bring him up, depending on how…" I swallowed. "How injured he is."

"Why can't we feel him?" Shane asked. "If he's right under our fucking feet?"

"I don't know," I murmured.

Clayton pulled me into his arms. "You may need more blood to feed him. Take mine."

"Do it fast," Shane said.

I bit Clayton without hesitation, taking his offering gladly. I was trembling with fear, fear that grew by the second. Now that we knew where he was—sort of—I was terrified of what we'd find when we got there.

I withdrew from Clayton. "I love you," I told him. "Tell the others we'll see them at dusk, and we'll be bringing the master with us."

Then I sank into the ground, Shane at my side, and let the earth tell me where my master was. Even if I couldn't find him, the ground could.

"Tell me," I whispered, and it did.

In complete darkness, I grasped onto the string of energy Amias had left below, and I let it pull me through the thick layers of dirt.

I wanted to sleep. We didn't go into the ground to stay awake—especially not that close to dawn—and I had to fight hard to keep my awareness.

I felt Shane lose his fight. I would tunnel on alone.

Down I went, deep, deeper still, farther down than I'd ever been. And finally, my reaching, desperate fingers touched something.

Not him, though. Silver.

No. God, no.

Silver chains.

They'd silver-wrapped the master and carried him as far down as they could, and they'd left him there, buried alive, starving, and alone.

Oh, motherfuckers. I will end you.

Humans often silvered and buried vampires. Often.

But not this fucking deep.

No human had hurt my master.

The silver wasn't touching his flesh—not yet. They hadn't put him in a box. They'd covered his body with layers of heavy tarp, then wound the chains around it.

It was as though they'd wanted to punish him, but weren't willing to add burns to the torture of the burial.

Maybe it was the coming dawn, my exhaustion, my fear, or the fact that I'd been without my dominant master, untended and uncomforted and unguided, but my mind began to creep back into its pre-Leo bite, and I became closer to the feral thing I'd been than the woman who'd been walking the earth a few short minutes earlier.

And nothing mattered but Amias.

Silver couldn't hurt me.

I broke the thick chains and unwound them from his body, then burrowed farther down so I could get them away from him. Their proximity would distress him. He'd feel their noxious, draining energy even if they weren't directly touching him—especially when he was so very weak.

I rushed back to him, willing myself awake, though dawn had come crashing into existence up top. Sluggish and almost numb I ripped the tarp from him, opened a vein in my wrist, wrapped my free arm around his cold, unmoving body, and shoved my bloody arm against his mouth.

The blood would find him.

Clayton's blood, my blood—it all belonged to Amias.

Now that the silver was gone, now that blood was in his mouth, bringing him back, I could feel him.

I could feel his struggle.

Even with the silver, he'd managed to move. To undulate through the ground, trying to find Willow-Wisp, because the graveyard earth would have made him stronger.

Trying to find his way to the top. To me.

I slept.

In the blink of an eye the sun was gone and I awakened. I had not moved in my sleep. My wrist still lay against his lips, and my arm was still around him.

He'd nearly drained me.

I was too empty to be helped by a supernatural. I needed the magic of human blood.

That was the first thing I felt.

The second thing was Amias's lips against mine. Unmoving, cold, but there.

I was dying.

I'd given myself to the master, and there was nothing left of me.

Then Shane wrapped us up in his embrace and propelled us to the surface. We broke through and lay like weighted, half-dead slugs.

"Hang on," Shane murmured.

He left us, but was back in minutes. He brought food.

It was contained in a mesmerized human woman, warm and strong and alive.

As I drank, the spark of life inside me flared, and when the human died, then almost immediately began to turn, I was touched by something I'd never felt before.

I was a mother, and she was my child. I was her maker,

and she was my rifter.

She was mine. Mine.

I would tend her. I'd put her in the ground and grow her, take care of her, teach her. Together we would—

Shane yanked her from me, ripped her heart from her chest, and took the pieces of her into the ground. He was back before I'd stopped moaning.

"You can't have kids, baby hunter," he murmured. "Stop it."

And Amias lay silent and unmoving upon the ground. Pain ripped through me—the pain of realization.

I'd murdered a human woman.

To deal with it, I shut my emotions right the fuck down.

I shoved the memory of what I'd done into the earth with the human, and I left it there as I crawled to Amias and once again fed him the blood inside me.

We would survive. No matter what.

And someday, the earth would be inundated with the strong, the supernatural, the vampire. No, that was wrong.

The rifter.

For us, it was the beginning.

A brand new beginning.

Chapter Thirty-Two

PUNISHMENT

"This is what the elders fight against," Himself said. "This is what we *all* fight against. The humans cannot end. If they end, we end. Can you not understand?"

"I do understand," I said, and sank a little further into my guilt. "But human blood was the only thing that would bring me back. Shane saved my life."

Shane and I had been getting a lecture from Himself and the elder since we'd made it back to the way station. I was high on the dead human's blood, worried about Amias, and terrified that the elders would hurt Shane for grabbing the human.

The elder pointed a long, bony finger at Shane. "He should not have killed a human to save you."

I dropped my gaze. He was right. We shouldn't have killed a human so I could live. There were no excuses.

I should have felt worse about it than I did.

Fucking rifter heart.

"This is your fault," the elder told Shane. "You, a vampire, have murdered an innocent."

"You will be punished and punished severely," Himself added.

I didn't move, but I looked at the King of Everything, and I could almost feel something dark inside me click into place. "He's not yours to punish."

"Then whose is he to punish, girl? Yours?" The elder stared at me, contempt in his little black eyes. "You cannot punish him. You cannot control him."

"He is mine," Amias said, stepping in through the open kitchen door. "And I will tend him."

It had only been a couple of hours since his rescue, and he had yet to tell me who'd put him in the ground—but I was nearly certain I knew who had done it. I just didn't know why.

No one but the elders would be powerful enough to neutralize and silver the master, then bury him so deep we couldn't feel him.

He looked good, though. He'd cleaned up and fed, and he was the very picture of glowing health.

Except for his eyes. They held only darkness.

"But *you* belong to me," the elder said, angry. "And all that is yours belongs to me. It is the council's responsibility to control the vampires."

"It won't happen again," I said. "We never meant for it to happen in the first place. Shane was thinking only of saving my life—not killing a human. I took too much."

Himself and the elder stared at me, silent. But I could see their revulsion. They no longer thought of me as a vampire. I was the rifter. The girl's murder had snuffed out the vampire. I knew what I was, and I accepted it, even if I didn't quite embrace it. My guilt wouldn't let me.

That was good enough. I needed a conscience to separate me from the monsters. And I had one.

So fuck them.

"Would it have been different if the human we'd killed had been a…" I waved my hand. "A bad human?"

"Of course," the elder answered, his eyes bright with pain. "You must not kill innocence. You must not kill *good*. What would remain to fight the evil?"

"The vampires?" I suggested.

He could only stare at me.

"It is the rifter," Himself said, finally. He put his fingers to his mouth, overcome, and turned away. "The elders are right. We made a mistake. You…"

But he could say nothing else.

"It was a fucking accident," Shane said, glaring. "The human was turning. I had to kill her. We went too far, took too much. We know that. What the fuck else do you want us to say?"

I reached out to take his arm and when his automatic reaction was to pull away, I squeezed hard and refused to let him. "No more of that," I told him.

"I will handle my house," Amias told the two ancient men. "Please. Leave me to my business."

The elder curled his fists. "Your disobedience will not be tolerated. That is why you were punished. I will see you replaced as master of this city."

"You silvered and buried him," I said, abruptly cold.

"He is not above punishment," the elder told me. "And this is not your concern. You have no knowledge of vampire ways. You are not really a vampire, are you?"

I shrugged. "I am not really *your* vampire. I am his." I jerked my thumb at Amias. "So what happens to him is my concern." I took a step toward him. "What did he do to deserve it?"

"You cannot understand."

"I understand that you can't suddenly reappear after deserting him for so very long and expect things to go back to how you left them. *You* should be punished. You abandoned the vampires. So lay the fuck off my master, asshole."

"Trinity," Himself roared, thumping his staff on the floor. "They sacrificed, they did not abandon! I will not allow such disrespect." He actually pointed the tip of his staff at me, and for a second, I thought he was going to kill me on the spot.

The elder nodded. "It is as we said. This one is beyond our help." He leveled a cold look at Himself. "You see, don't you?" Then he put his stare on Amias. "If you continue to refuse to consider our orders, we will have no choice but to end you both."

"What orders?" I asked. "Tell me."

"No," Amias said, but the elder ignored him.

"The rifter can be excised," he said. "Amias can kill

you, then put you in the ground and regrow you. It is then possible that you will reemerge as a vampire—not the vampires' enemy."

There was silence all around.

I looked at Himself. "You agreed with that?"

He sighed. "No, child. For you would return as something less than what you are fated to be."

"Only the elders agree that such a thing should occur," Amias said. "But it is a risk I am not willing to take."

"So they punished you for it."

"He is harming vampires because of his regard for you," the elder said. "He is willing to risk his people because of his love for you."

"It's all tangled up together," I realized. "Fate and rules and love and hate." I was suddenly tired. I wanted nothing to do with their politics or worries. But I would not let them harm Amias again.

I drew my sword and she lit up, causing the elder to throw an arm up to shield his face from her silver light.

"You threaten my master, you threaten me. And I *will* destroy you."

They could only gape.

"My love," Amias said, his voice so utterly empty that I knew he was as stunned as the elder and Himself. "No."

But I wasn't backing down. "Go rule your vampires," I told the elder. "And leave me and mine alone. We understand what needs to be done with the humans, the city, and the future. Amias and I and our little circle—we are, as of this moment, liberated from you, your council, and your rules. You aren't required to protect us, and you aren't permitted to discipline us. You will not rule us." I pointed at Amias, who stood like a statue, empty, blank, dark. "You will not rule *him*. Do you understand my words?"

The elder was as still as Amias. "You are going rogue. You wish to take the master with you."

I shrugged. "Call it what you want, but we are..." I

shook my head, searching for the words. "We are apart."

The elder looked at Amias. "She will cause the rift," he said. "The rifter will rift. *That* is predicted. And you will let her."

Amias finally moved. He came to stand at my side. "What she says is right. We are meant for other things. He knows." He gestured at Himself. "He understands. Now the council will, as well. It will be as she says."

"You will cause separation amongst the vampires," the elder whispered. He looked like his world was ending.

"Not if we aren't forced to," Amias said. "Do not force us to."

"The elders rule the vampires," the elder said.

"Not us," Amias replied. "Not anymore."

"You will allow a rifter to rule you." The elder trembled, and for a second, I felt sorry for him.

"I will allow a rifter to rule *with* me," Amias corrected, gently. "She is my queen, and that is how it was always meant to be."

I looked at Himself, remembering the words he'd spoken when he'd invaded my mind. *"Your king will be the one with whom you rule."*

I gave him a nod, which he returned.

"You must agree," the King of Everything said to the elder, softly. "There can be peace. We know your power, and we respect it. But Trinity is right. They are apart." And he came to stand with us. Together, we faced the elder. "And you shall not hurt them."

"We will not kill humans." The elder's voice shook with frustration. "We cannot interfere with their battles. It is not the right thing to do. Who will police this...this rogue group, if not the council?"

"We will police ourselves. And Safin isn't human." I lifted an eyebrow. "Will you kill him?"

"It would be an abuse of their power," Himself told me. "There are rules they must not break." His stare was soft even as he rebuked me. "They cannot use their power to wipe out everyone they do not agree with."

"Power," I said. "*What* power? They disappeared and allowed their vampires to be hunted and killed. They let vampires be silvered and buried and staked. Angus's daughter was just beaten and terrorized and lies in the Deluge attempting to heal because of Safin. The elders don't protect us. Power?" I snorted. "I don't see any fucking power. I just see a desire to rule, to be blindly followed, to be unquestionably obeyed. I don't see any power."

And by the end, my voice was full of tears and despair, and the old elder softened, at last.

"Trinity," he said, gently. "You *must* have faith."

Himself nodded. "As must you, my dear friend," he told the elder. "As must you."

Then they both looked at me, and something changed. Something was understood, and balance, it seemed, was restored.

They left without another word.

"My love," Amias said, and pulled me into his arms. "Oh, my love."

"What just happened?" Shane asked.

"The council will allow us our freedom," the master said thickly. "And they will allow her to live."

"Allow?" I asked. "We *took* our freedom."

A spark of anger lit Amias's eyes. "He could have turned Shane to ash with a look, Trinity. He could have commanded it and I would have burned as though the sun had touched me. He could have done that to punish you. So yes, he is allowing us our freedom."

I began to tremble with the sudden realization of what I had risked. Himself would have fought the elder, and the elder had known that, but still, it could have cost Shane and Amias their lives. And that would have cost me mine.

"Amias," I whispered. "I..." But there was nothing to say. It had ended well, even though it could just as easily have gone to hell.

"I must punish you for killing the human girl," Amias told Shane. "These are different times. New beginnings. Once the executioners have been dealt with, the ground will be waiting. You are a vampire now. It is time you began to live like it."

"What about me?" I asked. "I'm the one who drained her. You're not punishing me?"

His smile was tiny. "Am I not, Trinity?"

He turned on his heel and left, and we stayed frozen in place.

"Oh," I said.

Yes, he would punish me.

He would put Shane in the ground.

What would hurt me more than Shane's agony?

"You can refuse your punishment," I said, woodenly. "I will stand with you."

He shook his head. "You might rule with him, Trinity, but I don't. He's my maker. I can't do anything but obey him."

"I won't allow it," I murmured.

"You won't have a choice."

Jin stuck his head through the doorway, his eyes like big black holes in his face.

"You can come in," I said. "They're gone."

He swept the kitchen with that black stare, making sure I wasn't lying to him.

My cell rang and I jumped, then pulled it from my pocket. "Crawford?"

He was running as he talked—his voice was jerky. "Trinity, Safin just called me. They attacked the tunnels. Get there now."

Then he was gone.

"No," I cried, as rage began to rise inside me. Rage, not fear. There should have been fear.

Shane grabbed my shoulders. "What happened?"

Leo jogged into the kitchen, his hair still wet from the shower, smelling like power and strength. "Trinity?"

"Safin found the tunnels," I said. "He's going after the children."

Chapter Thirty-Three

TAKEN

Apparently, Safin healed quickly. With the damage he'd sustained from the battle, he should have been in bed, attempting to heal.

Instead, he was at the tunnels, attacking helpless supernatural kids.

I sped through the doorway, Shane at my back, screaming silently for Amias. If Safin stayed to fight, we were going to need the master.

The tunnels were covered with dozens of spells, protection and otherwise. One of the spells made it nearly impossible for humans—or outsiders—to find the entrances and exits.

Yet somehow, Safin had.

When we arrived at the tunnel entrance, no enemy was there.

"They're at one of the exits," Shane said.

The tunnels came out on the other side of Bay Town, deep in the woods. It wouldn't take us long to find which exit—once we were in the woods the sounds of battle would likely tip us off—but it was a delay we couldn't afford.

Supernaturals began to come out in force as the news spread. I tasted their panic, immediate and sharp, as they rushed to defend the most vulnerable among us.

Someone would hurry to the Deluge to tell Angus that as he sat at the bedside of one of his children, the others were under attack.

That would push him over the edge.

Exactly as Mikhail Safin wanted.

But there were no executioners. Not at the tunnels.

Dead bodies—I counted five of them—littered the ground.

A few wolves milled the area, and when word spread that help had arrived, children began spilling from the exit.

Crawford had arrived at very nearly the same time I had, and he strode toward me, his stare moving over the area, assessing the situation. I stared at him, feeling almost as if he were the only familiar thing—the only calm thing—in the jumble of confusion and discord.

For a second I felt the need to go to him. To stand with him so he wouldn't have to be alone. Because he seemed alone. He always seemed alone.

He met my gaze, and for maybe the first time since I'd come back, his eyes didn't waver or flinch or fill with pity over my circumstances or fear that I might mesmerize him. The guilt had also melted away. And what remained was the one thing that had lurked there since the beginning.

And I was the one to look away.

I took a deep breath, then another, and finally, the black rage began to weaken.

"How did he get in?" Crawford asked.

I shook my head. "I just arrived so I know nothing." I lifted a hand and gestured at a wolf, but as he began to jog toward me, Crawford pointed at something behind me.

"Angus had Jade and her crew guarding the tunnels," he said. "Those killed must have been her men."

I turned and spotted Amias crouching before a battered woman. I recognized Jade Noel even beneath the blood covering her face.

Alejandro knelt behind her and she reclined against him, her hands in her lap. I stepped on something as I neared her, and when I glanced down, I found her wand.

It hadn't done her any good—at least I thought it hadn't, until I spotted a dead executioner lying a few yards from her. Somehow, she'd managed to break through Safin's protection spell and had killed at least one of his men.

I placed the wand in her lap and glanced at Al, but I didn't ask him if she was okay—obviously she was not.

Her eyes were unfocused, her nose was bleeding copiously, and the fingers of her right hand—her wand-holding hand—were bent at odd angles.

The place was filling up with supernaturals and the ground was being trampled and muddied, but no one cared. There was no crime scene to preserve, no evidence to gather, no chain of command to worry over.

At least, that was what everyone thought until the new police captain—Wendy Knight—showed up and started shouting orders.

Apparently, she believed an investigation would be opened, and that there was a chance the executioners would be prosecuted for what they'd done.

That was what she said. She stood with Crawford at her side and yelled those things, as if they might somehow be believed, as if the shattered supernaturals might somehow care.

She had a lot of good intentions, and someday, perhaps, she'd make some changes.

I believed she would.

But that night, there was simply fear, violence, and the suffering of nonhumans.

"Trinity?"

I turned to find a short, dark-haired woman behind me, her hands clasped at her throat, her face so bloodless I was afraid she would pass out. I recognized her as one of the nannies who worked for Angus.

"Marie," I said. "Isn't it?"

She nodded. "I was with them when it happened."

I took her arm and led her toward Crawford and Captain Knight. They'd need an accounting of the events.

I introduced her, and Crawford and the new captain peered down at her. "Can you tell us exactly what happened?" Knight asked. "Were any of the children hurt?"

Supernatural healers—a doctor and two nurses, were calmly walking the area, assessing for damage, checking the children, and talking quietly amongst themselves.

The night's trauma was nothing new to them.

"They didn't come to hurt children," Marie said. "And the man who took Natalie promised he would keep her safe."

I swayed and Crawford shot a hand out to steady me. "Took Natalie," I repeated. "What the fuck do you *mean*, took Natalie?"

"I thought you all knew," she whispered. "The executioner said he was going to call and inform the mayor of his demands." She buried her face in her hands. "Angus is going to...he's just going to..."

But she couldn't finish her sentence. Angus was going to do a lot of things. He was going to break down, he was going to kill, he was going to feel the darkest terror of his life.

Shit. Little Natalie.

"Trinity!"

Harlan, Angus's son, rushed toward me. He had two small kids with him—not Angus's—and they clung to his hands, not making a sound.

"Harlan," I said. "What happened to Natalie?"

"I couldn't stop them," he said. He'd found a pair of pants a size too big for him, but the rest of his body was bare and smeared with bloodstains. He'd shifted during the attack, had tried his best to protect the others.

He wouldn't have had a chance.

I wrapped my arm around his shoulders. "It's not your fault."

He burst into tears, but the little ones with him clasped hands and stared solemnly, quietly.

"My father trusted me," he said, finally, as Crawford stood with his phone to his ear, listening to voicemails, hoping, perhaps, to find one from Darkness. "I let them hurt Derry, and I let the wolf take the baby. I'm fucking useless."

His despair was huge. He stood there, uncertain and agonized and guilty, and I didn't know what to do to help him.

Marie took his arm. "You protected us all as best you could," she told him. "You did everything you could and more. You didn't let them do anything."

"Harlan," I said. "What do you mean the wolf took Natalie?"

"He came in," Harlan said, as Marie nodded. "He was different. I asked him what was wrong, but he said nothing, he just wanted to check on us." He clenched his fists. "He asked specifically for Natalie, said he heard she was sick."

We stood there and listened as he told us that he'd pointed Natalie out to the wolf, said she was fine, not sick at all...

The attack had been sudden, quick, and brutal. The wolf had grabbed Natalie. She hadn't made a sound, just lay quietly in his arms as he'd sprinted back to the exit.

"I shifted and followed," Harlan said. "There were four of them fighting Jade and her guards. He killed them. Almost killed Jade. The wolf gave Nat to the big one."

"Safin?" I asked.

"No," Marie said. "The woman called him Edward or—"

"Edgar," I murmured.

"Yes, that's it. I'd followed Harlan out, and Edgar said he wouldn't let any harm come to Natalie." She buried her face in her hands and wept.

"Poor kid," I whispered. Angus's baby. His *last* baby.

"I tried to stop them," Harlan whispered. "A lot of us did. We shifted, but when we went after them, we couldn't do anything. They slipped away, and we couldn't do anything but batter ourselves against the invisible walls they left behind."

"He's a wizard," Marie said, lifting her tearstained face. "Their leader. And he's powerful."

"Why Natalie?" Captain Knight asked. "Was there a reason he took that particular child?"

"Safin saw her at the way station," I said.

"And he wants to hurt Angus," Crawford added grimly. "He sees Angus as…" He shook his head, unsure. "Competition, maybe."

Finally, one of the little kids broke the silence. "He's mean," she said. "That man."

"Yeah," I said. "He's mean."

The night was just beginning, and it was already shaping up to be the darkest one I'd seen for a long, long time.

Chapter Thirty-Four

FATE

"The wolf Safin captured led them here," Clayton said.

"I guess that was why they let me take him without a fight," Alejandro said. "He had his orders."

Jamie Stone stood a few steps behind him, watching us, not saying a word. Mostly, he watched Alejandro.

"Hey, Jamie," I said.

"Trinity." He gave me a smile, and I couldn't help but return it. The first time I'd seen that smile, I'd thought he'd been into me. But I couldn't give him what Alejandro could. Jamie Stone was exactly where he needed to be.

"What's the plan?" Al asked.

"Safin will offer an exchange," Crawford said. "The child for the dragon."

I nodded. And if Rhys were there, he'd make the trade willingly.

Crawford's phone buzzed. "Safin," he said. "You've gone too far."

He listened for a few minutes without saying another word, then finally, he murmured, "Do not hurt that little girl." Then he cut the connection and looked at me. "It's exactly as we thought. He wants you to bring the dragon to him. Says Natalie is in the care of some of his people, and they have orders to release her when he has you."

"We'll figure it out, Captain." Then I glanced at Captain Knight. "Sorry. Habit."

Leo stood a few yards away, his fists clenched, watching me. "When?" he asked.

Crawford glanced at his watch. "Three a.m. He didn't say why."

"It's a powerful hour," Jamie murmured. "He'll be at his strongest."

"And he actually believes we're going to stick to his fucking schedule." Shane said. "The man is psychotic."

"He absolutely will hurt that child. We'll do whatever he wants, if we can." I looked around. The wolves had melted away—gone home to their pack, but they were going to have to answer some questions, and they would have to turn the traitor over to Angus.

And Rhys...

His absence was becoming more worrisome by the second. "Where *is* he?" I muttered.

"He should have been back by now," Clayton told me, and there was something in his voice that made my stomach tighten.

"What are you thinking?" I asked him. Then without waiting for him to answer, I rushed on. "Rhys wouldn't run."

"Then where the hell is he?" Shane asked. "No one could take a dragon unless the dragon agreed to be taken."

I gestured at Amias. "Someone took a master vampire. Someone could take a dragon."

Amias narrowed his eyes, considering my words.

"He was suppressed for so long," Clayton said. "He lived with a need most people can't conceive of. He finally gets his freedom and now an asshole shows up and demands he give it away." He looked at me, his stare unwavering. "*I* might run."

"Yeah," I said. "I might, too. But Rhys wouldn't."

But he wasn't *there*.

I ran my hand over my face, craving, for the first time since I'd turned, something besides blood in my system. "I could use a drink."

Alejandro slid a flask from his coat pocket. "Here you go." At my look, he shrugged. "I once knew a vampire who could drink whiskey. Can't hurt to try."

I felt the master's incomparable presence at my back.

"It *can* hurt," he disagreed. "It will burn like drinking the sun."

I took the flask and with Amias and Shane looking on hopefully, I put it to my lips, tilted it, and let whiskey pour into my mouth.

Amias wasn't wrong. It burned like fire all the way to my belly, but the pain began to ease almost immediately. The sloshing of alcohol in my shriveled stomach was uncomfortable and strange.

I drank again.

"Let me try," Shane said.

I handed him the flask. He held it to his mouth, gave a tentative sip, then spat it out immediately, muttering and fanning his lips. "Asshole," he said. I didn't know if he was talking to me, Al, or the whiskey.

I grinned.

"How was it?" Al asked me, smiling.

"Not horrible. Kind of pleasant, actually. More because I could do it than—"

Abruptly my stomach rebelled and began to expel the whiskey, and that shit hurt worse coming up than it did going down.

I flew to the tree line, then stood heaving behind a particularly large oak. "God," I cried, when I was finished. "That hurts."

I pulled the cold night air into my mouth, letting it soothe my abused insides. Then I went back to the men, took the flask from Al, and drank again.

Crawford snorted and shook his head. Captain Knight watched him watching me, and there was something close to pity in her eyes. I wasn't sure who she felt sorry for—him, or me.

The whiskey burned more because of the rawness of my throat from the first attempt, but that time, it stayed down.

"Maybe you could try food," Leo suggested.

I clutched my stomach. "No. Just the thought makes

me sick."

Leo walked toward me, his tread purposeful and determined, his stare glued to mine.

"Leo?" I held out my hand to him. "Are you sick?"

His face was covered with a glossy sheen of sweat, his hands shook when he took mine, and his breathing was shallow.

"Clayton," I said. "Call the doctor over here."

"No," Leo said, without taking his stare from mine. "I need to talk to you, Trinity. Alone."

"All right," I agreed, concerned.

I pulled him toward the trees. We slipped into the quiet woods and then I turned to him, frowning. "What's on your mind?"

He continued to stare at me, saying nothing.

"Leo, you're acting a little freaky. What's up?"

His chest swelled as he took a deep, deep breath. "I want to..." He swallowed, then soldiered on. "I want to offer myself to you. You're going to face Darkness, and he's going to take you. It's my job to have your back. I'll feed you, and…" He stared over my head. "And whatever else you need."

A slow, uncontrollable smile slid across my face. I hoped he wouldn't think I was taking what he said lightly—I wasn't. But he pleased the hell out of me.

I ran my fingers over his arm. "I would love nothing more than to bring you officially into the group, Leo." And unable not to, I added, "And you will finally be mine."

"And you will be mine." His voice was fierce, for a second, and almost angry.

I pushed my fingers under the hem of his shirt. "Absolutely," I murmured. I remembered the inconceivable taste of him. The magic of him.

Hunger washed over me, sudden and intense, and there was nothing in the world but Leo Trask, the half-giant. My cravings were about to be satisfied.

He wasn't wrong. I'd need him. I'd need his blood. I'd need his…

Power, something whispered inside my mind. *You will need his power.*

And I could not wait to take it.

Clayton walked into the woods. "Trinity?"

I ran my tongue over the points of my fangs. "We'll be back in a few minutes," I told him.

His stare dropped to where my fingers disappeared under the hem of Leo's shirt.

Leo didn't move, didn't breathe, even, but I heard his throat click when he swallowed. "Trinity," he said, finally. "I…"

Amias joined Clayton and I sighed as the three men quietly stared at each other.

Apparently, they were going to need a minute. I hoped not more than that, because I was so close to getting what I wanted, what I *needed*, and they were making me wait.

I leaned against a tree and crossed my arms, tapping my toe impatiently.

The pre-rifter Trinity would have thought I was being selfish and greedy and cold. She'd have been correct—but the post-rifter Trinity didn't care.

I shook with the need to possess the half-giant, and the men continued to watch each other without saying a word. Like there was all the time in the world.

But I was done waiting.

I walked to Leo, pressed my palm against the covered ridge of his enormous dick, and squeezed.

"Men." My voice was thick, my words impatient. "You're welcome to join us."

Amias leaned forward to kiss me. "Next time. Gather all the power you can, my love. We're going to need it." Just before he melted into the shadows with Clayton, he turned back to face us. "There is no time for foreplay. Make it quick. When Angus arrives, there will be time only to kill."

"I'm sorry it has to be quick and dirty," I told Leo. I pulled my sword off my back and leaned her against a tree. "I know you'd like some romance, but—"

Then Leo shocked the hell out of me.

He took over.

I barely had time to gasp before he grabbed my throat, lifted me off my feet, and slammed me to the ground.

"You had your hand on my cock," he said. "Quick and dirty suits me just fine."

"Oh," I whispered. "Good, then."

"I hope you're prepared for some pain," he murmured.

Oh, he knew I liked a little pain. He knew.

He also knew I wasn't going to break.

Leo knew a lot of things. *I* had been the one in the dark.

Now that he'd made his decision, he was all in.

And he was *fierce*.

His greed exceeded mine, somehow.

He ripped my boots and jeans off me. My bare, sensitive skin rubbed against the rough fabric of his clothing, somehow more stimulating than if he'd been naked. His big hands shoved up my shirt and covered my breasts, his tongue raided my mouth, and suddenly blood wasn't the most delicious thing about the half-giant.

"I've wanted to do this since the day I met you." He muttered those words into my mouth and I swallowed them whole, hungry for anything he wanted to feed me.

I pushed him to his side, then ripped my lips from his as I released his hard cock from its confines. It sprang free and my eager thoughts stuttered to a halt for a few seconds as I absorbed the enormity of the situation.

Pun very much intended.

"It's like a fucking tree trunk," I whispered.

"Good thing you're like a fucking vampire," he whispered back, then shoved open my knees, flicked his thumb over my clit, and before I'd stopped moaning, he grabbed my knees, held them apart, and poised himself for entry. "Quick and dirty, yeah?"

"Yeah," I agreed. I was a mass of wet, throbbing need, but still, I was going to have some trouble taking him. Normal sized people weren't meant for sex with half-giants.

Once again, Leo shocked me.

I braced for pain, and there was pain.

He stretched me, his stare not leaving mine as he forced himself slowly and unhesitatingly into me, rocking his hips, driving himself deeper and deeper, and then, he conformed to me. He filled me up, and I felt him with every part of me. And it was *hot*.

Literally.

I stared down the length of my body, watching as he thrust into me, and it looked impossible. But it wasn't.

His stare was amused, but filled with heat, passion, and a hunger that would have matched the hunger in mine.

"Magic," I managed, then couldn't speak again.

Pleasure and pain. Fucking Leo was pleasure and pain, and it was exquisite.

"Taste me," he murmured. "Take my blood."

Oh.

Oh *God,* yes.

His blood filled my mouth, blood like nothing I'd ever tasted or imagined tasting, and finally, I lost control.

As did he.

He muttered something I didn't understand and plunged into me hard and fast, and I thought I was breaking and reknitting and maybe I was dying, and it felt better than any other moment in my life.

I could no longer tell the difference between pleasure and pain—it was simply one unending, excruciating, gorgeous sensation.

Once before, I'd caught a glimpse of Leo's bright soul. His perfect beauty. Only a glimpse. But now, that light shone from him, right *there,* and became part of me, engulfed me, bathed me.

What started out as quick and dirty turned into something spiritual and magical and unimaginable as we became one and our powers combined, our bodies connected, and our fates intertwined.

Leo was *mine*.

But he'd known, even if I hadn't, that I was his.

He'd taken my power as I'd taken his. He'd tasted the magic in my blood as I'd tasted his. We climaxed together, fingers grasping, tongues touching. I clenched around him, greedily milking every drop he had to give me, wanting more. Wanting everything he was.

Fate smiled, and my circle was complete.

I was one with all my men.

And together we would fight the darkness.

We would fight it every day for the rest of our lives.

Chapter Thirty-Five

CAGED

I heard the roar of Angus's truck seconds after I limped from the woods with Leo.

Maybe he didn't know that his child had been taken, but he'd know the possibilities.

I closed my eyes for a second, trying to gain strength for what was coming, and wished for the master. I needed him to keep my mind quiet.

"Where's Amias?" I asked Shane, grimacing at the tenderness of my body. I would recover quickly, but if I'd had my way about it, I would have lain in bed for a few days, basking in the afterglow of the half-giant's attention and the not unpleasant soreness he'd left behind.

"He went to search for Rhys," Shane answered.

Good. If anyone could discover what had happened to the dragon, Amias could.

The men—even Crawford—stood with me as we waited for Angus.

He slammed on his brakes, leapt from the truck, and strode toward us. I could tell he hadn't yet heard about Natalie. Whoever had reported to him had likely been too afraid to tell him his youngest was now in the hands of Mikhail Safin.

I gestured for Harlan to bring Angus's other children, and I went to meet the werebull. He was going to need us all.

When I was halfway to him, his cell rang. He frowned and ripped it from his pocket, then started to lift it to his ear.

"Angus," I yelled. "Wait."

But he didn't wait. His stare roved the area, distracted and searching as he looked for his kids, and without even glancing at the screen, he answered.

We gathered around him, and his kids clung to him, and they were what kept him calm when Safin's voice slid into his ear.

He met my stare as he listened.

"Angus," I whispered.

He dropped his phone back into his pocket and began hugging his kids, and his calm was so extreme that I was afraid for him.

"Dad," Harlan said, his voice breaking. "I'm sorry. I couldn't stop them."

"No one could," I said. "They're surrounded by an unbreakable magic."

"I will break it," Angus said.

My heart lightened. Safin was a dark, powerful force—there was no arguing that.

But Angus...

Angus would take death to Darkness.

And he would get his little girl back.

On my back, Silverlight buzzed.

Crawford excused himself to take a call, but he was back in seconds. "I sent men to Hyde Hill," he began.

"Safin won't be there," Angus said.

"No," Crawford agreed. "He was gone. Some of his men were there, but Safin took Aspen and Edgar and went into hiding."

"Where would they go?" I asked.

"Somewhere secluded," Crawford told me. "He was warned that deliberately putting the humans at such a high level of risk would not be tolerated. He's controlled—to a point. The government will not hinder him as long as he leaves the city, but they won't help him, either."

"We'll see if Clayton can track him," I said. "I need to get close enough to rip out his heart."

"You can't go up against him again," Crawford said.

"Especially not alone. Find someone who can break his protection spell, and then take him on. The last time you fought him, you ended up skinned alive by his whip. He's going to be even more prepared now that he knows what he's up against. If you—"

"Captain," Angus interrupted, almost gently. "Trin is immortal now. And she absolutely will fight Safin." He looked at me, his stare stark and blue in his pale face. "And If I'm not there, she'll keep him alive until I arrive."

I nodded. "I'll save him for you, Angus."

"She'll kick ass," Leo said, and though he sounded confident, I saw the worry on his face. "Every time she fights to victory, she comes back stronger."

"And colder," Shane muttered.

Jade, leaning on Jamie Stone's arm, stood behind us. "You can't treat her like she's human, Crawford. You have to treat her like she's badass." She grinned at me, though her eyes were flinching and bright with pain.

"Jade," Al said. "You'll need to sit this one out."

"Fuck off," she snapped. Then she gasped as her legs gave out, and only Jamie's supporting arm kept her upright. "Oh, that motherfucker."

Al took her other arm. "Jeremy," he called.

A young man jogged to us, and Al handed Jade off to him. "Take her to the Deluge."

"I don't need the fucking healer," Jade snarled. "I need a big bloody piece of Mikhail Safin."

Al didn't push it, but we all knew Jade wasn't going to be fighting. She couldn't even stand on her own.

"Anybody who wants a ride, get in the truck," Angus said. "Safin won't be calling back for a few hours."

"Where are you going?" I asked him.

"I'm going to see the wolves." Calm. So calm.

But as Angus turned to walk to his truck, Amias returned.

"I know where Rhys is," he said. "But I don't know how to free him."

"Free him?" Clayton asked.

And I understood what Amias was going to say before he said it. "The elders."

He nodded. "Yes, my love. The elders have taken it upon themselves to *protect* the dragon. No one can touch him now, and he cannot exchange himself for the child."

"We need him," I said. "Safin's protection can't withstand a dragon's fire."

"Rhys can't burn them," Angus said. "Not while they have Natalie."

And not even I was cold enough to sacrifice a child so I could kill the enemy. Not if I could help it.

Himself walked from the shadows, surprising all of us.

"If you cannot kill Darkness," he told me, "it will not be done. We cannot risk the dragon. You must not attempt to free him."

"None of us can do anything alone," I said. "My men and I will kill Darkness. It was never just me and my sword."

Clayton stood next to me, his body brushing mine. I knew he would always crave the touch of another person. Miriam had created that need inside him, and it would never die.

"Fate," Himself muttered, as though he would like to strangle said fate, and then he slipped through the dark night and left us to it.

None of us tried convincing him to free Rhys—not even Angus. We knew he would not be convinced. If we wanted Rhys free, we would have to find a way to do it ourselves.

Once again, Angus turned to go.

"Angus," Leo said, stopping him.

Angus turned to the half-giant, and in that instant realized that not only was Leo truly one of us, but that he was afraid Angus doubted him.

I saw the dawning realization in the werebull's eyes.

Angus glanced at me, then clapped Leo on the back.

217

"Good," was all he said, but Leo's entire face lit up. He straightened his shoulders and gave Angus a nod, then he, Angus, and Clayton strode on to Angus's truck.

I grabbed Al's arm when he would have hurried to his own car. "Alejandro." I pointed my chin at Jamie. "Can he weaken the walls and free Rhys the way his mother did the rifters?"

I waited for his answer, and Amias, Shane, and Crawford waited with me.

"He's getting stronger every day," Al said. "But I don't think he's strong enough to break an elder's wall."

Jamie kept his calm gaze on Al, but said nothing.

"For you," I said, "he'd be strong enough." He'd do it or die trying—but I didn't voice that part.

Finally, Alejandro nodded. "He'll try."

We left him there, his arms around Jamie, murmuring into his ear, and we raced to the wolves' village to stand with Angus.

Chapter Thirty-Six

WOLVES

The pack was waiting for us. They'd known we'd come. Because he'd harmed Angus the most by taking his child, Angus had the right to retaliate.

He wouldn't take the wolf's child. He'd take the wolf's life.

The wolf pack's main cabins were built in a crude semi-circle with a large clearing in the middle. They used the clearing for most things—meetings, fights, parties, punishments, and the like—and the ground had been worn smooth and packed hard by hundreds of feet over the years.

Nearby, a wolf's howl rose, and I rubbed the gooseflesh from my arms.

Their alpha stepped out of her little cabin, flanked by two rather large male wolves, and her stare went straight to Angus.

"Let me save you some time, Stark. I won't give my wolf to you. His punishment will be decided by me—and I can assure you he *will* be punished." And she turned to leave, dismissing us all.

Her arrogance was astounding.

"Vonda," Angus growled, and again, gooseflesh dotted my skin.

The wolf hesitated, but didn't turn to face him. "Carlos had a reason for what he did. Safin had taken Carlos' brother. He could have withstood his own torture, but he couldn't bear his brother's. I will punish him. Go home, Angus."

But I'd gotten a hazy glimpse into Safin's house of

horrors. "There was only one wolf in that motel," I said. "And Alejandro freed him."

"There was only one wolf *alive,*" she told me. "Safin killed the brother—but Carlos didn't realize it at the time."

Angus took a step toward her. "None of that matters. There is no excuse for a grown wolf harming a child. The wolf will die, and I will be the one to kill him."

Apparently, the alpha wasn't above using children to get what she wanted. She muttered a command, and wolves began creeping from their tiny houses. They spread out beside the alpha, and their children peered around their legs.

The alpha sent Angus a satisfied smile. "Go home, Angus," she repeated.

And he would have. He would have figured out another way to get the wolf who'd taken Natalie, because Angus wasn't ever going to hurt a child.

We turned at the sound of an engine and watched as Alejandro braked to a stop beside Angus's truck. He got out but didn't join us—just leaned against the hood of his car and waited to see what we would need.

Shane leaned over to whisper into my ear. "The bastard is in the cabin on her left. I saw him peeking through the curtain like a fucking little old lady."

Angus wasn't willing to so much as scare the children.

But Shane and I...

We were assholes.

We streaked to the cabin on the left—Shane couldn't get inside without an invite, but rifters could go wherever the fuck they pleased. The door crumbled when I kicked it, and I sprinted inside, then grabbed the wolf almost before he'd realized the door had been turned into kindling.

I tossed him through the doorway to Shane before turning to fight the two wolves who'd been in the room with him.

I didn't kill them, but I made sure they would stay down for a while. I ran back outside just in time to watch

Shane fling the wolf to the ground at Angus's feet.

Seconds, that was all it took.

I turned to the wolf alpha and smirked. "Fuck you," I said. "This wolf belongs to us now."

"Get your babies back inside," Amias told her, "before you get them hurt."

Maybe we needed the wolves as allies—but as long as Vonda was their alpha, we would be enemies.

Not that the vampires and wolves were friendly to begin with.

Vonda's wolves were poised to fight. Some of them shifted and stood trembling with eagerness, heads low, growls floating from between pulled back lips, teeth showing.

But Vonda didn't give the command. "You will pay for this," she told me, "with your blood."

"No, she will not," Amias said. "But I will reimburse you for the wolf. Name your price. We should not fight amongst ourselves. How much for peace?"

Vonda squinted at him. "You want to give me cash money for my wolf?"

"Yes."

Everyone knew the wolves were not rolling in money. She put her hands on her hips and considered his offer. "Five thousand dollars."

"Done."

"Then I will let your two vampires live."

Amias was not without pride. He curled his lip. "My vampires would destroy you," he said. "And you know that."

She looked like she might argue the point, but in the end, as her wolves stared out at us from eyes that had become stark and hopeless in expressionless faces, she inclined her head. "Five thousand dollars. Tomorrow." And when she turned to go back inside, I heard her mutter, "I should have asked for more."

I felt bad for her wolves.

Angus threw Carlos the wolf into his truck and peeled out, off to get information and vengeance.

"Give Clayton and me a ride back home?" Leo asked Alejandro.

"I'm happy to. Want a ride, Trinity?"

I shook my head. "Cars make my head hurt."

"You'll be okay after you get used to it."

"Yeah," I said. "Like with the whiskey."

He smiled, then walked to his car, Clayton and Leo at his side.

I tossed a look in the direction Angus had gone. "I wonder if the wolf has any information."

"Not likely," Amias replied, "but Angus will get it if he does."

"Yeah," I said. "I hope killing Carlos makes him feel better."

But we all knew it wouldn't.

Only getting Natalie back—alive—would make Angus feel better.

And freeing Rhys.

And ending Safin.

Call me pessimistic, but I was pretty sure Angus wasn't going to be feeling better anytime soon.

"What's the endgame?" Shane asked, as we walked home. "Even if Safin gets the dragon's power, what's he going to do with it?"

"Own it," I said grimly. "And that's enough for him."

Amias agreed. "The conquest is why he lives. When he has nothing left to take, the blackness inside him will destroy him."

"Depression?" I asked.

Amias shrugged. "Blackness."

In the distance, a wolf's long, lonely howl ended in a scream.

I couldn't help but shudder.

"I guess there's blackness in everybody," Shane said quietly.

Indeed.

"When dawn arrives," Amias said, "I will want both of you with me."

The night had become bleak and sad, and we would end it in each other's arms.

I hated the thought of dawn because I would be forced to sleep, and Angus would be without me. Without the vampires.

And he'd be without Rhys.

That left only Clayton, Leo, and Alejandro. And I was terribly afraid they just wouldn't be enough.

Not against Safin.

We went back to the way station to check on Jamie Stone's progress, and to wait for Mikhail Safin to call Angus with his demands.

But Safin didn't call Angus.

He called me.

Chapter Thirty-Seven

HUNT

"Hello, Trinity."

"Mikhail." I remained calm, but rage rose up inside me at his voice. If he'd been in front of me, I'd have killed him—captive child or not.

I put Safin on speaker so the others could hear, then paced the kitchen floor as he talked. I figured nothing he said would be a surprise, and I was right.

"This sweet child is terrified," he told me. "I'm afraid that if she's here much longer, she will simply collapse."

"The dragon is gone," I snarled. "If he were here, he'd turn himself over to you."

Jamie Stone ended up in Willow-Wisp. There was more power there, he'd said, and we'd left him there with Alejandro watching over him. We could only hope he'd free Rhys, because Safin wasn't going to settle for anything less than the dragon.

Angus had yet to return. Clayton and Leo sat at the table shoving protein and carbs down their throats. It was going to come down to a battle, and they'd need their strength.

Amias and Shane stood at the open kitchen door, letting the cold air in as they stared into the darkness.

"I want the dragon, of course," Safin said. "He is the entire reason I've come to Red Valley. But you knew that."

"We don't have him. The vampire elders took him. They knew he'd—"

"You must be wondering why I've called you instead of Stark," he interrupted, not at all interested in my excuses.

"Why did you?"

"Because you'll be the one to neutralize the dragon before you bring him."

"How would I do that?"

"Your sword, Trinity. Do you know where dragons are most vulnerable?"

I didn't, but because Rhys's sex was all tangled up in his dragon, I expected it was his cock.

"His eye," Safin said, dispelling that notion. "If you slide a powerful enough weapon into a dragon's eye, he will be unable to function. Certainly unable to shift. And your sword is powerful enough." He paused. "And also, I would like the sword."

I'd known he was going to want Silverlight, so I wasn't surprised by his request. "You weren't listening," I told him. "There is no dragon. There is no dragon eye. The vampire elders have hidden him in a prison between worlds. Surely you heard about our recent circumstances—the elders' return, the rifters, the reason I'm no longer human…?"

He said nothing for a few long seconds, then, "The rifter prison. You expect me to believe they've captured the dragon and are holding him in a rifter prison."

"It's the truth."

A child screamed, her voice so sharp and sudden and shocking that I dropped the phone. Someone yelled—Edgar, I thought—and finally, the screams turned to sobs. I picked the phone up with a shaking hand, thankful Angus wasn't there to hear his little girl's torment.

"Now, Trinity," Safin said, over the quiet sobs. "Do the elders still have the dragon?"

"Yes," I whispered. "Motherfucker. They still have the dragon. I can't get to him. I'm trying."

He didn't believe me. "I'll call again soon to see if you've retrieved him. If you haven't, there's really no reason to keep this little one alive, is there?"

"I will kill you," I murmured, unable to keep the rage from my voice.

"No," he disagreed. "You will bring me the dragon. *That* is what you will do."

I cut the connection, then turned to my men. They stood at the table, their food forgotten, their faces pale. Shane quietly closed the kitchen door, then sat down, not looking at anybody, but Amias walked to me and put his arms around me. He must have known I needed the comfort.

I heard the rumble of Angus's truck as he neared the house.

Jin turned from the stove. "You cannot give him what he wants."

"Yeah, no shit, Jin," Shane said.

"I have to," I told them. "He's hurting her."

"He'll believe you when his continued torture achieves nothing but a suffering child," Leo said.

"Fuck a dragon," Shane said. "We have to find Safin."

Clayton nodded. "And we have to find him now. Trinity, I'll try to track him. I need something with his scent."

Angus's footsteps were heavy as he walked toward the kitchen. He was bloody, and his stare was empty. "News?"

I swallowed hard, then lied to him. "No." I went to him and despite his grime, I wrapped my arms around him and held him. "Nothing yet. But Clayton thinks he can track Safin if we can find something with his scent on it."

"And Jamie is still attempting to break the walls," Leo said.

Angus nodded, then extracted himself gently from my arms. "I'm going to clean up." He turned back at the doorway, looking from one of us to the other. "I didn't kill the wolf." Then he walked away.

My heart broke for him.

"Let's go," I told Clayton. "Safin will have left his scent on something at the motel. We'll find it, and then we'll find him."

"Trinity," Leo said. "What did you do with the clothes

you were wearing when you fought Safin?"

I put my hand to my chest. "I left them on my bathroom floor."

"Perfect," Clayton said. "Go get them."

But Jin cleared his throat and stared at the floor when we looked at him. "They are in the barrel out back. I threw them away, but I have not burned them yet."

I headed for the back door. "Let's go sift through the trash."

Alejandro joined us when he heard us at the trash barrel. "Lose something?"

"The clothes I wore when Safin and I fought," I told him. "How's Jamie coming along?"

He shook his head. "Nothing yet."

Maybe I didn't really want Jamie to be successful. And maybe I wouldn't admit that to anyone but myself.

I held up a bag triumphantly after a few minutes of digging. "Found them."

Clayton took the strip of cloth that had once been a shirt from my fingers, and delicately held it to his nose. He shuddered.

"What?" I asked.

"I smell your stripped flesh," he said, lowering the filthy cloth. "It's...harsh."

"Try again," I urged. "Catch what lies beneath my scent."

But he crumpled the cloth in his fist and buried the fingers of his free hand in my hair. "I'm sorry." He lowered his mouth to mine.

"For what?" I murmured, against the lusciousness of his lips.

"For your pain," he said. "That I didn't stop it."

He wasn't just talking about my fight with Safin.

I cupped his cheek and caressed his smooth, cake-scented skin. "And I'm sorry I didn't stop yours."

He drew back, just a little. "You did, Trinity."

"Get Safin's scent," Shane said, his voice rough,

"before dawn makes us useless."

After one last lingering kiss, Clayton once again put the strip of cloth to his nose. He closed his eyes and pulled the scents deep into his brain.

I remembered well how it felt to catch a scent and follow it all the way to my prey. The thrill of that chase, the satisfaction of the kill. I remembered. The memory was not lost to me, and someday, I would track again. I believed I would.

Angus walked up behind me and slid a hand around my waist.

I leaned back against him, wishing we could go inside and lie in each other's arms. It seemed like forever since we'd had a moment to ourselves that wasn't wrapped in fear or worry.

"I have his scent," Clayton murmured. "But I can't..." He sniffed the air, his eyes closed. "I can't smell it past this cloth."

"It's the protection surrounding him," I said. "You can't touch him, smell him, hurt him. And we can't find him."

Angus said nothing.

"Wolf," Amias warned, and then a wolf, huge and raging, raced toward us.

Not *us*, really. He wanted Angus.

Angus snarled as he turned to face the attacker, but he didn't bother shifting.

The wolf leapt, flew through the air, and collided with the object of his wrath.

Teeth snapping, he went for Angus's throat.

"Dumbass," Shane muttered.

Angus buried his fingers in the wolf's fur, slung him to the ground, and proceeded to beat the hell out of him.

My cell rang. "Fuck," I muttered, then yanked it from my pocket as I left Angus to punish the wolf. "Crawford?"

"Trinity, Safin is attacking the city."

I put a hand to my chest and stopped walking, stunned.

"What?"

"We need you," he said, and then was gone.

But I'd heard the sounds loud and clear. Screams, gunshots, sirens.

Safin was attacking the fucking *humans*.

He'd gone mad.

"The humans are under attack," I told the men. "Safin is in the city."

Amias straightened. "He's gone mad," he said, echoing my exact thoughts. "We must go."

"Go," I said, my stare on Angus, who continued punching the wolf. He appeared not to have heard me. "I'll follow you in."

He sprinted away, already calling for the vampires. I felt that call the same as they would.

Clayton and Alejandro jogged toward their cars around front. Leo started after them, then paused at my side. He looked at Angus. "Should I—"

"No." I reached out to squeeze his arm. "Go kill some executioners. I'll take care of Angus."

Leo nodded. "Shane?"

Shane shook his head. "I'll come in with Trinity."

I strode to Angus and leaned over to get in his face. "Angus, the city is under attack."

He stared down at his victim, his fist raised. I didn't know what he was seeing, but I was pretty sure it wasn't the wolf.

"Angus," I said, my voice sharp enough to cut through his bloodlust. I put my palms on either side of his face. "Safin is in the city."

The wolf passed out, and automatically shifted back to his human form. He was unconscious for only a few seconds. When he opened his eyes his rage had fled, leaving only a hopeless sadness in its place.

"You killed my brother," he said, dully. "And I can't even avenge his death."

"He's not dead," I said, wondering just how many

brothers Carlos had. "Angus kicked his ass, but he didn't kill him."

Hope crept into the wolf's widening eyes. "Not dead?"

Angus gave his head a hard shake to clear it, then got off the wolf. When he looked at me, his eyes were clearer.

"The executioners are attacking the humans?"

I nodded.

"You didn't kill my brother?" The wolf cried. "Where is he?"

"It is my right to kill him," Angus growled. "But he can't suffer in death, can he?"

"You should also blame our alpha," the wolf said, his words thick and mangled through his swollen, split lips. "She forced my brother to lead Safin to the tunnels. She made Carlos go in and get the child. *She* is the one you should kill."

"Angus," I said. "We have to get to the city."

"Please," the wolf said. "We need help. None of us is strong enough to challenge her." He glanced at Angus and then away, and though his thoughts remained unspoken, he was easy to read. He wanted Angus to go after the alpha.

Angus curled his lip and turned away.

"I can tell you where Darkness is hiding," the wolf whispered. "If you will kill my alpha." He lifted his chin and managed, despite sprawling on the ground, naked and bloody, to show a bit of spirit. "Is that a trade you are willing to make?"

Angus yanked him from the ground and held him dangling in midair. "Safin is in the city, attacking the humans."

"No," the wolf said, his voice thick. "That's a distraction. He's gone to the Deluge. He will prepare for you there. His final attempt." Then he squealed and kicked his legs when Angus's grip tightened.

Angus dropped the wolf, then turned to look at Shane and me, the hapless wolf already forgotten. "He's likely lying, but we have to check."

"Shane and I will meet you there," I said. We didn't really believe Safin was hiding in the swamp with the healers while his men attacked the city, but we would see for ourselves.

I doubted Angus heard me. He was already running to his truck.

I'd get to the Deluge before he did. Still, I would wait for him at the entrance. If the enemy was there, we'd go in and face him together, as we should.

There were only a couple of hours before dawn arrived. That's how long I had to kill Mikhail Safin—and I *had* to kill him. I had to find him, and I had to kill him.

I absolutely could not fall into sleep and leave my men to face him alone.

Chapter Thirty-Eight

DELUGE

I worried about Rhys.

I imagined him battering himself against the invisible walls of his prison, screaming words no one would hear. The elders would release him after we'd succeeded in destroying the threat, but I had to wonder...

Would he remain unbroken when they did? Or would his sudden and confusing confinement have driven him mad?

It had changed the rifters. I didn't like to think of Rhys there—wherever *there* was—alone and confused.

The barely visible dirt path leading to the Deluge veered abruptly off the main road. If a person didn't know what they were looking for, they would likely miss the turn—especially in the darkness. There were no signs, only overgrown weeds, potholes, dampness, and deep ditches.

I slowed to a walk and Shane and I silently jumped the ditch at the side of the road, then continued on through the deep woods.

"It feels good to run like that," I said.

"I can't remember what it was like not to," he told me.

"Me neither." It was as though we'd always been vampires.

In the distance, the angry roar of an automobile grew louder. Angus was coming.

We crept on in silence for a few seconds. "The heaviness of this area feels like Raeven's Road," I said. "Do you remember..."

I trailed off, because there were so many things to remember about Raeven's Road. And most of them involved Shane.

I caught his stare, memories of a not so distant past strong in my mind. I'd fallen in love with him there. Had fought vampires with him, and demons, and had fucked him for the first time there. I'd nearly gotten him killed on that road, and had given him to Amias to save his life.

Raeven's Road held little but violence and pain and desolation; still, I would always feel a bittersweet nostalgia when I thought of it.

Shane didn't look away, perhaps as lost in the memories as I was. The cold moon watched us, kindly lending a mellow brightness to the night, and the air was fresh and chilly. But nothing could dispel the heavy dread of the swamp. It was a harsh place.

The Deluge, despite its similar heaviness, was about to add another dark chapter to its grim story, and I knew I would never think of it with nostalgia. Safin had already seen to that.

Shane held out a hand and I hesitated, unsure of what he wanted. Then I realized he wanted to touch me, and with a quiet sigh of relief, I went to him.

"Baby hunter," he murmured.

I held him as tightly as I could without hurting him, and I imagined he was doing the same to me. I buried my face against his warm neck and forced myself to remain quiet, but I couldn't stop a few wayward tears from wetting his skin.

No one knew what would happen that night.

And not even Shane could maintain a grip on his rage when he knew that night might see us all destroyed.

Angus surprised me. As overflowing with worry as he was, as much as he needed to rush the Deluge, find Safin, and save his daughters, he came in quiet.

He'd parked his truck away from the swamp, and we continued to the Deluge together.

"He may not be here," I said. "Why would he send his men to the city without him?"

Shane shrugged. "Why would he attack the humans at all?"

"Maybe there's no reason," Angus said, his voice a quiet rumble. "Maybe he's just lost his mind and is going on a rampage to kill everyone in his path."

"I don't like this," I said. "It doesn't feel right."

But we continued grimly on.

I pulled Silverlight from her sheath, holding my breath as I willed her to remain dark and quiet. She did, and there was only a soft *snick* when she left the scabbard.

"Shane and I will go in, find the girls, and get them to safety," Angus said.

"I'll handle Safin." Then I added, "And if I can, I'll save him for you."

He shook his head. "If you can kill him, kill him."

Angus no longer cared about revenge. He just wanted the son of a bitch dead.

The healers had chosen their seclusion well. The swamp was unfriendly. Dense, wet, and tricky, the closer we got to the healers' cabins, the harder it was to walk.

A rustic, slightly treacherous road led to the cabins, but it was an easily ambushed road, and anyone traveling it would be seen from those in the cabins. We did not want Safin, if he was indeed there, to see us coming.

The tangled vegetation was thick and rife with long, sharp briars, and sucking mudholes gobbled at our shoes like greedy monsters. I stood in muddy water to my thighs and felt flashes of pain, there and gone, and realized that buried silver, combined with the water, would make it difficult for vampires to set foot near the cabins.

And I wondered what the healers were hiding from. No one but people desperate to hide would choose to live in such a hostile place.

The area thinned out and abruptly, the healers' cabins appeared. We crouched behind the trees, watching, listening, getting the feel of the place.

"He's in there," I whispered, finally, and both Angus

and Shane nodded.

Safin was in that house.

We had a chance to surprise him, and all we could do was take it.

The thought had barely entered my mind when a *crack* echoed through the night.

The second before someone shot at us, Angus, standing in front of Shane, leaned over to look at something on the ground. The bullet meant for him hit Shane, instead.

Shane was flung backward from the force of it entering his head, and the last thing I heard before my mind flew into chaos was the maniacal sound of someone laughing.

I screamed, sure that Shane was dead before I remembered he was a vampire—he would survive a bullet wound to the head. I fell to my knees beside him even as he opened his eyes and began to heal.

He would be okay.

But if Angus had taken the bullet, he would most certainly not have been.

Angus had already shifted. With his hooves kicking up great clumps of wet earth, he raced into the clearing.

The next shot took me in the arm as I leaned over Shane. I heard a distant, strangled scream as I half fell atop my downed hunter, and I knew Angus had found the shooter.

But there were others.

Safin had known we'd come.

It was time to fight.

To kill.

To take back our city from the darkness.

A zing of joy shot through me, and I didn't feel bad about it.

I freed the rifter much as Jamie would free the dragon—I hoped. I shattered the walls around that dark beast and she rushed out to engulf me, and I was ecstatic.

The rifter wasn't so afraid.

The rifter was simply a bloodthirsty killer.
Like Mikhail Safin.

Chapter Thirty-Nine

POSSESSION

The main cabin was surprisingly large and possessed a wide, wraparound porch, and was surrounded by three smaller buildings. All of them were raised off the damp ground and were accessible by what seemed like miles of old, wooden steps leading up to the front doors. Even if Safin and his crew hadn't been there, shooting as us, I would have thought the place was grim and creepy.

There were too many sounds—roars, shouts, screams, gunshots, barking dogs, distant sirens—and they battered my sensitive ears until I was unable to really hear anything. I couldn't separate the sounds, couldn't absorb what I needed and toss the others to the side, but I rushed on through the mud and splashed through the water, my mind in chaos but my stare steady on the cabin.

Safin was in there. The only thing that would end the battle was his death, and I meant to make that happen.

He walked out of the house, bold and calm, and stood on the porch. "Aspen," he called.

Aspen and Edgar walked to the edge of the roof of the neighboring cabin with Angus's daughters. Both girls were silent, and neither one of them struggled. Edgar held Derry, and Aspen gripped the smaller Natalie. Aspen shoved Natalie dangerously close to the edge. "If you can take her, she's yours," she yelled.

Angus roared and rushed the cabin, no thought in his mind but saving his girls.

"Angus, no," I screamed.

I reached him in mere seconds, but I didn't get to him before Safin's whip did. Darkness flicked his wrist and the whip streaked through the air, wrapped around the werebull's neck, and began to behead him.

Safin was counting on shock and awe to give him the advantage, had planned for it, and in the end, he got exactly what he wanted.

Someone I would throw down my weapon for.

He got Angus.

Angus didn't shift back to human form. As his animal, he had a much better chance at surviving the constricting whip. But for a second, his eyes met mine, and I saw his rage. He wasn't giving up. He wasn't going to die.

He was too pissed off for that.

All around us, men were fighting. All around us, men were shooting, dying, bleeding.

The supernats had arrived, sometime, somehow, and I hadn't even been aware of it.

The vampires, too, but they couldn't get into the battle.

Over the years, the healers had vampire-proofed their property. They'd laced the ground near their house with silver, had hung it in their trees, had even placed silver-plated sculptures at odd intervals. The vampires tried to get through it, but it repelled them, hurt them, and forced them to hang back. There was simply too much of it.

The healers were apparently very anti-vampire. Safin had discovered that and was planning to use it to his advantage.

His backup kept the supernats occupied while Safin attempted to get what he really wanted.

Angus's dead body, and me.

I didn't try to cut through the whip. It would have taken too much time, and we didn't have time. I raced toward Safin. I jumped, leapt over the porch railing, and lifted Silverlight, preparing to thrust her into his vulnerable chest.

"Stop or they all die," Mikhail said. "One at a time."

Edgar might have a soft spot for children, but his boss did not.

LIGHTBRINGER

He would kill both of Angus's children, and he would make Angus watch. There was no flinching in his eyes, no softness, no doubt.

"I will kill them," he said.

"I know," I murmured.

Then I flung Silverlight at his heart—because that was my one fucking chance, and I figured he'd kill the children anyway.

But whatever he had surrounding him was too strong. Given time, the sword would have broken through.

Too bad we had no time.

Darkness smiled

"Trinity," Derry screamed. "My *dad!*"

Everything seemed to slow down. The sounds, only a moment ago loud and discordant, dimmed and fell away. I honed in on Safin's eyes, the sweat beading on his nose, the soft breath hissing from between his teeth. I concentrated on the muffled *thump, thump* of his heartbeat and the thundering rush of blood through his veins.

He held out his hand. "You for them. Edgar will be happy to save the little ones. You know that. And I swear to you, I give you my word, I will release the werebull."

"Why?" I murmured. "Why do you want me?"

"Because you can get the dragon." He peered at me, curious. "You can, can't you?"

"I don't know how."

He shrugged. "I *believe* you can free the dragon. If I have your power, I can free the dragon. At the very least, if I take you and the sword, I will not leave this godforsaken place empty-handed."

He snapped his fingers. "The sword, please. For the sword I will drop the werebull."

I would give him my sword and my power, and perhaps he would kill them anyway.

The cabin shook when Safin flung Angus against the side of it. "I will slice his head off in thirty seconds. Make your choice."

239

"Trinity," Derry moaned. "My dad."

I felt my men watching me from below, I felt their helplessness, their anger, their fear. Mostly, I felt their love.

I closed my eyes and blew out a soft breath. Then I thrust Silverlight into her sheath and held her out to Safin. "Trade."

Safin dropped Angus, flung him to the ground, and I heard the thump of his body like a death knell.

He took Silverlight gently and slung the strap of her sheath over his shoulder. "Come here," he told me. "I won't hurt you."

But before I gave myself to Mikhail Safin, I stepped to the edge of the porch and peered over.

"Angus," I called.

"He's alive," Clayton said. "Trinity, you can't…"

"I have no choice," I told him.

"Let them go?" Edgar yelled. "Mikhail, let them go?"

"Not just yet," Safin said.

Natalie began crying, and the sound droned on and on, endless and heartrending. It drilled into my brain, sank into my memory, and I knew it would not fade away for a very long time.

"Nat." Angus tried to yell, but his voice came out croaky and rusty. "Let her go. Let her go."

"Not just yet," Safin repeated.

"If you do this," Amias said, "we won't let you leave the Deluge."

The silver should have kept him out as it kept out the other vampires, but Amias bore his pain silently and stood with us despite his rapidly weakening strength. The silver was draining him, but he would not leave the ones he loved.

Safin threw back his head and guffawed, genuinely amused. "Master vampire, if you could stop me, you would have already." He looked at me and dropped his smile. "Come here. No more delays."

I glanced to where Edgar and Aspen waited with the

girls.

"Aspen," Mikhail said. "Kill the little one."

"No." I'd already handed over Silverlight, the only thing that could kill him. I walked to him.

"Good," he said. He coiled his whip around my body. The end of it, a throbbing, rubbery tentacle, caressed my throat. I could feel Angus's blood on that tentacle.

"Safin," Crawford yelled. "Your life is over. You have to know that. Let her go."

He shouldn't have come to the scene of a supernatural fight. He was human, as much as he seemed determined to prove otherwise, and one of these nights he was going to come into Bay Town and get himself killed trying to help us.

Trying to help me.

And I wasn't sure that wouldn't just break my cold rifter heart—which was turning out not to be that cold after all, unfortunately.

Safin didn't bother replying to Crawford. "I need power," he told me, his voice soft. "But this is not a power trip. I don't want to rule the world. I simply must have power to live. To kill. You understand that."

The whip moved from my throat to my lips, rubbing back and forth, and I could barely resist the urge to open my mouth and bite a chunk off it.

"You understand," Safin continued, "the urge to kill, don't you?"

"Oh, yes," I replied, shuddering when my tongue touched the tip of the whip. "I understand completely."

He hesitated. "I wish you could join me," he said, finally. "If I didn't need to absorb you, I would partner with you. Imagine what we could do, together. What we could chase. What we could *possess.*"

"I'm flattered."

He nodded, untouched by my sarcasm. "And afraid?"

It was my turn to hesitate. "I'm afraid to fail."

He lifted an eyebrow. "But you *have* failed, Trinity. So

you don't need to be afraid of that anymore."

"It's not over yet, Darkness."

"For you," he said, "it is over."

But then Rhys, leaning on Jamie Stone's arm, walked into the clearing. "No," he said, "it is not."

I smiled. "I'm glad you made it, Dragon."

Safin's eyes widened and he wrapped the whip tight around my throat, strode to the edge of the porch and peered over. "You lie."

I snorted. "You hoped he'd come to save me, didn't you? That's the only reason you didn't stop talking long enough to suck me dry. You knew."

He glanced at me and the whip tightened a little too much. "I hoped, yes. But I am not gullible enough to believe you've brought him to me."

"He brought himself," I said. "Rhys?"

"I'm all right, love," he replied, "but I fear I now have the urge to kill Himself and the elders."

"Understandable," I said.

"Shut *up,*" Mikhail yelled, and the abrupt change from calm to emotional was startling. "You haven't brought the dragon in that sad, ragged man. You have brought more delays, and I will not have it."

He was raging, and he believed we were trying to dupe him. He believed we were laughing at him. But he also had the tiniest sliver of hope that maybe we really had brought the dragon.

"Mikhail," Aspen yelled. "This kid's fucking crying is driving me crazy. Let her go or let me kill her."

"Bitch," I whispered.

"Kill her," Safin said. "Kill them all."

And then everything happened at once.

Safin yanked the whip from around my throat and drilled it into the base of my neck. It went in with a shocking ease, and began to wrap around my spinal cord. I felt it like an icy heat, spreading from my neck to my lower back, and just that quickly, I could not move.

I was paralyzed.

I'd planned to fight him at the last minute—to open my hand and call Silverlight to me, to plunge her into his heart, over and over, until that black, cold thing was shredded, bloody meat and he was dead at my feet.

Sometimes plans go awry.

I could not move, but I could feel.

Oh, I could feel.

Safin was pulling out my insides. He was taking everything I was and would leave only a shell behind.

I had no words for that feeling. Safin's possession was unfathomable.

There was chaos below as my people fought his people—and I could only hope that the girls had been saved and the healers, if they lived, had been rescued.

Because the dragon was there, and he had come to burn the place down.

Chapter Forty

TRAPPED

Safin wasn't taking only me.

He was absorbing everyone and everything there.

I didn't believe he knew he was or that he could, but I absorbed what he absorbed. I felt it. We were connected through his living whip.

It was unpleasant.

And that was the understatement of my life.

Silverlight fought his thievery. Her struggles were my struggles. The only difference was, she was succeeding in her fight.

I was not.

Then I felt the heat from the dragon, and Safin's shock. He tried to pull out of me, because he realized his mistake.

He hadn't trapped me.

I had trapped him.

I couldn't have done it without Leo's blood inside me. Without his power, I could not have held Darkness.

And despite the black horror of the situation, despite my paralysis, the feeling that my insides were rotting into a reeking, slimy mess and being siphoned out by a fucking snake whip in my spinal column, I smiled.

"Oh," Safin whispered. "I made a mistake."

Indeed.

Would Silverlight and I survive the night? I wasn't sure. But Mikhail Safin, executioner, supernat tormentor, power thief, would not.

It was not only for us, for Bay Town, or for the world of supernaturals that it was important to emerge victorious from this night. It was important for the humans.

I heard someone—Crawford, I thought—scream a horrified *"No!"* and that scream echoed inside my mind as I lay in Safin's arms and kept him trapped inside me.

And then I felt the dragon's fire.

It was the fire of magic.

He washed me in it, and Darkness with me.

It only burned for a little while.

Blue, sizzling flames, tall and fat with red tips, danced merrily as they engulfed us, and the dragon did what Darkness had meant to do. He stole our fucking power.

All of it.

Safin's, Silverlight's, and mine.

Enraged, I fought, even as I neared death, because I was not quite sane in that scorching, magical mess. I was not quite sane.

Rhys's whisper flared inside my mind.

Shhhh, love. I must. I must.

I lost everything I was.

Rhys took it when he took Safin.

With my sword's light and his dragon fire, he killed the darkness.

Then something hit my palm, hot and hard, and I wrapped my hand around Silverlight and burst from the flames, naked, shiny, and clean, like a newly minted penny.

And I was mad as hell.

I went after the dragon with my sword, determined to take back my power. My speed, my strength, my fucking immortality. He'd taken it all.

I was just a woman with a sword.

Once again.

"Trin," Angus roared, and oh, the pain in his voice. The disbelief. The joy.

I was on the ground, and they were trying to reach me, but fire was everywhere. The mud bubbled, the water boiled, and the ground was ash and hot coals. The trees had become columns of gray smoke, and the moss strings of streaming lava.

I was fire. And the dragon filled the sky.

He lowered his head and even as I shook Silverlight at him, laughably ineffectual and raging, he sent a stream of blue fire to once again engulf me. But that was not a fire of taking. It was a fire of giving.

Like a sponge, I absorbed what he returned to me, what was rightly mine, and I slurped up the little something extra he added.

And when he withdrew, I was whole.

I was me. The good, the bad, and the truly fucking hideous.

Angus was the first to reach me. His throat bore deep, mottled marks from the whip, and his bare body was burnt in places, raw in others, but he was alive. All my men were alive.

Even Mikhail lived. But he lived inside the dragon. He and his power belonged to Rhys now.

I guess Darkness sort of got what he wanted, in the end.

I guess we all did.

Chapter Forty-One

TWO WEEKS LATER

I fell asleep at dawn in my own bed, wrapped up in Amias and Shane's arms.

When I awakened at dusk, Rhys and Clayton had piled on the bed with us, and Leo sat in the chair beside the bed, his arms crossed across his mighty chest, dozing.

The master and Shane woke when I did, but lay quietly with me, getting the feel of the room and the world outside the room. It was not unusual to wake up and know immediately that the world had gone nuts or that someone we loved was hurting.

But there was only peace inside that room.

I turned my head slightly, darted out my tongue, and tasted the master's skin.

His eyes crinkled at the corners as he smiled, and my heart lurched at his beauty.

"Hi," he murmured, heat and hunger in his eyes.

"All is well," I said, as I did every night since Darkness had been destroyed. "Isn't it?"

"All is well, my love."

"Still no sign of Aspen," Clayton told me, before I could ask.

Aspen had escaped the Deluge. Perhaps she would stay gone forever, or maybe someday she'd reappear and try to attach herself to someone else of power now that Mikhail was gone. I didn't really care.

If she returned, we would handle her.

"Where's our werebull?" I asked. He'd been spending more time at his house. His children wanted him near.

"With his kids," Rhys told me, his voice soft. He gave

me a slow smile when I looked at him, and once again, my heart lurched.

"You all are too, too pretty," I said.

Leo stretched. "Some of us are prettier than others."

I laughed, then lost my breath when Shane slid his hand across my bare abdomen. "We should take advantage of the peace and quiet," he suggested.

"Oh, absolutely." I gasped when Clayton dipped his fingers between my thighs and began rubbing languidly, as though he had all the time in the world.

And he did. There was nothing pressing outside that room, no terrible enemies to defeat, no one calling for our help.

At that moment, there was only peace.

Well, not only. There was sex, as well. And hunger. And love.

Rhys crawled under the sheets and I felt his lips on my inner thigh, then his teeth, gentle but with enough of a bite to make me shudder.

Amias pulled the sheets off my body and let them slide to the floor, and I stared down my nude body, fascinated by the darkness of Rhys against the paleness of my skin.

Rhys had changed since his dragon had taken on Mikhail Safin. I wondered if it was because that dark power lived inside him. He'd become gradually and subtly withdrawn. When I asked him about it, he told me "*nothing is wrong, love.*" But there was distant look in his eyes when he said it.

He looked up at me. "Tonight, you'll feed from me." He switched his gaze to Amias. "You, as well."

Why did I feel like it was an order?

And why did I feel like it would be the last time?

Amias sighed, then nodded. "It is an honor to partake of dragon blood," he said, almost formally. "We thank you for the gift."

I frowned. "What is—"

But Rhys wrapped his lips around my clit, and I forgot

to care about his intentions. He lifted his head once more, as I arched my back and cried out. "Just me this time," he told the others. "But you are welcome to watch." He flashed a grin and the old Rhys was there, but...changed. He'd made a decision of some sort, and I was terrified about what that might mean.

I reached down and buried my fingers in his hair. "Rhys, don't leave me."

"Never, Trinity. I'll always be here."

Funny how that didn't really reassure me. I didn't believe his idea of "being here" was quite the same as mine.

His stare softened. "I will always *be* here," he promised. "I love you. You know that, don't you?"

"Yes," I whispered.

But I didn't want him to change.

Too bad that wasn't up to me.

He turned his head to kiss my thigh.

"I can't enjoy something that feels this sad," I said.

He laughed. "Oh, I believe you can."

But surely my heart was too heavy, my brain too filled with dread. I couldn't think about sex. Not even—

Oh.

Maybe I could, after all.

Rhys began doing things with his mouth that drove everything from my mind but the pleasure of his sex.

The *power* of his sex.

I couldn't lie still. I half sat up, my hands at the back of his head, pressing his mouth harder against my center, gasping as the heat from his mouth slid inside me. His mouth was like fire, but it didn't burn me. He flicked his tongue and sent sparks of fire into me, sparks of pleasure, and I lost my breath as I came with my entire body.

"Hold her." I heard his words dimly, but they held no real meaning. Someone slid his arms around my waist and pulled me back against his body, and both my hands were taken forcefully from Rhys's head and held tightly in strong grips.

I could have broken free had I been able to concentrate for a second, but Rhys was killing me with power, magic, sex.

He sucked, licked, and bit me through orgasm after orgasm. They never weakened, those orgasms. Each one was like the first. And I kept coming.

I kept coming, because his *mouth*.

God, his mouth.

I couldn't move. My men held me, and Rhys's glorious mouth kept me pinned to the bed, my limbs heavy, my body jerking from pleasure that only seemed to grow more intense with each hot stroke of his tongue.

I opened my eyes when he slid up my body and positioned his cock at my throbbing, wet, eager sex, and for a second, fear tried to overwhelm the pleasure. It wasn't possible, but it tried.

His eyes were red, and smoke drifted from his nose and mouth. There was something dark and primal in his eyes, and I didn't know him at all.

Then the fear and pleasure combined and I could only stare mutely into his red eyes, waiting, waiting...

With one fierce thrust, he shoved his cock inside me.

At the same time, someone—Amias, maybe—pushed my mouth against Rhys's throat. "Drink," he commanded.

Blood, sex, power.

It filled me. It filled the room.

It overflowed to all my men, even the one not there. Then I realized Angus *was* there. He whispered in my ear, kissed my neck, caressed my body.

They were all there, touched by Rhys.

And I was being fucked by the dragon.

His magical blood filled my mouth as his thrusting cock filled my body, as everything he was filled everything I was.

My cries blended with his as we climaxed, and I understood then, though I would forget later, that *still* the dragon held back. Rhys was coming into his final power, and he was going to need a dragon to match it. To handle him. To free him.

Not me. A dragon.

If he'd have given me everything he was, I would have gone into the despair. He would have killed me. I was immortal—except when it came to the dragon.

The dragon could kill anything.

Except another dragon.

I wanted to reject that, to deny it, to rail against it.

All I could do was scream in pleasure.

His blood kept me from dying. Had he not fed me as he fucked me, I wouldn't have survived.

Amias, too.

The connection was immediate and sharp when he took the dragon inside himself—the blood, the power, the sex—and it gave us both something we would need to rule the vampires. To protect Bay Town.

To control the humans.

Pure power.

The elders would have their rules. They would have their boundaries.

Amias and I…

We would not.

And we could thank our dragon for that.

Chapter Forty-Two

ENDING

"My end has come to fetch me," Himself said.

We all stood inside Willow-Wisp where he'd summoned us, and despite my issues with the King of Everything, I could only look at him with softness.

He was dressed in red ceremonial clothes—his burial clothes, perhaps—and his staff glowed with a pearly shine. His hair flowed like wispy floss over his shoulders, and his black eyes were bright and lively.

If he were dying, he wasn't sad about it.

He was ready.

But he hadn't called us there so that we might usher him out of the world. He'd called us there to witness his appointment of a new king.

He held out a hand to me. "Bloodhunter. Caretaker. Peacemaker. Lightbringer. Come."

I didn't want to rule the supernats.

"Don't be ridiculous," he snapped, as though I'd spoken my thoughts aloud. "Come here, child."

Jin stood behind me, and without warning, he shoved me toward Himself. "Go," he hissed.

Jin figured everyone should be as afraid of Himself as he was.

The supernaturals of Bay Town had all come to what was likely the last meeting Himself would ever call, and my men and I stood in the front row. I felt like I was ten years old and in the principal's office—a principal who might rip my head off at any moment.

I threw a glare at Jin, then straightened my shoulders and joined Himself, who was flanked by two of the vampire elders.

Vampire elders who, I'd learned, had taken up residence high in the dark hills of Red Valley. Amias had told me. He'd also told me that Jade lived in those hills. Jade and her crew. Amanda Hammer had survived the Deluge, but she was still not back to normal. I never found out what had happened to her to begin with, but that was her story, and she was unwilling to share it.

Safin had killed the healers. The swamp was empty, now. Empty, dark, sad.

When I reached Himself, one of the elders took a step to the side, indicating that I should squeeze between him and the king. I wasn't comfortable there. I didn't belong with the old ones, with their mystery and unfathomable logic.

I certainly didn't belong on Himself's abandoned throne.

"This woman," Himself said, causing me to jump, "is one of the champions of Bay Town. She will forever protect you; that is her purpose. Do not forget." He looked at me. "Do not forget."

I nodded, my throat dry.

Derry caught my stare and grinned, as though she were amused by my awkwardness. Angus was at her side, Natalie in his arms. When I turned my gaze to him, he gave me a wink—a rather wicked one—and I couldn't help but relax. No matter what had passed or what would come, there was one beautiful constant in my life.

My men.

"I'm afraid we will always face adversity in one form or the other," Himself continued. "But we will grow stronger with each victory. The circle surrounding us…" He paused to nod at Angus and the men at his back. "Will grow stronger. Bay Town is not destined to fall."

No one moved, as captivated by their ancient leader as they'd always been. They trusted him—a bit too blindly, in my opinion—and they believed in him completely.

Himself took my hand. "Thank you, Trinity." He squeezed my fingers, gently. "Thank you. You continue to impress me with your heart, even though it has been somewhat blackened by the monstrous rifter." His eyes twinkled as he stared up at me, but I figured he was only partially joking.

"I can't be King of Everything," I murmured.

He lifted an eyebrow. "My dear, of course you can't. You are not meant to rule. You are meant to fight." He released my hand. "I simply wanted to acknowledge your bravery and your sacrifices."

I was dismissed.

I walked sheepishly back to my place with the supernaturals.

"I will announce my replacement," Himself said, his voice booming. "And then I must leave you."

There were murmurs of denial, and a few of the supernats wiped at their eyes.

He pursed his lips, satisfied, and then continued. "There is one who can protect you more completely than I could. He will not be bound by the rules that controlled me and that continue to control the vampires and their elders."

The two old vampires at his side nodded soberly in agreement.

"The world is changing," Himself said. "And quickly. This is the time of greatness, of joy, of peace for the supernaturals. But do not think it will remain so forever. Life can—and will—change in an instant. Be ready." Again, he looked at me, and I couldn't help but feel those last words were for me alone.

I nodded. I would be ready, and I would never forget.

Himself turned his eyes from me and thumped his staff upon the ground, then pointed it at someone in the crowd. "Come, my friend. Allow me to anoint the new King of the Bay Town Supernaturals. The new King of the Red Valley Humans. The King of the World." He paused. "The

King of Everything."

There was movement behind me, and even before I looked to see who would walk to Himself, I knew. My chest tightened, my eyes filled immediately with tears, and I wanted to fling myself in front of him and forbid him to change, to leave, to become something other than the man I loved.

I took a step, meaning to do exactly that, but Angus wrapped his arm around my shoulders and pulled me to him. "No, sweetheart," he said, gently. "It's his right."

His right? Who would *want* to be the King of Everything?

Rhys Graver, apparently.

His shoulders straight, chin up, eyes shining, Rhys strode to Himself. He took the old man's hand and knelt before him, and I put my fingers over my mouth to keep myself quiet as I watched.

I was losing Rhys.

My beautiful Rhys.

That was what it felt like.

Loss.

The supernats were gaining an amazing new ruler. Rhys was gaining power and the responsibility of protecting his people. But I was losing the love of my life.

I didn't care if that was selfish of me.

"I won't give him up," I cried, suddenly and totally unintentionally. "He's mine."

Himself didn't grow angry or impatient, simply shook his head and raised his hand to quieten the uneasy murmuring that swept through the crowd. "No, dear child. You are his. You are *all* his."

And I understood why the elders had trapped him inside the rifter prison. He had to be protected from a man who could have absorbed some of his power, could have made the dragon just a little less. They'd had to protect him until he was so strong that no one could take him.

He was that strong now.

The naming of the new king was relatively quick. The transference of power would come later, and in private. I was glad. I couldn't have watched.

"I will name your assistant," Himself said, jolly.

I frowned. If he thought he was taking two of my men, he was mistaken.

"Alejandro Rodríguez," the old man called. "Your bravery, talent, and loyalty are unmatched. I will give you the honor of serving as the new king's assistant. Will you have it?"

Jamie, staring at the ground, paled.

I knew exactly how he felt.

"I will." Al beamed, his chest swelling with pride. "I am honored, sir."

"Now," Himself said, "we celebrate. Jin?"

"It's ready. I have prepared a feast."

"To the house," Angus roared, then strode to Rhys and clapped him on the back. The others surrounded him, some touching him, some hanging back shyly, as the man they'd known for so long became something almost…untouchable.

"Where are you going, baby hunter?" Shane asked, as I turned to slip away.

"I'll be back in a little while. I just…" I didn't know, though, so I shrugged and hurried away. I'd said my goodbyes to Rhys the night he'd given me his blood and had promised he would never leave me, even if I hadn't really known it was goodbye at the time. He was inside me. He would always be there.

And as I'd feared, it hadn't meant the same thing to him as it had to me.

I walked to the city, hoping the fresh air would clear my head and maybe blow away some of the pain I felt at the thought of losing Rhys.

It didn't.

A new vampire bar had been constructed on Montgomery Street, as Crawford had promised. The place wasn't crowded, but it wasn't empty, either. The humans were coming around.

"Whiskey," I told the bartender.

He looked behind me, saw I was alone, and raised an eyebrow. He hadn't retracted his fangs—for the benefit of the mostly drunk humans—and was suitably attired in black, his hair long and slicked back. He also wore thick eyeliner, and the slightest touch of red lipstick. "Whiskey?"

"Yeah. Whiskey."

He poured it. "What are you going to do with that?"

"I'm going to drink it." I saluted him with the glass, then went to sit at a table in the corner. Before I could lift the glass to my lips, Frank Crawford walked in.

"Man walks into a bar," I murmured.

He didn't look surprised when he saw me, which made me think he'd either seen me enter the place, or one of the men—Shane, probably—had called to see if he could keep an eye out for me.

He bypassed the bar and came to my table. "Trinity," he said.

"Captain." I eyed his crisp suit. "You're looking spiffy."

"Thanks. May I join you?"

I pointed at the chair across from me. "Sure."

I downed the whiskey, concentrating on the path it burned to my stomach. I found it strangely pleasurable.

"What?" I asked, when I caught Crawford staring at me.

He shrugged. "I've never seen a whiskey-drinking vampire before."

"I can't eat," I told him. "At least not without losing it a few minutes later. But I don't seem to have a problem with whiskey." I grinned.

His stare grew sad at my grin. "God, Trinity."

"What?" I asked, again.

He shook his head, and I didn't think he'd answer, but finally, he did. "It's a little fucking sad. Your existence. Everything that happened to you, because of you, and for

257

you. It's all just a little fucking sad."

I looked away. "You're not going to cry, are you, Captain?"

He stood, sending his chair scraping back across the floor, and walked around to stand at my side.

I looked up at him. "What?"

His smile was small, but genuine. "You keep asking that."

"Yeah. So...what?"

He held out his hand. "Dance with me."

I was too surprised, for a second, to say anything.

He didn't move, just stood there with his hand out, and before I could tell him *no, not a good idea, Captain*, I glimpsed something in his eyes.

I wasn't the only one who was a little fucking sad.

I stood without a word and placed my hand into his. It felt...wrong. But in the end, Frank was an uneasy friend and I was willing to let him hold me for a minute.

It wouldn't hurt anything.

I stepped into his arms and we barely moved, just gently swayed, his breath on my forehead, his fingers inching across my lower back, our gazes meeting, then sliding away.

The music was something slow, sang by a man with a haunting voice, and I shivered to hear it. I'd forever associate that song with Frank Crawford.

"Frank," I said.

But he shook his head. "Shhh."

He pulled me closer, and his lips brushed my hair and maybe he didn't think I'd feel it, that stolen kiss, but I did.

I closed my eyes and leaned into him. I wrapped my arms around his waist and pressed my lips against his warm throat and I thought about how it might feel to bite him, kiss him, kill him.

He shuddered when my darkness seeped into him. Frank Crawford was a little something more than he realized. I believed that deep in his DNA lived a hint of supernatural, and in another time, he'd have belonged with me. To me.

But not now. Not now that I was turned. Not now that the rifter in me would make him into something completely nonhuman, something like me.

Even if I had good intentions, I would eventually lose control and hurt a man like Frank. A *human* like Frank. I would bite him. I just would.

And I was a decent enough person to keep my fangs to myself. I cared about the captain.

Without thinking it through, I slid my fingers to the back of his neck, lifted my lips to his, and kissed him. I put everything I had into that kiss.

We both knew it was all I could give him.

He knew it was all he could take.

His lips were warm and firm on mine, and we moved in tandem, bodies pressing, lips brushing, fingers squeezing, hearts wishing.

When the music ended, we parted, as though it were an order. But just before we did, he put his lips to my ear. "I love you, Sinclair."

"I know, Captain," I whispered.

That was hard. That was fucking hard.

I guess the rifter hadn't eaten my heart after all.

"Now we're sad together," I said.

His eyes crinkled when he smiled. "We always were."

"If things were different…"

"Yeah."

I hesitated. "Could you ever—"

He recoiled. "God, no, Trinity. Never."

I'd known, but still. "I want you to be okay."

He leaned forward and kissed my cheek. "I'm okay."

Then he turned and walked away, and I was pretty sure he was smiling.

My heart inexplicably and abruptly light, I followed him out, eager to get home to the way station.

I'd left my heart there.

I hope you enjoyed the Silverlight series.

If you loved this book, please <u>leave a review</u> on Amazon. <3

-Laken

Laken's books:

The Rune Alexander series

The Waifwater Chronicles

We, the Forsaken (Get this book for free by subscribing to my mailing list at www.lakencane.com.

Harbinger Bend

Silverlight series

You can find Laken on her Facebook page at www.facebook.com/authorlakencane. For a full list of links, book list, reading order, and blog, visit her website at www.lakencane.com.

Reviews are always appreciated!

ABOUT LAKEN CANE

Paranormal/urban fantasy author Laken Cane went the indie route with Shiv Crew in 2013. Since then, she has published seventeen books and a short story, including urban fantasy, paranormal romance, and paranormal post-apocalyptic.

Laken shares her Ohio home with three spoiled dogs and a tenacious African Violet, drinks too much coffee, and continues to explore all the worlds that live inside her mind.

Laken loves to hear from her fans! You can email her at laken@lakencane.com or come talk to her on her Facebook page.